DATE DUE		
NOV 15 1985	AUG 26 1992	
NOV 26 1985	JUL 5 1995	
DEC 13 1985		
JAN 3 1986		
JAN 31 1986		
FEB 26 1986		
FEB 9 1987		
MAR 20 1987		
FEB 15 '88		
APR 30 '88		
APR 2 [...]		

BYTE BEAUTIFUL

EIGHT SCIENCE FICTION
STORIES

By James Tiptree, Jr.

TEN THOUSAND LIGHT-YEARS FROM HOME
WARM WORLDS AND OTHERWISE
STAR SONGS OF AN OLD PRIMATE
UP THE WALLS OF THE WORLD

BYTE BEAUTIFUL

Eight Science Fiction Stories

JAMES TIPTREE, JR.

DOUBLEDAY & COMPANY, INC.
GARDEN CITY, NEW YORK
1985

Acknowledgments

Introduction: Bringing It All Back Home Copyright © 1985 by Michael Bishop

Grateful acknowledgment is made for permission to reprint the following:

Excerpts from "The Death of the Hired Man," from *The Poetry of Robert Frost*, Edited by Edward Connery Lathem. Copyright 1930, 1939, © 1969 by Holt, Rinehart and Winston. Copyright © 1958 by Robert Frost. Copyright © 1967 by Lesley Frost Ballantine. Reprinted by permission of Holt, Rinehart and Winston, Publishers.

"With Delicate Mad Hands" Copyright © 1981 by James Tiptree, Jr.

"Beam Us Home" Copyright © 1969 by James Tiptree, Jr.

"Love Is the Plan the Plan Is Death" Copyright © 1973 by James Tiptree, Jr.

"The Man Who Walked Home" Copyright © 1972 by James Tiptree, Jr.

"Your Faces, O My Sisters! Your Faces Filled of Light!" Copyright © 1976 by Alice B. Sheldon

"The Peacefulness of Vivyan" Copyright © 1971 by James Tiptree, Jr.

"Excursion Fare" Copyright © 1981 by James Tiptree, Jr.

"I'll Be Waiting for You When the Swimming Pool Is Empty" Copyright © 1971 by James Tiptree, Jr.

Library of Congress Cataloging in Publication Data

Tiptree, James

    Byte beautiful.

    Contents: Introduction/by Michael Bishop—With delicate mad hands—Beam us home—[etc.]

    1. Science fiction, American. I. Title.

PS3570.I66B9   1985   813'.54

ISBN 0-385-19653-9

Library of Congress Catalog Card Number 85-10185

Copyright © 1985 by James Tiptree, Jr.

ALL RIGHTS RESERVED

PRINTED IN THE UNITED STATES OF AMERICA

First Edition

To Charles A. Schehl, M.D., true son of Galen, whose great skill and compassion have for so many years kept Tip's Edsel of a body from the junk heap it so richly merits.

CONTENTS

INTRODUCTION
Bringing It All Back Home

Much could be—indeed, has been—written about the woman who, when she sends the lovely wares of her imagination into the world as stories, so often styles herself "James Tiptree, Jr."

For a long time, of course, everyone thought that Tiptree was a man, even those who had been carrying on correspondences with her. As Ursula K. Le Guin confesses in an introduction to *Star Songs of an Old Primate* (Del Rey, 1978), Alice Sheldon's third collection of eloquent and moving stories, "I don't think I have ever been so completely surprised in my life —or so happily," as when she learned that "Tip," too, was a woman.

The delightful shock of a delightful recognition.

Others may not have been so happily surprised, however, and I am sure that at least a few received the news with a brief inner sinking. In any event, the aftertremors of the revelation rumbled through the terra cognita of the science fiction field—where everybody, it too often seems, knows absolutely *everything* about everybody else—for months. All that quake-riven ground, as I say, has been surveyed before and will undoubtedly get stepped off and marveled at again, every time that a curious reader with an abiding affection for truly *human* SF stories tries to come to terms with Tiptree territory. As I am doing now.

My own reaction to the startling news that James Tiptree, Jr., had undergone a change of sex?

First, I have no clear recollection of the year. 1975? 1976? 1977? Somewhere in there, maybe '77. Nor do I remember whether I first read the story in a newsletter or heard it from a colleague in a telephone conversation. What I do recall is afterward going to the bookcase here in my study and picking out from it the only two paperbacks bearing the magical Tiptree byline, a pair of story collections (for "he" had not yet published a novel): *Ten Thousand Light-Years from Home* (Ace, 1973) and *Warm World and Otherwise* (Ballantine, 1975). Some of my favorite stories in the field sat shoulder to shoulder in these two books, elbowing one another with their diverse styles and storytelling approaches but somehow achieving a unity of theme and vision that made them . . . well, unmistakably Tiptree-esque.

From the early Ace volume, let me cite such titles as "Beam Us Home," "The Peacefulness of Vivyan," "The Man Who Walked Home," and "I'll Be Waiting for You When the Swimming Pool Is Empty" (all four included here), which is not even to mention "And I Awoke and Found Me Here on the Cold Hill's Side," "Painwise," and "Forever to a Hudson Bay Blanket." And from *Warm Worlds and Otherwise*, "The Milk of Paradise," the Hugo-Award-winning "The Girl Who Was Plugged In," the Nebula-Award-winning "Love Is the Plan the Plan Is Death" (included here), "On the Last Afternoon," and the uncannily fine "The Women Men Don't See," this last title, as Le Guin, with amused approval, was later to note, now redolent of irony.

Anyway, I thumbed through these two books, savoring the titles, rereading certain passages, and now and again closing my eyes and shaking my head. The inimitable Tiptree a woman? One of my fleeting first responses to the news may have been a *small* twinge of dismay.

A decade ago, you see, it was popular among some fans and critics to argue that all the best new writers to have made their debut in the SF field since '62 or so were women, with maybe three or four exceptions. In the early to mid-1970s, I was sometimes singled out as an exception, and sometimes not, but James Tiptree, Jr., *always* made that grudging list, and I was proud of him for showing the feminist movers and shakers and their supporters (among whom I enthusiastically counted myself) that a man could indeed write as perceptively and sympathetically about women as women could write about themselves. "The Women Men Don't See," in particular, proved the point; and in a story called "Allegiances," whose narrator is a young woman named Clio Noble, I had even gone so far as to write my own version of the confrontation with aliens that gives the Tiptree story so much of its impact.

Think, then, about the irony implicit in my (first) (fleeting) reaction to news that James Tiptree, Jr., was in astonishing fact of the, uh, contrary gender. Michael Bishop, enlightened male feminist and science fiction writer, had just lost an ally in his secret struggle to prove that "a man could indeed write as perceptively and sympathetically," etc., etc. In other words, my (initial) (evanescent) reaction was both selfish and sexist. Yes, Alli/Tip, S-E-X-I-S-T, *sexist*, and I suddenly had a picture of myself snapping my suspenders, smoking a big green cigar, and shouting down the stairs at my wife to bring me, double-damn-quick, a cup of coffee and a Danish.

And then I leaned my head back and laughed. I was laughing at myself, I was laughing at the perfection with which Alice Sheldon had disguised her workaday identity without really playing anyone false, and I was laughing at the immense, rotten scaffolding of prejudices, assumptions, half-truths, and outright lies that bigots and believers alike so often erect around themselves to give their hatreds or their hobbyhorse a home. I may have even done a giddy little tapdance, who knows? For in having once claimed "James Tiptree, Jr." as an exemplar of the fact that men can "write as perceptively and sympathetically about women," etc., etc., I now saw that the obverse was manifestly true—namely, that women can write as perceptively and sympathetically about men as men can about themselves. And yet that was no revelation at all, for I had believed *that* almost intuitively—for a long time. Why, then, had I such a strong need to garner praise for creating believable female characters in my own work?

The answer to that question says more about me, and about the profound social corrective of the women's movement from the late 1960s to today, than it does about James Tiptree, Jr., or about the stories in this book, and I do not want to go into the matter here. Instead, let me point out that those writers with the most humane understanding of the species are those with either a built-in or an arduously acquired empathy for people of *every* race, age, faith, nationality, and sex (there may be more than two sexes, you know) under our tiny sun. Alice Sheldon demonstrably possesses this kind of empathy, and her stories reflect it. They reflect it in a way that enriches the science fiction field by bringing humanity—not, specifically, either maleness or femaleness—to settings beyond our experience, to conflicts beyond our unaided imagination, and to characters of alien as well as earthly origin.

Which was one of the points I had intended to make by calling this introduction "Bringing It All Back Home." For even in her most high-flying and far-flung fantasies, Alice James Raccoona Tiptree Sheldon, Jr. (to borrow once more from Ursula Le Guin), always takes care to bring the story home. To make it, even as it soars, sing and belch and weep and sweat and somersault. She does this by guying it securely to the upright and/or crooked constants of the human heart. Which is a fancy way of saying that no matter how strange the place that Tiptree takes us, or how distant, or how lightless, we will ultimately find our way to both comprehension and compassion because she makes us want to understand and she encourages us to care. And that of course is what a real writer must do, bring her stories home by never forgetting where home actually lies. Tiptree, bless her, never forgets.

> Abominations, that's what they are: afterwords, introductions, all the dribble around the story.
> —J. Tiptree, Jr., 1971

Le Guin prefaced her introduction to *Star Songs of an Old Primate* with the daunting little epigram you see above. She got around the problem of dribbling on the stories themselves by discussing instead the *significance* of the revelation that James Tiptree, Jr., was also Alice Sheldon. Her remarks there bear reading, or re-reading, and if I had Le Guin's grace and wisdom, I would quit the field without another word. But Tip, or Alli, asked me to do this, and I am unable to retire without dribbling, maybe in a fashion *forgivably* abominable, over the contents of this new book, *Byte Beautiful* (Doubleday, 1985).

You see, I am one of those people who *like* introductions, prefaces, forewords, afterwords, auctorial asides, and gratuitous oh-by-the-ways. I used to go to the movies early so that I could see the previews of coming attractions and stayed late to catch the trailers. If you are not a person similarly afflicted, you probably bailed out of "Bringing It All Back Home" long ago, assuming that you even stopped to sniff its first page; you are now flying high on the wings of the Good Stuff that follows. But if you are a fellow forewordphile, intent on getting a little extra for your dollar, even if what you get is really only the literary equivalent of a Cracker Jack prize (a Chinese finger cuff, say, whose grip is feeble and easily broken), let me try to hold you for another two or three minutes.

(Delaying gratification, I have been informed by experts, is sometimes a means of heightening one's pleasure.)

(Of course, even experts have their off-days.)

Consider "Excursion Fare," a story first published in Judy-Lynn del Rey's *Stellar # 7 Science-Fiction Stories* in August 1981. Previously uncollected and unaccountably not much remarked in its only previous appearance, this novelette demonstrates the patented attention-grabbing Tiptree technique to a fare-thee-well. Two downed balloonists, with whom the reader willy-nilly sympathizes, face what seems an inescapable death in a storm at sea. I give very little away reporting that they are rescued—for the worried reader, helplessly flipping ahead, can see that this is a *long* story, with dialogue, and not a survival-experience tale in the mode of Stephen Crane's "The Open Boat." A shift of mental gears, then, as the reader, gratified by the rescue, settles in to enjoy a tale that now appears designed to illuminate what the author herself may consider the most viable and humane approach to caring for people who are terminally ill. In other words, "Excursion Fare" has made a sudden but apt transition from pure adventure story to the kind of information-imparting narrative favored by utopian didacticists from Sir Thomas More to H. G. Wells to B. F. Skinner. How do these happy, as opposed to terrifying, "death ships" work? What impact are they likely to have on the laws and customs of the "civilized" nations that the mercy ships have sailed to escape? And so on.

Tiptree, however, complicates the story yet again, and this time I leave it to you to encounter the unexpected and gripping twist for yourself. In many ways an old-fashioned story, as even its *Astounding/Analog*-ish title forthrightly suggests, "Excursion Fare" derives its power from our concern for Dag and Philippa, and for all the other people aboard the *Charon*, and from Tiptree's ability to underscore the human dimension of an event that might in other hands assume vast and impersonal proportions. As nearly always in a Tiptree tale, we are brought home to the indefatigable resources of the human spirit—without being swamped by mere rote or Pollyannaish sentiment.

Now consider all the stories in *Byte Beautiful* that deal in one way or another with the deep-seated human homing impulse. I think that with only a little effort I could make a case for putting every story herein gathered into that category, not omitting the aforementioned "Excursion Fare" and the hilariously satirical "I'll Be Waiting for You When the Swimming Pool Is Empty." Two stories in this collection—significantly, to my mind—have the word *home* in their titles, "Beam Us Home" and "The Man Who Walked Home." The former takes the *Star Trek* phenomenon, which began in the late 1960s and has lately obtained new impetus from the success of three feature films, and uses one of its lovely but hackneyed premises—the technological fellowship of the starship *Enterprise*—to shine a caustic light upon the contrasting reality of our own malodorous and hate-filled times. Who among us feels comfortably at home strolling through the antique furniture of our twentieth-century condominum? Certainly not Hobie, the protagonist of "Beam Us Home," a story that ends on a note of such ironic poignancy that you may find yourself torn between laughing and crying. "The Man Who Walked Home," on the other hand, upends Hobie's wish (the desire to realize, *now*, a conjectural future of love and sanitized adventure) in its documentary portrait of the victim of a gone-awry scientific experiment struggling as valiantly as Sisyphus to reach again the imperfect world from which the mishap evicted him.

Robert Frost has written: "Home is the place where, when you have to go there,/They have to take you in," and also "I should have called it/ Something you somehow haven't to deserve"—but Tiptree's people, almost always deserving, characteristically have to think, fight, suffer, scheme, and endure simply to *find,* or refind, the place that they can recognize spiritually as home. This is true of Hobie in "Beam Us Home," John Delgano in "The Man Who Walked Home," the crazy female courier in "Your Faces, O My Sisters!", the mind-wiped title character in "The Peacefulness of Vivyan," the alien Moggadeet in "Love Is the Plan," and the facially deformed Carol Page in the extraordinary novella "With Delicate Mad Hands," printed previously only in the Tiptree collection *Out of the Everywhere* (Del Rey, 1981).

Indeed, "With Delicate Mad Hands" contains one passage of headlong movement and urgency—the approach of the spacecraft *Calgary* on the veiled radioactive world called Auln—that bears out Robert Silverberg's contention that one of the identifying talents of Tiptree is the "ability to create a scene of sustained and prolonged movement, a juggernaut." And it is telling that the scene here in question describes a movement that the reader comes to view in retrospect as a *homing,* for Carol Page (a/k/a Cold Pig), like Hobie in "Beam Us Home" and John Delgano in "The Man Who Walked Home," has had to travel wide and far to find a place in spiritual consonance with her own modest, and altogether human, longings.

It sounds almost corny to say so, but what almost all Tiptree characters are searching for, the "home" toward which the private tropisms of their hearts invariably orient them, is a four-letter word, *love.* A foolish introducer, which I have already proved myself, could milk from this conclusion another five or six stodgy pages of dribble, but even I am not *that* pathetically lacking in grace and wisdom. Therefore, reader, if you are perusing this introduction in a bookstore or a library, do the sensible thing and either buy the book or check it out. Then go home.

Go home and read the stories.

—Michael Bishop

Pine Mountain, Georgia
January 11–13, 1985

WITH DELICATE MAD HANDS

Carol Page, or CP as she was usually known, was an expert at being unloved.

She was a sweetly formed, smallish girl of the red-hair-green-eyes-and-freckles kind, but her face was entirely spoiled and dominated by a huge, fleshy, obscenely pugged nose.

A nurse at the State Orphans' Crèche told her that a student OB had crushed it, in the birthing that killed her mother. What resulted was a truly hideous snout, the nostrils gaping level with her squinted eyes, showing hair and mucus. The other children called her Snotface.

As she grew older she became CP, and later yet, when her natural fastidiousness was known, the spacers called her Cold Pig, sometimes to her face.

Had CP been officially born to one of the world's ruling Managers, a few passes with a scalpel would have returned that snout to its dainty pixie form; her eyes would have been as nature intended, provocatively tilted green stars, and her lips would have retained their delicious curves. Then, too, her skin would have remained cream and rose petal, instead of its dry angry workhouse red, and her slim fingers would have stayed delightful. The lack of these amenities cost the world a girl of delicate, impish beauty —but this world was precariously recovering from many and much more terrible losses, and individual desolations counted for little.

CP was, in fact, lucky to be alive at all.

At fifteen her mother had been assigned to a visiting Manager who fancied virgins. She became pregnant through an unexpected delay in his schedules. He had become fond enough of the child so that when he saw how passionately she wanted her baby, and how she dreaded her destined future, he took the trouble to find a place for her in a State hospital. Here, of course, she died, but the baby, CP, retained her place-rights in the State Enclave.

This Enclave was one of a small number of city-form complexes on clean ground, where a shadowy form of old-style middle-class life was maintained. It served as a source of skilled labor and very occasional potential Managers. CP's basic health needs were attended to and she was placed in the Enclave's Orphans' School, where she became Snotface.

Here CP developed two traits, the first well known and the second totally secret.

What was known to all was that she was a hard, smart worker—tireless, unstoppable. Whatever came her way, she drove herself into the first percentile at it, and looked for more. It presently became clear what she was aiming at—in a school where mere survival was a feat, CP was dreaming of an all but impossible achievement: Space Crew Training.

She was doing it by simple hard work, undistracted, of course, by anyone who wanted personal relations with a Snotface. Whatever could conceivably be of help she learned, fast and well. She plowed from arithmetic through calculus into vector math, she tackled metallurgy, electronics, computers of any and all kinds. Astronomy she devoured. Being a realist, she neglected no menial art—metal-cleaning, nutrition, space cookery, nursing, massage, the twenty-seven basic sexual stimulations, how to fix any common appliance, space laundry. She took a minor in space medicine. And always she went at engines, engines more engines, and whatever she could find on orbital flight and thrust maneuvers. Her meager State allowance she saved from childhood until she could afford simple flying lessons at the Enclave strip.

And she made it—the incredible quantum leap into Basic Space Crew Training. A mathematician who had never touched a woman pushed her name; a State test administrator who wanted to up his school averages was of use. A general shortage of support personnel for the vital asteroid mining program helped. But basically it was her own unquenchable drive for the stars that carried her up.

Lots of people longed to go to space, of course; among other things, the spacers' life was thought to be a privileged one. And people admired the stars, when they could be seen. CP's longing wasn't unusual; it was only of another order of intensity. She didn't talk about it much—in fact, she didn't talk much at all—because she learned her fellows thought it was comical: Snotface in the stars. But, as one of them put it, "Better there than here."

In Basic Crew Training the story repeated itself; she simply worked twice as hard. And her next small savings went for a medical operation—not on her nose, as any normal girl would, but on the sterilization required of female students, for which they had to pay, if they wanted to get to actual flight. (For space-station workers it was desirable too, but not compulsory.)

And she made it there too, relatively easily. At nineteen she certified for work in space. She was ready to be assigned off-planet. Here, oddly, her dreadful looks helped. In her interview she had asked particularly for the far-out exploratory flights.

"Holy Haig," the young interviewer said to his superiors on the Assignment Board. "Imagine being cooped up for a year with that face! Stick her in the far end of station sewage reclamation, I say."

"And you'd be a damn fool, sonny. What caused the abort on the last Titan trip? Why were there three fatal so-called accidents on the last six Trojan runs? Why do so many computers 'accidentally' dump parts of the log on a lot of the long missions? We lost the whole mineralogical analysis of that good-looking bunch of rocks on the far side of the Belt. If you recall, we still don't know where we'll get our cesium. Why, junior?"

The young Personnel man sobered quickly.

"Ah . . . personality tensions, sir. Stress clashes, unavoidable over long periods to men in confined quarters. The capsule-design people are working on privacy provisions; I understand they have some new concepts—"

"And to these tinderboxes you want to add an even reasonably attractive woman, sonny? We know the men do better with a female along, not only for physiological needs but for a low-status, noncompetitive servant and rudimentary mother figure. What we do *not* need is a female who could incite competition or any hint of tension for her services. We have plenty of exciting-looking women back at the stations and the R & R depots; the men can dream of them and work to get back to them. But on board a long flight, what we need sexually is a human waste can. This—who is it? —Carol Page fits the bill like a glove, and she has all these skills as a bonus, if her marks mean anything. Talk about imagining a year with 'that face'— can you imagine any crew who wasn't blind or absolutely crazy experiencing the faintest additional tension over *her?*"

"I certainly see what you mean, sir—I was dead wrong. Thank you, sir."

"Okay, skip it. Hell, if she works out at all she may actually be a fair asset."

And so it was that CP went out to space, with a clause in her Articles certifying her for trial on long-run work.

On her very first run, a check on a large new incoming asteroid apparently dislodged from cis-Plutonian orbit, she proved the senior Personnel man right. She cleaned and dumped garbage and kept the capsule orderly and in repair at all times, she managed to make the food tastier than the

men believed possible, she helped everybody do anything disagreeable, she
nursed two men through space dysentery and massaged the pain out of
another's sprained back; she kept her mouth strictly shut at all times, and
performed her sexual duties as a "human waste can" with competence,
although she could not quite successfully simulate real desire. (It was after
this trip that she began to be known as Cold Pig.) She provoked no personal tensions; in fact, two of the crew forgot even to say good-bye to her,
although they gave her superior marks in their report forms.

After several repetitions of this performance she began to be regarded
by the Planners as something of an asset, as the Personnel chief had
predicted. The crews didn't exactly love her, and made a great exhibition
of groaning when Cold Pig showed up on their trip rosters; but secretly
they were not displeased. Cold Pig missions were known to go well and be
as comfortable as possible. And she could fill in for half a dozen specialties
in emergencies. Things never went totally wrong with Cold Pig aboard.
The Pig began to be privately regarded as lucky. She achieved a shadowy
kind of status in the growing space network.

But not with Captain Bob Meich, on whose ship, *Calgary*, her story
begins. Captain Bob Meich loathed her, and despised a certain fact about
Cold Pig that was the most precious possession of her life.

Among the various Articles of Contract by which she was bound, there
were two unusual clauses that were all she had worked for, and which she
prized above life: Cold Pig, almost alone among thousands of women in
space, was fully certified for solo flight.

She had insisted on a general flight clause at first signing, and she had
the attested experience to back it up. Authority showed no particular resistance: space work includes thousands of hours of dull routine ferrying of
stuff from here to there, which the men disliked, and quite a few station
women were allowed to help out. Cold Pig's looks were helpful here too;
clearly her goings and comings would never cause a ripple. But Cold Pig
had her sights set higher than this.

Once in space, she set out to achieve a solo cert for every type of rocket
going. She piled up flight time between all her assignments. She would fly
anything anywhere, even if it meant three months done in foul air, herding
a rock in an old torch with a broken-down air regenerator she could barely
keep functional. Her eagerness to fly the lousiest trips slowly made her an
asset here, too.

The payoff came when there was a bad rock-hit on a hot new short-run
mission; Cold Pig not only saved a couple of lives, but flew the new model
home alone and docked it like a pro. The wounded captain she had saved

was grateful enough to help her get the second Article she coveted, the big one: it was formally stipulated that if a scout became disabled on a multi-ship mission, Carol Page would be assigned as replacement to take over his mission and ship, solo, until he recovered. This was extended to include flying the mother ship itself should all other crew be totally disabled.

Thus it was that one day Cold Pig came head-to-head with Captain Bob Meich of the *Calgary*, on the extreme-range mission on the far side of Uranus, with four of the ship's five scouts out on long exploratory flights. Don Lamb, the fifth and last, lay stranded helpless in his sleeper with a broken hip, and his scout ship idled in its berth.

"No c—t is going to fly off my ship while I'm breathing," Meich said levelly. "I don't give a flying f—k what your Articles say. If you want to make a point of it back at Station, you can try. Or you can have a little accident and go out the waste hole, too. I am the captain and what I say goes."

"But, sir, that data Don's ship was assigned to is supposed to be crucial—"

He glared coldly at her; not sane, she saw. Nor was she, but she didn't know that.

"I'll show you once and for all what's crucial. Follow me, Pig." He spat out the name.

She followed him to the scout access tunnel; all the ports but one were empty. He opened the port of Don's scouter and crawled into the small capsule. *Calgary*'s pseudo-gravity of rotation was heavy out here; she could hear him grunting.

"Watch." He jerked the keys from the console and pocketed them. Then he yanked free the heavy pry-bar, and deliberately smashed it again and again into the on-board computer. Cold Pig was gasping.

He crawled out.

"Take your pants off."

He used her there on the cold grids beside the wreckage of her hopes, used her hard and with pain, holding her pants across her ugly face so she nearly smothered.

At one point a bulge in her shirt pocket attracted his notice: her note-book. He jerked it out, kneeling his weight hurtfully on her shoulders, and flipped through it.

"What's the hell's this? *Poetry?*" He read in ferocious flasetto scorn: " '*With delicate mad hands against his sordid bars*'—aagh!" He flung the little book savagely toward the waster. It went skittering heavily across the grids, tearing pages.

Cold Pig, supine and in pain, twisted to see it, could not suppress a cry.

Meich was not normally a sexual man; several times she had felt him failing, and each time he slapped her head or invented some new indignity; but now he grinned jubilantly, not knowing that he had sealed his own fate. He jerked her head forward and, finally, ejaculated.

"All right. That's as close as you get to flying, Pig. Just remember that. Now get my dinner."

He was tired and withdrawn; he hit her covered face once more and left her. Cold Pig was grateful for the cover; she hadn't cried before in space— not, in fact, for years. Before dressing she rescued the little notebook, put it in a different pocket.

"Pig!" He may have had a moment's worry that he'd killed her. "Get that food."

"Yes, sir."

Quite insane now, she smiled—a doubly horrible effect on her bloodied face—and went to do as he ordered, smoothly, efficiently as always. Don was awake, too, by now, looking curiously at her. She offered no explanation, merely inquired what he'd like to eat.

The dinner she produced was particularly tasty; she used some of her carefully hoarded spices to disguise any possible taste from another carefully hoarded ingredient—though she knew from long-ago paramed school it was tasteless.

The fact that she was crazy was made clear by her choice. She had other capabilities; she could have served a meal from which neither Don nor the captain would ever have wakened. In fact, she did give one such to Don, who had always been minimally decent to her. But for the captain she had another, and as it turned out, more perilous plan. Cold Pig was human; she wanted him to *know.*

He ate heartily. Another type of person might have been made slightly suspicious by the niceness, comprising just the foods she knew he was fondest of. Or by her compliant, quietly agreeable manner. To Bob Meich it only confirmed what his father had taught him, that all women needed was a little knocking about, to be shown who was boss. He announced thickly something to this effect to Don, on his bunk in the next "room"; expecting no answer and getting none.

Don was young, the captain mused. Too soft. He still talked about his mother. When Don got better he would teach him a thing or two about handling women.

Presently he began to slump toward the special dessert CP served him. Feeling some irony, she put his "nightcap" bottle where he liked it, within

easy reach. She was impatient now, there was much to do. Waiting, she
had to admire his extraordinary physical vitality. A dose that ought to have
brought quick oblivion took a few minutes to work fully on him. She began
to worry that he might hear Don begin to hyperventilate, but he gave no
sign of this. Finally Meich stared about, focused on her, shouted
"Wha—?", and half rose before he went down for good.

She should have been warned.

But he *was* completely unconscious—she snapped her fingers by his ear,
sprinkled salt on his exposed eye to make sure. She could get to work.

First she wanted to check on Don. She had saved enough of the substance she had fed him to serve her own necessities, and she wanted to see
how painful it might be.

Don was half off his bunk, the last spasms subsiding into occasional leg
jerks. His face was not excessively distorted, only sweat-covered, and the
mouth was bloody. He'd bitten almost through his tongue, she found. But
it did seem to have been quick. There was no heartbeat now except for one
last faint thud that came during the minute she listened. Despite herself,
she wiped his face a little, closed his eyes, and laid a hand for an instant on
his soft brown hair. He *had* been considerate once.

Then she went to work, hard and fast. She blunted one scalpel and
another—those suits and air tubes were tough—and had to go to pliers and
other tools before she had things to her satisfaction. Next she got all
essentials tied or taped in place. She also disconnected a few alarms to keep
bedlam from breaking out prematurely. Early in the process, Meich startled her by sliding out of his chair, ending head down under the table.

One of the air canisters she'd wrestled loose rolled under the table too,
the cut end of its hose wagging. This she noticed only subliminally; it
didn't seem to matter. She was busy undogging heavy seals.

The main air-pressure alarm in the pilot's chamber was very loud. It
roused Bob Meich.

He rolled convulsively, and pushed himself half upright, overturning
table and seats, opening, closing, opening his eyes wide with obvious effort.

What he saw would probably have stunned a lesser man to fatal hesi-
tancy. The room was in a gale—papers, clothes, objects of all description
were flying past him, snapping out of the half-open main port.

The port was opening farther. As he looked, the suited, helmeted figure
of Cold Pig pulled the great circular port seal back to its widest extent and
calmly latched it. Alarms were howling and warbling all over the ship as air
left from everywhere at once and pressure dropped—total uproar. Then
the sounds faded as the air to carry them went out. The last to remain

audible was a far faint squeal from the interior of Don's scouter. Then near-silence.

CP had wondered whether Meich would go first for his suit or directly to the door and herself.

His reflexes carried him, already gasping in airlessness, to the suit that hung on the wall behind, standing straight out as it tugged to fly. One heavy boot had already rolled and shot out the port—no matter, the helmet was there. Emergency suits were emplaced throughout *Calgary*, which was partly what had taken her so long.

He was halfway into it, staggered against the wall, when he saw the cuts. He grunted—or perhaps shouted; the air was now too thin to carry sound —and fell to his knees clasping the helmet. But he couldn't or didn't put it on—his dying eyes were still sharp enough to catch the neatly sliced air hoses. The helmet couldn't help him; it was now connected to nothing.

His mouth opening and closing, perhaps yelling curses, he toppled to the floor, taking great strangled gulps of near-vacuum. Finally he rolled again beneath the table. His last gesture was to grab the bolted-down table leg with one strong pink hand, to fight the pull that would carry him out the port. He held there through the last spasm CP decided was death. She couldn't see him fully, she wanted neither to touch him nor to peer, but he was totally moveless. Man cannot live without air. Not even a Meich, she told herself.

In her savage heart she was a shade disappointed that he had not put on the useless helmet. Further, she would have been better pleased never to have to see that face.

The gale was subsiding, the pull from the port was almost gone. CP waited impatiently until the VACUUM light flashed on the console; it was time to get to work. Don should go first.

Outside the port was a rushing, flickering grayness—the starfields flashing by as *Calgary* rolled. Only ahead and astern was there relatively stable vision. Ahead lay steadier stars, she knew—she dared not, of course, lean out to look—while behind lay the great dim starlit disk of Uranus, flame-edged on one limb. They were orbiting in outward-facing attitude, to maximize the chance of observing any events on the planet. By chance— she hadn't had endurance enough to plan—*Calgary* was just coming into that arc of her orbit where the sun and the world of men were almost directly in line beyond the planet.

Good. She hooked a safety web across the open port, and walked, cautious of any remaining air pockets, into the chamber where Don lay.

She had prepared jato units to send the corpses as fast as possible down out of orbit and falling into Uranus. There would of course be no science fiction nonsense about macabre objects orbiting *Calgary;* certainly not after she was on her way out and away forever—how she longed to start!— but more practically, she wanted no accidental discovery of the corpses. It would be, of course, a million-to-one freak. But freaks happen. CP knew that. In *Calgary*'s attitude, the temptation to set the jets directly at Uranus was strong, but she must arrange them to decelerate instead—most efficient.

She was figuring out the settings as she bent over Don. The hypo she had prepared in case Meich went for her was still clenched, almost hidden, in one glove. She must put it down somewhere safe.

As she reached toward a locker, her body was touched from behind. Terror. *What—*

An arm clamped hard around her neck.

As it passed her faceplate, she had a glimpse of muscles and unmistakably pink, hairless skin.

A dead man had come after her. Meich had come back from death to kill her—was killing her now.

It would indeed have been Meich's impulse and delight to maul and kill her with his bare hands. But he was impeded. One hand was pressing the cut end of an air-tank hose to his mouth. And it is not easy in vacuum to batter a body in a pressure suit, nor to choke a neck enclosed in a hard helmet base. So he was contenting himself with yanking out her air hoses first, intending to get at her when she weakened, and keep her alive long enough to fully feel his wrath.

His first great jerk almost sent her reeling, but he had a leg hard about hers, holding her close.

Cold Pig, aghast to the bones, didn't keep her head. Adrenaline rush almost stopped her heart.

All was gone from her save only reflexes. The hand holding the hypo came round in one drive of horror-heightened power and precision—the needle he hadn't seen was there went straight in, against all likelihood not bending, not breaking, not striking plastic or bone, right through the suit he had pulled up, through liner, skin, and visceral sheath, while CP's clumsy gloved fingers found the triggers and her terrified muscles exerted impossible strength. The discharge shot directly into liver and stomach and ran out lodged in the lining of his renal vein. The strike was so clean Meich may never have felt it. He didn't know he was now truly a dead man. Or would be in seconds.

And seconds counted.

He had torn her air tubes loose; she was without air save only for the tiny amount lodged in her helmet and suit. And he was clamped to her, arm and leg. She began to choke, partly from sheer panic, as she twisted in his dying grasp, not understanding at first what was happening. The force of her turning blow had carried her partway round; she contorted frantically, and finally saw the air tank he was holding and the hose end he breathed from.

It took precious instants for her to understand that she must open her faceplate and get that air hose to her mouth.

Somehow, in spite of his mad battering and wrenching, she opened up. Dying girl fought with dead man for the hose end. She could not possibly pry loose his fingers, though she broke one. But the lethal drug was telling on him—she finally butted his head aside with her helmeted one, and managed to gulp air hissing from the hose he held.

In one last spasm of hate he tried to fling the air tank away from them both. But the tank struck her body. She held on.

And then it was over, really over at last. Meich lay slumped grotesquely at her feet, against Don's bunk.

It took infinite time for her to stop shaking. She vomited twice, fouling herself, but since the hose end was free she didn't aspirate it. She watched, watched for any motion or breath from the twice-dead man. Only the fear that the wildly escaping air—so precious—would give out finally got her moving rationally.

It was almost more than her fingers could do to reconnect her hoses, fit a spare for the damaged one, wipe out and close her faceplate. She would have to live and work for a time in her own vomit, which she found appropriate.

And there was much work to do, in vacuum, before she could reseal *Calgary*. It was now getting very cold.

She had a message to send, and she wanted to dump everything of the men's before repressurizing, to use the waste flush later as little as possible. The bodies she would send out first, right now.

This time there was no question of Don preceding; she laid shuddering hands on Meich's legs and dragged him to the port and the jato rig. She managed to stop herself from leaning out to make sure he had jetted clean away, not caught on some part of *Calgary* to clamber back at her. But she did permit herself to go to the stern port and watch his jet dwindle among the whirling stars.

Then Don. Then everything she could lay hands on or dump from lockers, even to letters, private caches, the pinups on walls, even the duty roster. All, all went out, and did orbit *Calgary*, but only for a time.

Finally she unlatched and wrestled shut the cold main port.

Then without waiting to repressurize, she was free to yield to heart's desire. She didn't even bother to sit down, she simply ran through the basic emergency ignition sequence—*Calgary* was already in perfect attitude—and slammed the main thrust over and on.

Softly, with slowly growing, inexorable power, *Calgary* departed orbit and headed at maximum acceleration away from Uranus, away from Sol behind it, away from humanity, outward toward empty space and the unreachable stars.

Now the message.

She activated the high-gain transmitter, and plugged her suit mike in. And then Cold Pig undertook the first and last literary-dramatic exercise of her life. She was, after all, as noted, human.

First she keyed in the call signals for *Calgary*'s four other scouts, plus a general alarm. Next, gasping realistically, "—All scouts, do not try to return to *Calgary;* repeat, do not . . . try return to *Calgary* . . . there's nothing . . . there . . . Head for . . . the . . . *Churchill.* —Wait, maybe *Calhoun* closer . . . repeat, *Calgary* . . . is not on station . . . do not try to return. . . . Wounded, will try to return log . . . so much blood . . . Cause: Captain Robert Meich dead, self-inflicted . . . gunshot . . . Lieutenant . . . Donald Lamb also dead by gunshot . . . inflicted by Captain Meich. . . . Both bodies lost in space . . . Captain Meich shot Don and . . . unsealed . . . main port. . . . He took Don's body, and . . . shot himself in the abdomen before . . . going out. . . . Cause: Captain Meich said we were docked at invisible spy station, when Don tried to stop him . . . open port he said." Here her words were coming in a soft fainting rush, but clearly, oh clear: "He said Don might be an alien and shot him, he was carrying gun three days . . . sleeping with it. . . . Cold, blood . . . he made me strip and tied me to galley post but Don threw me . . . helmet and air tank but I—have . . . shot wounds in body . . . since yesterday . . . fear *Calgary* lost, Captain Meich fired escape course, broke computer . . . cold . . . trans . . . mission . . . ends . . . will try . . ." And then very weakly, "Don't repeat don't return . . ."

After a few more deathly sounds, she unplugged, leaving the transmitter on. It was voice-activated, it wouldn't waste power, but she must be careful about any sounds she made, especially when air came back.

Then she went carefully around the ship, sealing off everything but necessary living space, to conserve air, and turned the main air valves to pressurize.

Finally she snapped out the log cassette in a realistically fumbling manner, carefully tearing the tape head off before where she knew her argument with Meich began. It would look as if she had simply torn it clumsily loose. To add verisimilitude—they would test, oh yes—she reopened one of the cuts Meich's blows had left on her face and dabbed her fresh blood on cassette and canister. The canister went into a wall slot, which would, when activated, encase it in its own small jato device with homing signal to Base. She fired it off.

The date from *Calgary*'s exploratory mission would arrive, some day or year, near Base, beeping for pickup. That much, she thought, she owed the world of men. That much and no more.

The air pressure was rising slowly. No leaks so far, but it was not yet safe to unsuit. She checked the scanners once, to make sure Uranus and Sol were dwindling straight astern, and set the burn to turn off in an hour. If the fuel lasted that long.

Then she simply sat down in the co-pilot's chair, leaned back in her filthy helmet in the comfortless suit, and let herself lose consciousness. When she awoke she would be far enough away to turn the transmitter off.

She was headed for the Empire. Whose name, she knew quite rationally, was Death.

When she came to, the main torch was off. Had it run out of fuel? No, turned off, she saw, checking the console; there was still some energy left. Her eyes, nose, and lips were crusted, almost closed. Air pressure was back to cabin-normal.

Gratefully she opened her faceplate, unlatched and lifted off the heavy helmet assembly that had saved her life from Meich. Don't think of all that, she told herself. Never again. Never ever again to suffer anything of man. Think of the fact that you're dehydrated and ravenous and dirty.

Gulping juice and water alternately, she checked position. She must have been unconscious a long, long time, they had passed Neptune's orbit; still accelerating slightly. She should have saved the main burn till she was freer of Sol's gravity; she was glad she hadn't.

She got herself unsuited and minimally washed. There was a big cleanup to do. But first she'd better make herself count up her supplies, which was to say, her life.

She had long ago made the rough calculation that it was somewhere in the range of a hundred to a hundred fifty Earth-days.

Food—no problem. The dehydrated supplies were ample to take six men and herself another year.

Water was more serious. But the reclamation unit was new and worked well, all tanks were full. She would be drinking H_2O that had passed through all their kidneys and bladders the rest of her life, she thought. But in the humans of her Earth such thoughts no longer could evoke revulsion. She had drunk unrecycled water only a few times in her whole life; it had been desalinated water from a far sea. The importation of water-ice asteriods to Earth had been one of Base's routine jobs.

Calgary even had a small potential supply of fresh water, if she could reach it without too much loss of air. They had encountered a clean ice rock and lashed it to the substructure of the hull.

She was gazing about, checking around the main console, at which she had never been allowed to sit before, deferring calculation of oxygen, when an odd glint above caught her eye. She stood up in the seat to peer at the thing embedded in the ceiling. A camouflaged lens.

She had stumbled onto one of the secret spy-eyes and spy-ears placed in all ships. She put a screwdriver between its rim and her ear, and caught a faint whirring. Somewhere in the walls a tape deck reeled. It had of course recorded the true events on *Calgary*, and the fish-eye lens was set so that her present course-and-position readings would be recorded.

It was not, she was sure from former tales and trials at Base, transmitting now. People had confided that the eyes and ears sent off their main data in supercompressed blips, at rather long, random intervals. The detailed reading would wait until *Calgary* was back in human hands.

For that, they would have to catch her first. She smiled grimly through cracked lips.

But had it already sent off a data blip while she was unconscious? Or in the time before, for that matter? No way to tell. If so, her story would be only an addition to the catalog of her crimes. If not, good.

How to deactivate it, without tearing out the walls, or causing it to transmit in terminal alarm? Others must have tried it before her. She would have to think hard, and discard her first impulses.

Meanwhile she contented herself with taping over the lens. Then she thought for a moment, and continued searching. Sure enough, now that she knew what to look for, she found the backup—or perhaps the main one; it was much more skillfully hidden. She taped it, thinking too late that perhaps the blanking-out itself was a trigger to it to blip. Well, no help for that now. At least she was free of the feeling of being watched. This was actually a strange new sensation. People took the fact of being covertly observed almost for granted. Brash souls made jokes about what must be mountains of unread spy-eye data stored who knew where and how, perhaps an asteroid full.

She sank back down in the comfortable pilot's couch. If there was a third backup on her now, good luck to it.

The oxygen.

Even before she had dumped a shipful of air, the oxygen situation had not been very healthy. The regeneration system was old-style, dependent on at least some outside sunlight. The weak light at Uranus's orbit hadn't been enough for it; some of the bionic compounds had gone bad, and the regenerator was near the end of its life.

This had been well understood before the . . . incident. It had been planned to cut short the time in total shadow by establishing a semipolar semiorbit—Uranus rotated almost "lying down" relative to the solar plane —so as to maximize light. And the *Calhoun* was headed to an emergency rendezvous with them as far out as possible, to pass over oxygen and regenerator equipment. The water-ice rock might have had to be used inefficiently for air; they were on the lookout for others. Not a crisis, as such things went, but a potentially uncomfortable prospect.

Now she dreaded to think what a period of cold vacuum might have done to the system, and made herself go check. Damage, all right—some trays that had been photosynthesizing showed brown edges. Not a total wipeout, though, as she had feared. It would take care of some of her CO_2, more if she rigged emergency lights. She counted and recounted the suit tanks, and checked the high-compression ship supply of oxygen.

The answer came out surprisingly near her rough guess—oxygen for 140 days max, ten weeks. Actually the CO_2 buildup would probably sicken her seriously before that, unless she could contrive some help.

First was to supply all possible light of the correct wavelengths to the regenerator trays. She sorted out filters, power cords, and robbed all the lights she could spare from the rest of the ship, until she had all trays as fully lit as possible. She even found a packet of presumably long-dead culture starter—"seeds"—and planted them in the hope of restarting two dead trays.

That took hours, perhaps days; she kept no track, only stopping to eat and drink when the need was strong. The trays were huge and heavy, and she was sore. But she felt nothing but joy—joy in her perfect freedom. For the first time in years she was alone and unsupervised. But more: for the first time in her life she was truly free for good, accountable to no one but herself. Alone and *free* among her beloved stars.

The job completed, too tired to clean up herself and *Calgary,* she staggered back to the pilot's couch with a cold meal, and alternately ate and gazed out at those starfields straight ahead that could be seen through the gyro-stabilized scope.

It wasn't enough. She wanted it all. What did she have to fear from the physical deterioration of zero gee?

She sank into sleep in the big pilot's chair, planning.

Over the next two Earth-days she cleaned ship intermittently, between work on her main task: to stop the rotation that gave *Calgary* it's "gravity." She was careful to use as little energy as possible, letting every tiny burst take fullest possible effect before thrusting more.

Outside, the stars changed from a rushing gray tapestry to a whirl of streaks, shorter and shorter, steadying and condensing to blazing stubs against perpetual night.

Her touch was very accurate. At the end she scarcely had to brake. The bright blurs and stubs shrank and brightened—until, with a perceptible jolt, there they were! Stars of all colors and brilliances, clouds dark and light, galaxies—tier beyond tier, a universe of glory.

CP toured the ship, unscreening every viewport. *Calgary* had many; she was an old belly-lander built originally to shuttle from the Mars sling, in the days when seeing outside with the living eyes was still important to men. *Calgary* even had a retracted delta wing, unused for who knew how long.

There were more cleanup chores to do as all gravity faded out and objects began to float. But always CP would pause as she passed a port, and revel silently in the wonders and beauties on every side. Her own wretched reflection in the vitrex bothered her; soon she turned off even the last lights, so that *Calgary's* interior became a dark starlit pocket of space-night.

Ahead of *Calgary* lay, relatively, nothing. She was flying to Galactic North, toward a region where the stars were few and very far, without even a dust drift or any object closer than many human lifetimes. This didn't trouble her. She turned off most of the forward scanners and sensors, wanting to spend her last days studying and dwelling mentally in the richer, wondrous starfields on all sides.

The condition of weightlessness didn't bother her at all. She was one of those rare ones who found sustained pleasure in the odd life of free-fall. The exasperations of toolboxes squirmily unpacking themselves when opened merely amused her. And *Calgary* had many ingenious old zero-gee life and work aids. While CP's body healed, she was happy to be free of anything pressing her.

She was indeed grateful for all the comforts of the big mother ship. She'd never intended to steal it. A scout, the scout Meich had denied her, would have sufficed. This trans-Uranus trip was the farthest out she could ever have expected to be allowed to go. When Don broke his hip it was simply luck: she had been debating how most humanely to incapacitate the last pilot, so that she could take his scout as her Articles promised. The small capsules weren't comfortable, little more than flying torches, but their ample power would have served to carry her out, and not been worth pursuit.

Out was all she craved. Out, outward forever, past Oort's cloud—would she be alive and lucky enough to detect a "sleeping comet"?—outward at greatest acceleration from Sol and all the world of men—out free, in freedom dying, all too soon dead—but her body still flying free. Never to be pursued, touched, known of by man or humanity.

Out to end among the stars. It was all she had dreamed of, worked and endured for; rationally.

No, not quite.

CP was not always rational, or rather, never "rational" at the core. There was always the thing she called, for short, "the Empire."

It was noted before that CP had one total secret. The fact that she planned to steal a ship and fly out to her death she of course kept secret. But it was not her Secret, and it wasn't even unique. Others before her had now and then gone berserk under the strains of man's world, and taken off on death-flights to nowhere. Such loss of valuable equipment was spoken of rarely but very disparagingly, and accounted for much of the Managers' endless, stringent screening, testing, and rechecking practices in space. But this plan was not her Secret.

"The Empire" was. The Empire of the Pigs.

The Empire was everything and nothing. It was basically only a story, a voice unreeling endlessly in her head. It had started before she could remember, and gone on ever since. It accounted for the inhuman sanity of her behavior, for her unshakable endurance under intolerable stress. It was an insanity that kept her functioning with superior competence and rationality, and it was known or suspected by nobody at all.

Not even the prespace test psychologists with all their truth serums and hypnotic techniques and secret, ceaseless spy records over every private, drug-relaxed hour of her test month, not even their most artfully sympathetic human-to-human congratulatory wind-downs, which had in the end brought so many secrets to so many hard-guarded lips; none of it had unsealed CP's. Her Secret lived unsuspected, unhinted-at to any other human soul.

Somewhere in her early years she had seized a chance to study the disapproved findings of psychology. What she really wanted was to know if the voice in her head meant she was truly crazy, although she didn't admit that to herself. It probably did, she decided subliminally, and buried her Secret deeper. As usual, she also studied hard and efficiently in the brief time allowed, and this knowledge helped her later to fend off assaults on her mind and to gratify those who controlled her fate.

The story had started very early.

She'd always been told she looked like a pig. One day the honors children were given a great treat—a visit to the city zoo. Here she saw a real pig; in fact, a great boar and sow. She lingered to read every word on the cage-card. It told her how intelligent pigs were—and by nature cleanly, too. And somehow there started in her small head the story of the Empire of the Pigs.

The Empire was very far away on Earth, perhaps beyond the Chicago Pits. At first everyone in the Empire looked just like her, and life was simply very good. Every night, no matter how exhausted she was, Snotface would live there for a few instants. It took months of such instants to develop each satisfying aspect or event.

In the tale she always referred to herself as the Pig Person. At some early point things changed a little: she had volunteered to be surgically altered for temporary exile among Yumans.

And then one day she was taught about the stars. Right in the classroom her world gave a sort of silent snap, and the Empire moved off Earth, forever. Perhaps the Voice started too, she never troubled to make sure. She couldn't think then; she feared being inattentive.

But that night excitement fought off fatigue as she thought of the Empire in the stars. It was relatively quiet in the dormitory; she remembered that a star or something said, very, very faintly but clearly, "Yes."

She fell asleep.

This starward move gave whole new dimensions to the physical Empire. She busied herself with adjustments and composing new delicious stories of life there and the joys she would later return to.

Another quiet night the Voice said, stronger, "Come."

Such events she accepted tranquilly but happily. She would certainly come. Although even then a tiny part of her mind knew too that her return would also mean her end. This didn't disturb her; dying wasn't uncommon in Snotface's world.

The story soon grew very complicated, developed and abandoned sub-branches, and changed greatly over the years.

Quite early the Empire people changed from being literal pigs to a somewhat shadowy physical form—though always entirely real. In one phase they ceased to be of two sexes. About that time her unexplained exile also changed, first to an exciting spy mission. Real Earthly pigs were sometimes failed spies, or persons being punished by some power. In one episode the Pig Person rescued them and helped them resume their real forms. "Pig" also took on an acronymic meaning, which she didn't use much: "Persons in Greatness." One of the main branches of the story, which tended to take over as she grew older, also had a title: "The Adventures (or Reports) of the Pig Person on Terra."

All this complex activity kept the deep inside of CP's head very busy, without in the least interfering with all her learning and work.

By the time she went to space, a typical entry might transcribe thus (in this branch she wasn't primarily a spy but a stranded, ship-wrecked traveler trying—successfully—to work out her way home):

> Today the Pig Person judged best to open her legs twice to accommodate the hard, fleshy protuberances characterizing two male Yumans. One Yuman requested her to conceal her face during the procedure, so she improvised a mask from her underwear (see note on male-female Yuman attire). The Yuman appeared gratified. This is important because on return from this flight he will be promoted to Personnel Assignment, where he could help the Pig Person acquire more skills on some of these Yuman-type spacecraft. The Pig Person also made a mental note to improve this technique by making a real mask—better, masks of several types—as soon as materials can be procured. How her friends in the Empire will enjoy the notion that some poor Yumans cannot look at her fine Pig face without losing the ability to erect their absurd organs! But however amusing this is, the Pig Person must positively bend all efforts to returning to the Empire before all her information becomes obsolete.

So spoke the true, silent Voice of Cold Pig nightly—sometimes, in bad periods, hourly—in the dark shell under her shining red hair.

Or was it her voice?

Mostly, yes. By it she changed almost unbearable humiliation and pain into "funny" stories.

But there was another real Voice, too. The main one.

It didn't always speak in words. At first, and much of the time since, it "spoke" like a feeling, a sense of being listened to encouragingly, and responded to, quietly and often volubly, just beyond her hearing range.

But more and more, in those early years, the Voice rose to blend exactly with her own, as she composed-recited to herself the life and events of the Empire of the Pigs. Sometimes the Voice came alone into a mental silence, though what it told her wasn't usually quite clear. Very occasionally it rose to complete clarity; for example, it had four times given her the answers during her myriad academic exams.

Since the answers the Voice provided were actually known to CP, only lost from tiredness, she was subconsciously reassured. This proved that the Voice wasn't a craziness, but merely what the book had called a "projection" of her own memories, seeming to come from outside.

Such projections, she learned, weren't uncommon, especially under stress. And in dreams.

As for the Voice giving her new ideas, elaborating details about the Empire, she read that creators, artists, and writers—usually the mediocre ones—often projected their inspirations onto some outside source like their "Muse."

CP was wholly Noncreative in any normal way, a personality deficit considered valuable, even essential, among non-Managers. Her secret Empire-story and the Voice must be some rudimentary Creativeness, leaking out, luckily in a private way.

She took care to memorize every possible Noncreative test response and attitude, and sealed her Secret tighter.

And the Voice only rarely gave her totally new information. On a few occasions it had seemed to pull her from the Empire to tell her about—she was not quite sure what, only that there was often an accompanying large visual impression of blue or lavender, and once, very clear, a gray hand. It was doing something with a complex of fabric. . . . All meaningless, afterward.

What wasn't meaningless was an indescribable personalreference "transmission." The Voice *knew her.* And now and then it repeated, "Come."

Twice it said very clearly, "Waiting."

All this concerned space too, she was sure. Well, her one wish in life was to go to space. Projection again, nothing to worry about.

"I will. I will. I will. I will . . . The Pig Person shall go to the stars," she told the Voice. "The Pig Person will end among the stars. Soon. Soon."

Now, as she settled to her last days on *Calgary*, she—or the Voice—composed as usual a succinct account of all that had passed. But it was cast in quite new terms. Gone were the flat hard tones of unutterable sadness, the terse descriptions of the intolerable. She still spoke as the "Pig Person" —but this person had at last found freedom and joy, found her way to the stars. A way that would lead her back to the Empire, could her human life be long enough to reach it. It would not be. But she would at least end on her free way home.

Thinking this, it came to her that her chance-determined course might not be quite right. Perhaps this was even told her. Conscious with most of her mind that she was giving way to real insanity, she carefully scanned the forward field. Empty, of course, save for the faint far stars. And yes—the Voice was right—she was not quite on course. She must correct just a trifle. It was important.

On course for *where?*

For the first time she faced her madness abruptly, hard. *What* "right" course, en route to *what?* To nothing—nothing but icy vacuum and nothingness and dying. She proposed to waste fuel "correcting" to an insane delusion? A delusion she knew perfectly well was born of her human need for support amid ugliness, rejection, and pain?

But if nothing lay ahead, how could the spent fuel matter?

Slowly, almost but not quite amused at herself, she gave in.

Her fingers played delicately over the thrust-angle keys, her eyes went back to the scope. Where? Where shall I come; show me! She let her eyelids almost close, feeling for it. *Where, where?*

And dreamily, but clear, it came to her: there. *Here* . . .

Random nonsense, she told herself angrily, almost turning away.

But the shadowy vector persisted clearly in her mind. She peered through her strongest scope, scanned every band of EM radiation. Absolutely nothing lay *there.*

"Come," the Voice sighed in her head. "Come. I have waited so long."

"Death calling," she muttered harshly. But the fact was, she couldn't be truly comfortable until she turned *Calgary* to head precisely that way.

Carefully, deliberately, she set in the course correction for Nowhere. She punched to activate. The burn was very brief; she had been, as usual, accurate. *Calgary* shuddered imperceptibly, the starfield crawled slowly slightly slantwise, then steadied to a rest with almost no braking necessary, pointing exactly *there.*

And as it did so, the Empire died.

For the first time she could remember, the story that had run ceaselessly in her brain, the Voice that was mostly a feeling, fell silent. What had hit her? What had silenced her? Startled, yet somehow accepting, she stared about. Nothing had changed; it was simply gone. There was no Empire, no one to "report" to, ever again. She was alone. Or . . . was she? It didn't matter. Everything was all right. Had not the Voice been commanding her too in its way? Now she was truly free of the very last outside orders.

She went back to her quiet routine of gazing, observing, using the scope and other analyzers on interesting objects. Of them all, she preferred the eye. She found an old but serviceable computer-enhanceable high-power scope in a rear locker, left unused in recent years when no one had desire nor time to look at things too far to give promise of gain. To her joy, with a bit of work it proved functional. She pored over star charts, identifying and memorizing. In some peculiar way, this activity was all right too, beyond her own personal fascination.

By using all the ports, she had a 360-degree field of view in all directions —the universe—and she scanned at least briefly, but systematically, over it all. A feeling almost like the old voice-in-her-head encouraged her. Habit, she knew. I'm projecting my own pleasure back at myself.

As the early days stretched to weeks—she kept only the vaguest track of time—she experienced only comfort. Small events: one of the regenerator trays she had planted "took," the other stayed dead. She scraped together a last sprinkle of seeds and tried again. She also arranged a contraption, a double-inlet tube that would carry her breath from her habitual seat and bunk directly to the trays, which at this time were actually short of CO_2. The later buildup to saturation and ensuing degeneration would go fast; she installed a gas sampler and alarm to give ample warning of the rise.

Absurdly, she minded the prospect of dying from simple oxygen lack less than the notion of positive poisoning by her own wastes. This was non-sense, because what she knew of physiology told her that internal CO_2 would be an agent of her death anyhow.

Despite her comfort, she made every possible effort at conservation. The possibilities were pitifully few, consisting primarily of minimal use of the waste flusher, which lost air. Even when she had collected quite a pile of the men's overlooked leavings—including souvenirs of Meich—she denied herself the luxury of flushing them out.

Aside from the star work, and simply indulging in a rest she'd never known, she occupied herself with recalling and writing down such words as had once struck her as wise, witty, or beautiful: sayings, doggerel, poetry, a few short descriptions of old-Earth phenomena no one she knew had ever seen—a clear sunrise, a waterfall—the names of a few people, mainly women, she'd respected. Effortfully, she even composed a short account of a striking memory—an eclipse she and other children had been allowed to see in the open.

She mulled unhurriedly over practical matters, such as whether the expenditure of oxygen necessary to bring in that ice-rock lashed to the hull would repay her in oxygen theoretically extractible from it. Quiet . . . a blissful life.

But one day came disturbance. The lone bow scanner chirped. Doubtless a malfunction; she moved to turn it off, then paused. This might signal an oncoming rock; she didn't want to die so. She activated another. To her surprise it lit in confirmation. For one horrifying instant fear seized her—could the human world have somehow pursued her here?

She turned on more pickups, was reassured—and then so amazed that she peered out visually to orient the scopes. Not a rock, or a rocket, not small but vast: ahead and slightly "above" her floated something world-seized—no, nearly sun-sized—very dimly lavender, glowing and ringed.

For another sickening instant she feared she had, incredibly, flown a circle and was coming back among Sol's outposts. But no; the scanners told her that the body occulting the forward field was nothing in Sol's family. Huge, her sensors told her, but relatively small-massed. The surface gravity, if she was seeing the surface, would be a little less than Earth-normal. It was definitely, though faintly, self-luminous—a beautiful blue-rosy shade she had no name for.

And very highly radioactive.

Was she looking at a dead or dying star? Possible; yet this body conformed to nothing she knew of in the processes of star-death. Perhaps a star not dead, but still below the threshold of interior ignition? A star coming slowly to be born? Or one destined to remain thus, never to ignite to birth at all?

Without even considering it, she had automatically activated thrust and set in a course correction that would fly her straight at the body. Equally automatically, she noted that *Calgary*'s pile was so used out that she hadn't possibly enough fuel to shed her now tremendous velocity and slow *Calgary* into any kind of close orbit. She ignited thrust.

What was she doing—unconsciously planning to die by crashing into this silent mystery? Or, if it had atmosphere, be roasted to death in the friction of her fall? It was not the quiet death she had intended, among the eternal stars.

Yet approach she must. Approach, see, and know it, orbit closely if only for a last fiery instant.

She lost track of all time, as the mystery grew in the ports, with her terrible speed, from dim point to far disk to closer, larger, port-filling nearness. She was retrofiring repeatedly, trying to get effect from every precious erg, willing *Calgary* to slow as if her naked desire could affect the laws of physics.

Finally the time came when she felt uncomfortably upside down to the great surface; she expended a precious minimum of energy slowly righting *Calgary*'s attitude. On crazy impulse, she suited up, leaving only the faceplate open, and strapped herself in the pilot's cocoon. It was all futile madness—despite everything she could do, her velocity was impossibly too great. Still she retrofired intermittently, trying to judge exactly optimum angles of thrust, fighting the temptation to torch everything once and for all, straining back in the cocoon, willing, commanding, imploring aloud to *Calgary* to slow—slow—slow—slow—

And luck, or something logically nonexistent, was with her. She was still moving lethally, hopelessly too fast, but *Calgary* seemed to have shed more velocity than the computer predicted possible. The thing must be faulty; she took over completely from it, and against all calculated chance, achieved a brief quasi-orbit in what seemed to be the equatorial plane.

She could see the "surface" now—a smooth, softly glowing, vast-dappled, racing shield, which the sensors told her was cloud. Two hundred kilometers beneath that lay solid "ground," some of which registered as liquid. Expecting nothing but nitrogen-methane at best, CP glanced at the spectroscope—and lunged against her straps to slap on the backup comparators.

Same readings!

That cloud cover was oxygen-hydrogen: water vapor. And the basic atmosphere was 25 percent oxygen on a nitrogen base. She was looking at an atmosphere of Earth-normal quality.

Hastily she ran through the tests for various poisons; they were not there. This was preindustrial, prewar air such as CP had never breathed on Earth!

Except, of course, for its appalling radioactivity, which apparently emanated from ground level. It would quickly destroy her or any Earth-born living thing. To walk on this world, to breathe its sweet air, would be to die. In days, perhaps only hours.

Her orbit was decaying fast. The visible cloud was no more than a few thousand kilometers below her now. Soon she would hit the upper atmosphere—hit it like a skipped rock, and perhaps break open before *Calgary* burst to flame. The ship's old ablatives had been designed only for Mars, and deteriorated since. Slower; slow down, she pleaded, using the last full thrust of the pile. In her mind was a vivid picture of her oncoming doom at her present inexorable speed. Only moments of life remained to her— yet she was content, to have found, in freedom, this great wondrous world.

Belatedly recalling that Don's scout capsule was still on umbilical, she managed to reverse-drain its small fuel supply into two of *Calgary's* back boosters that weren't operated off the pile. Slow down—slow! she willed, firing.

The small backfire did seem to slow her a trifle. She had abandoned the instruments, which foretold only her death, and was watching the cloud tear by below. *Slow down, slow down!* She pushed herself back so hard she ached, sensing, dreaming that the death clouds were rushing imperceptibly slower. The atmosphere that would kill her extended, of course, far above them. She was all but in it; the molecule counter was going red.

Then, while she noticed they were over "land," *Calgary* seemed actually, undeniably to slow further. The clouds below changed from a featureless stream to show perceptible dark-light gradients flashing by. Still far too fast, of course; but it was as if she was passing through the backward tug of some unknown field. Perhaps the effect of the denser molecules around her? But *Calgary* wasn't heating up. Some utterly alien energy was at work. Whatever it was, she needed more. Slow, much more. Desperately she urged it.

And *Calgary* slowed.

What mystery was helping her kill velocity? It had to be physical, explicable. But CP, knowing with part of her mind that she had gone crazy, gave herself over to a deep conviction that this was no impersonal "field." She *knew* it was connected in some way with her need, and with her visualizing—"broadcasting" mentally—her plight. Mad, she was. But she was being helped to slow.

Perhaps I'm already dead, she thought. Or perhaps she would come to, drugged and manacled, in Base Detention. What matter? She had reached her Empire's power; it was saving her at last.

Over and over again she "showed" the unknown her needs, her vulnerability, the onrushing terrors of impact and heat, all the while draining every tiniest output from the dying pile, which seemed to have regenerated slightly while she'd rested it.

And *Calgary* slowed, slowed, slowed as if flying through invisible cold molasses—so that the first wisps of atmosphere came past her at little more than common supersonic speeds. A miracle. There were no smashing impacts, only a jostling of loose objects, and very little heat. And then she was down to where the first visible tendrils of cloud rushed by.

It was so beautiful she laughed out loud—the blue-lavender-pearl streamers against the star-blazed night. For an instant she looked for *Calgary*'s shadow, and then checked herself and laughed again; this world had no sun, it had never known a shadow from the sky—all its light came from below, within.

Then she was in it, blinded, dependent only on her instruments. *Calgary* was barreling down, its orbital direction curving to a fall. It occurred to her that the delta wings would help now. Would they extend, and if so, would they tear off? She had an instant's neutral memory of another life, in which a captain's potential madness had driven him to a compulsive predeparture checkout of *Calgary*, even to the old, never-used wing, even to insisting that it be serviced to function. Strange.

She activated the extensors, pulled with all her strength on the manual backup. Gratings, groans—and the delta lurched from its slots and extended in the alien air, slowing *Calgary* into a yawing roll. She thanked fate that she had strapped in where she could reach the old flight controls. Now her hard Earthside flight training served her well; she soon had *Calgary* on a rough downward glide. The wings vibrated violently, but stayed on, even at this wild speed.

Down, down through two hundred kilometers of brightening cloud. Until she burst abruptly out of the lowest, lightest layer, and saw—yes—a world-ocean far below. This ocean glowed. She looked up and saw the cloud ceiling lit grape-blue, krypton-green, by its reflection.

Next moment she was over land, too high to see anything but swaths of new luminous colors. Glowing orange, smoky turquoise, brilliant creams and crimsons, with rich dark-purple curves and flowings here and there; a sublime downscape, with tantalizing illusions of pattern. Above her the solid sky was lit up varicolored reflecting it, as if an immense stained-glass window were shining from below.

The ocean under her again, this time much lower. She could see the lucent pale-green V where it broke on a small island. The surface seemed very calm, save for long, smooth swells. More V's of green-blue light came under her—an archipelago? Or—wait—was there *movement* down there? Impossible. She strained to see—and suddenly there could be no doubt. Twenty or thirty somethings were each trailing its brilliant V of wake, moving contrary to others.

Life.

Life! Whalelike mythical beasts? Or was this perhaps a warm, shallow puddle-ocean, in which great creatures, like the Earth's cretaceous saurians, sported? Or—she dared not think it—ships? Whatever, minutes from her death, she had found, or been found by, the first alien life known to humanity; on a dark, solitary, unseeable almost-sun.

She prayed aloud to no god to let her slow enough to have one sight of this marvel. To the unknown power that had helped her she sent desperate, fear-lit images of her onrushing crash, explosion, death—unless *Calgary* could be slowed enough for her to belly-land it in one piece. She had the momentary sense that the power was reluctant, perhaps tired—but desire to know more of this wonder drove her shamelessly. She pled with all her soul to slow more.

And sluggishly, but in time, response came. Once the slowing was so abrupt that her glide fell below *Calgary*'s high stall speed. She went tail down and began to drop like a stone, until she found one last unbelievable gulp of fuel to send the ship back into level flight. She tried to send in careful detail the image of her needs. They were almost unfillable—to glide *Calgary* to some sort of bare, level landing place, large enough to absorb what would be her ground momentum. If only she could, once, *see* these marvels! No matter how injured she was, she longed only to die with her eyes filled with them.

Nothing but death lay ahead, but CP was in ecstasy such as she'd never dreamed of.

Releasing the controls for an instant, she flung her arms wide. "I name thee Cold Pig's Planet!" she said to Auln. (Auln? Whence did that come to her?) But no, she was not falling to the satellite of any sun. "I name thee Cold Pig's Dark Star!"

Appropriate, she thought wryly, grabbing the controls, and strapping in tighter. All those weary hours of Earth-flight kept returning to her aid. Skillfully she nursed the awkward old ship over the pale fires of this shoreless sea; she was too low to see beyond the far, high horizon to where land might lie. She could only fly straight with the direction of revolution toward where she remembered the continent bulged seaward.

Unsteady breezes tossed her, sometimes bringing her so low that *Calgary* barely skimmed the crests—and once she all but nosedived in, as she caught a flash of strange life, dark-bodied, playing in the waves. Too fast, too low, *Calgary* could not survive splashdown here. Resolutely she ignored all wonders, made herself concentrate on staying airborne, above what seemed a world on fire. The horizon was so weirdly high! This world was huge.

And then a line of brighter fire showed on the horizon ahead, seeming almost above her. Shore! But forested, she saw. Those lighted shapes were a solid wall of trees—she was hurtling toward a fatal crash. Frantically she pictured, pled for what she needed—and then saw that the forest wall was not solid, there was a great opening, an estuary slanting out. She swung *Calgary* to aim into it; she could see now that it wasn't a wide river, but a relatively small stream edged with swamp, almost treeless. Perfect. But coming at her fast, too fast—if only there could be headwind! She was prepared for anything now, had no wonder left but only gratitude as the sudden shore wind struck and slowed her.

Into the opening they tore, over the margin that appeared barest. Then *Calgary*'s belly structures hit sticky marshland, crushed clangorously—the ship bounced and careened past flying trees—flat-spun twice, throwing CP about in her straps—and went wing up, the down wing breaking off as it plowed fountains. And finally, incredibly, all motion stopped.

CP slowly, dizzily, stared around her at the cabin. No broken walls or glass, air pressure reading constant. The cabin seemed to be intact. Intact. She was down safe! And, apart from a few bruises, herself uninjured.

Her hearing was deadened by pressure change. When her ears opened, she could hear only the clanks of cooling metal, and the crackle of a small flame by the jets, which died as she watched. No hiss of escaping air. But the silence outside had the unmistakable sense of density and resonance that told her the *Calgary* was no longer in vacuum but in air.

Weak almost to fainting, CP wiped her breath from the vitrex to peer out. It was confusing—a world like a color negative, all light coming from below, with strange-hued shadows above. So beautiful. Only trees and shrubs were around her—a wilderness of trees; CP had never seen so many trees all in one place. And they stretched on and on, she knew, to the horizon. Beyond them she could just see the lighted sparkle of running river water, *free water*, presumably fresh.

A paradise—save only for the lethal radioactivity, which had her scanning dial stuck against its high edge. A paradise, but not for her.

Nevertheless her prayers were granted. She was seeing a New World. She could touch it if she wished. A deep, extraordinary happiness she could scarcely recognize filled her. Her lips trembled with a constant smile she'd never felt before. But she could no longer keep her eyes open. She knew she had spent some hours fighting *Calgary* down; she didn't realize it had taken her three Earth-days.

As she lost consciousness, hanging sideways in the straps, from somewhere outside a living creature gave a single, unearthly, echoing hoot, loud enough to penetrate the sealed cabin.

Her last thought was that she would probably awaken, if she did, in the bonds and cuffs of Base prison.

She woke up painfully stiff and thirsty, but with the same marvelous alien world outside the port. And the air-pressure reading had stayed constant! All essential seals were intact—a final miracle.

Calgary had come to rest nose down on its broken wing stub; the "floor" was at a 40-degree angle. As CP unstrapped and slid down, she saw how good this was: the big port at her chair gave her the view outside right down to ground level, and so did one end of the bow window. The opposite port gave her the treetops. She paused curiously to study their strange adaptations of form to utilize light coming primarily from below. There seemed to be two general types, a pad-leaved sort, and a big tree fern, but there was extraordinary intervariation.

How much sealed airspace was left her? Gone, of course, was the whole underbody, the scouter dock, and the trailing space equipment—including the ice rock. But she had the pilotage and observation chambers, and the door to the galley had sprung askew without causing leaks. So had the wash-and-wastes roomlet, and even the door of her own bad-memoried little cubicle—no leaks in there.

Gratefully she pulled off her heavy helmet and shook out her flaming hair. Her last days would be not only sublimely interesting but actually comfortable!

Her water supply was intact too; she had checked that when first slaking her huge thirst. She would have to conserve, but she would have quite enough for the twenty days or so of oxygen left to her. That lack would be her end, as had been foretold from the start.

Just as she settled by the window to open a food pouch, movement outside drew her eyes. *Calgary* had plowed a long open avenue through the swamp brush, and was turned so she could look right back down it to the far, high, green glimmer of the sea.

Now something she had taken for vegetation moved, moved again, and became a long, willowy, pale animal. It was clambering down from a low fork in a tree by the "avenue," where it had perhaps spent the night. Had it been watching *Calgary*, shocked by the crashing intrusion of the ship? Even at this distance she could see that its eyes were enormous. They were shining with reflected light, set very far apart on a thin whitish head. The head resembled that of a goat or sheep which CP had seen alive in the zoo. It was definitely watching her now. She held her breath.

As it swung down, she could see that its side-skin hung in folds, and a long-ago memory of her one picture book came back. Earth had once had "flying" squirrels and other gliding animals. Perhaps this creature was a giant form like that, and used its flaps for gliding between trees?

Down from the tree, it sat on its haunches for a moment, still watching her. *Please don't be frightened,* she begged it mentally, not daring even to close her mouth, which was open for a first bite of breakfast bar. The creature didn't seem alarmed. It stretched, in a laughably human way, and dropped its short forelimbs to the ground. It had a short, stout, upcurled tail.

Now CP remembered a picture that was closest of all—the kangaroo. Like the kangaroo, this animal's rear end was higher than its shoulders on all fours, because of its long, strong hind limbs; and its neck was curved up to carry its long head level. Only its tail was much smaller and shorter than the picture she recalled.

To her delight, it began calmly to amble, or walk-hop, right toward *Calgary*. As it came closer, she could see its draped pelt clearly.

It wasn't fur.

It wasn't bare hide or leather.

It was—yes, unmistakably—and CP's mind seemed to explode with silent excitement—it was *fabric*.

As it came closer still, she could make out that around the neck and along the back-ridge ran a pattern of what could only be embroidery. It was set with knots and small shiny stones or shells.

She simply stared at the approaching form, unable to take in all the implications at once.

A world not only bearing life, but bearing intelligent life.

Too much, that she had stumbled on *this*.

And yet—was she really so surprised? The feeling that something . . . or someone . . . was "hearing" and helping her down had been so strong. . . . Was she looking at the one who—?

Impossible. She could think no further, only stare.

The creature—no, the *person*—calmly returned her gaze, and then sat down again, upright. With delicate spatulate fingers, it unfastened the throat of its cloak—CP could clearly see its thumbs—and removed it, revealing its actual pelt, which was cream-white and short. It folded the cloak deftly into a long strip and tied it around its body, then dropped back on all fours and resumed its amble toward her.

But it did not head to her window; it detoured around *Calgary* on higher ground. As it passed, twitching one of its tall "ears" toward her, CP had a confused, faint mental impression of others—very diverse others—somewhere nearby, whom this one was going to meet. The notion vanished so quickly she decided she had made it up. Her visitor was passing out of sight from that port, into the undisturbed forest ahead of *Calgary*'s stopping place.

She clambered quickly to the side post, but the stranger was already beyond sight among the trees. Perhaps someone or something else would come from that direction? She made herself comfortable by the vitrex, and at last began to eat her bar, studying all she could see. She was over the broken wing stub now. *Calgary* had come to rest against a dry hillock; this side made a natural approach. Slowly, so as not to alarm anything, she extended the auditory pickup and tested it. It worked! A world of varied rustlings, soft tweets, a croak or grunt, filled the cabin.

After a moment's thought, she tested the sound transmitter and extruded that too, so that her voice could be heard outside.

Presently she became aware of a periodic crackling or crashing sound coming from the woods beyond the hillock. She watched, and saw a far treetop sway violently and go down. Soon another followed, a little closer, and then yet another smaller tree jumped high and disappeared. A big herbivore, perhaps, feeding?

But as the sounds came closer, they seemed clearly deliberate. Perhaps a path or road to *Calgary* was being cleared. If so, what would appear? An alien bulldozer? A siege ram? A weapon carrier brought to blast her and *Calgary* out of existence?

Yet she waited unafraid, only glad and fascinated. This world did not feel hostile. And had they not already helped her, saved her life? *Calgary* had rudimentary defenses, mainly of a ballistic sort, which in recent decades had been occasionally used only to break up rocks, but it never occurred to her to deploy them. Life here had saved her life, and she had intruded a great shipwreck upon them. Even if they wished to be rid of her now, whatever came she would accept.

And suddenly it was there—so different from her expectations that she didn't at first take it in. One—no, two tall-humped forms were pushing through the trees. Their sides and tops seemed hard; she could hear thuds as they brushed against stems. Why, they were great tortoises, or turtles! She had once seen a tiny live one, much flatter in outline. Or could these carapaces be, like the Watcher's cloak, artificial shells? No, she decided. Their limbs and necks were formed to them; she seemed to see attachment in the openings' depths. Could they be trained beasts, used here instead of inorganic machines?

As she watched, mesmerized, one of them backed ponderously into a tangle of tree trunks, sending them down like paper trees. Then it turned, reared up, and began neatly to break up, sort, and pile the debris. Just behind it, the other was doing the same. Then it came past the first, selected an obstructive giant tree, and repeated the process. She realized how very big they were; the tops of their shells would be higher than her head, and their push-force must be in tons.

As she saw the results of their work, she realized these couldn't be animals, however trained. They weren't merely clearing a way; they were creating order. Behind them stretched a neat, attractive clearway, without the edging tangle of damage usual on Earth. It wound away quite far; she could see perhaps a kilometer.

As the creatures reared up, worked, dropped down to push, it was evident to CP that they had a generic resemblance to the first one, whom she thought of as the Watcher. The same heavier hind limbs, here ponderous and half-hidden by their carapaces; the same shorter forelimbs, here massively muscled. When they extended their necks, these too were long, though thickly muscular, coming from very large front openings in the shell. They walked with heads high and level. The heads, now retracted to their shells, were somewhat similar to the Watcher's. Not at all reptilian, with upstanding "ears," heavy frontals, and protectively lidded eyes.

As they came closer, working rapidly but always neatly, she could see that their carapaces carried decorations. Some self-luminous pebbles or seeds had been set among the designs; their undershells, seen brightly illumined, were beautifully scrolled, and seemed to have straps or tool pockets mounted on them. Logical, she thought; frees the front limbs to walk. And finally, as the closest one rose up to grapple a tree fern, came the most bizarre touch of all—she could clearly see that it was wearing cuffed, decorated work gloves.

This perception set off her overloaded nerves—she nearly dropped the kaffy from her shaking hands as a gale of giggles swept her, turned into peals of laughter that rang through the speaker into the swamp. Abashed, she thought how inappropriate this was, that the first human voice heard on this world should be not a proper formal speech, but laughing. She couldn't help herself. She had laughed little in her life. No one had told her the sound was very sweet.

She had it under control in a moment. Wiping her eyes, she saw that the turtlelike workers had dropped their logs and come closer for a look-in. She hoped the sound she had made wasn't displeasing or ugly to them.

"Excuse me," she said absurdly through the speaker.

A vague feeling of all-rightness suffused her; one of the "turtles" made what was clearly an attempt at imitating her laugh, and they went back to their labor, now almost at the ship.

And when her vision cleared, she could see, in the distance, six or seven new shapes approaching up the path the "turtles" had made.

She finally bethought herself the binoculars, and peered with all her might. The glasses were of course set for celestial use, with a very small field, and she had trouble at first in counting how many were in the group.

Four—no, three of them closely resembled the Watcher, but she could pick him, or her, out by the paler fur, and the color of the tied-up cloak. This method of transporting stuff seemed to be common. The other two kangaroolike ones diffused among themselves too—she had a glimpse of more strangely formed heads, possibly even an extra very small set of forelimbs—but she was too busy trying to see all the others to check.

Another of the turtle or tortoise types was with them, its carapace heavy with encrustments. She gained a quick impression that it was quite old. It was even larger, and differed from the tree movers in its eyes, which were enormous and very bright beneath the heavy lids. Indeed, her first sight of the group had featured eyes—huge eyes, so bright and reflective that some seemed almost self-luminous. She noticed that all of them, as they advanced, looked about continuously and carefully, but with their major attention on *Calgary*—almost like a group of advancing headlamps.

Touching, partly leaning upon the carapaced one, came a short figure so swathed in red fabric veils that CP could make nothing of it, except for the great eyes in a face much shorter and more pugged than the Watcher's. The fur on its skin was pale, too. CP had the impression that this creature —no, this *person*—was somewhat ill or weak, perhaps old, too. She or he paced upright, much of the time leaning on the big "tortoise," only now and then dropping to a quadrupedal amble. Their slower movements seemed to be setting the pace for all.

Another veiled person of the same general type, but taller and blue-veiled, came behind, moving strongly, so that the limbs often thrust through its veils. CP could definitely make out two pairs of upper "arms"; the lower pair seemed to be used for walking. Its upper body was upright so that, walking, it resembled a creature CP had only once seen a child's picture of—a being half-horse and half-human. But its face was neither horse nor human—the features were so snarled that only the big eyes, and four tall feathery protrusions that might be ears, or other sensory organs, could be identified.

Two more figures with gray pelts brought up the rear. One of them attracted CP's attention by swerving off the path into a pool of water, and drinking deeply with webbed hands held to a kind of bill or beak. She guessed that it might be at least partly aquatic. Its companion waited for it. Behind this one's shoulders were two hard-looking humps that might be vestigial wings.

The party was close now; CP had discarded the binoculars. As they passed the tree-moving turtles, the personages she thought of as the Senior Tortoise and its veiled companion paused, and the others halted with them.

There was a brief interchange, consisting of some short, voiced phrases mingled with odd, meaningful silences. CP could not tell which voices belonged to whom; only one was melodious, but they were not unpleasing. Nor did they sound tense, agitated, or hostile. She gleaned the notion that this visit was in some weird way routine, and also that the road had been constructed voluntarily, by nearby residents, perhaps.

Could it be that people were *used* to spaceships landing here? But no; the party gave no sign of familiarity with anything like *Calgary*.

Their first act was to tour deliberately around the ship—CP saw that the ground had been cleared around her while she slept—looking gravely at every detail. CP followed them around from inside. On impulse, when they could see both her and the remaining wing, she raised her hand and moved an aileron control.

There was a general, surprised backward start.

By this time, CP was sure that some at least were telepathic. She sent them the strongest feeling of friendship she could project, and then pictures of herself moving controls. The "kangaroo" types seemed to respond with eagerness, as did the "Senior Tortoise." They moved closer, eyeing her keenly. So CP spent a happy time moving and wiggling everything that functioned, at the same time naming it and its function through the speaker. The small red-veiled alien seemed particularly interested in her voice, often attempting to repeat words after her.

They all had no hesitation in touching anything and everything; the agile web-footed ones clambered over the remains of *Calgary*'s top, and all came up and peered into all the cabin ports by turn.

Several times CP stopped herself from trying to warn them not to approach the "hot" thrust vents, or the debris of the reactor chamber. It was hard to realize that any residual radioactivity from *Calgary* was as nothing compared to the normal blizzard of hard radiation just outside, in which these visitors had evolved and lived.

Presently the small red-veiled alien limped, or hobbled, to the extended speaker and laid a fragile, pale, apparently deformed hand on it. At the same time, a very clear image came to CP; she closed her eyes to concentrate on it, and "saw" herself with opening and moving mouth. The image flickered oddly. The alien had made the connection between her voice and the speaker. But how to transmit "yes" by mental imagery? She nodded her head vigorously—a meaningless gesture here, no doubt—and said verbally, "Yes! Yes. Uh . . . hello!," pointing to her mouth and the speaker.

The little alien made a peculiar sound; was that a laugh? Next moment its hand moved to the auditory pickup, and CP experienced something new—a strikingly sharp image of the microphone, followed by a literal blanking of the mind—indescribable. As if an invisible blindfold had descended. Next instant came the mike image again, and again the blank—and back to the image; faster and faster, these two impressions alternated in her mind, to a flicker sequence that made her dizzy.

But she grasped it—as clearly as a human voice, the alien was saying, "And this thing is—what?"

So that was how questions were asked!

How to answer? She tried everything she could think of, pointing to the alien, to her own ears (which were doubtless not ears to the alien), saying "Hello" repeatedly like a parrot, all the while trying to picture an alien's mouth speaking. She'd never seen the red-veiled mouth, so she imaged another's.

Something worked—with apparent eagerness, the small alien put its face to the mike, and nearly blasted CP from her chair with "ER-ROW! ER-ROW! ES!"

CP was childishly delighted. She and the alien exchanged several "Hellos" and "Errows" through speaker and mike.

But shortly a new question emerged. She began to receive a strengthening picture—as if from several minds joining in—of herself coming out of *Calgary* and moving among them. After a few moments of her nonresponse, this image began to alternate slowly with a scene of the aliens inside *Calgary* with her. Again, the two images alternated faster and faster, to confusing flashes. But the meaning was plain—"Will you come out, or shall we come in?"

It took her a long, laborious effort to try to transmit the impossibility. She concentrated hard on forming images of the port opening and air coming in, herself falling down, pictures of radiation (she hoped) coming from the ground. Suddenly, at those last pictures the old tortoise seemed to understand. He advanced and laid one heavy paw on *Calgary*, and then made a sweeping gesture that CP read as negation. Of course: *Calgary*, alone of most of this world, was inert, nonradioactive.

At this point they seemed to have had enough, or were tired; in very human fashion they drew off to sit in a group at the edge of the clearing with the tree-fellers, and produced packets of edibles. CP stared eagerly, wishing she could see and taste. As far as she could make out, most of them ate with more or less Earthlike mouths, but the veiled persons inserted their food beneath their throat veils.

Then the small red-clad alien seemed to notice her staring and CP suddenly felt her mouth and nose filled with an extraordinary alien sensation—neither good nor bad, but quite unknown—which must be the taste of what they were eating. She laughed again, and daringly transmitted a faint replica of the cheese-and-peanut-butter packet she was eating.

Refreshments were soon over. Now the large blue-veiled alien and the kangaroo types came forward to the window. Looking directly at CP, the veiled one stood up and made motions of turning. CP understood; it was her time to be inspected. Obediently she turned, extended an arm, opened her mouth to show her teeth, wiggled her fingers.

Then the veiled one raised her top arm, unfastened something, and deliberately let drop a veil. The implication was plain: undress. For a moment CP was overcome with an ugly memory of Meich, the countless other humiliations she had undergone. She hesitated. But the alien eyes were insistent and seemed friendly. When CP didn't move, the big alien pulled off another veil, exposing this time its own bare and furless belly and haunches. A strong feeling of reassurance came to her—of course, to these people her body was as neutral as a mollusk or a map. She unzipped her suit and stepped out of it and her underclothes. At the same time, as if to encourage her, the alien removed its own upper-body covering. CP noticed that the others in its group had turned tactfully away.

CP was amazed—in the crotch where human sex and excretory organs would be, the alien had nothing but smooth muscle. But its chest region was as complex as a group of sea creatures; valves, lips, unidentifiable moist flaps and protrusions—clearly its intimate parts. CP could form no idea of its gender, if any.

Not to be outdone in scientific detachment, CP demonstrated her own nude self, and made an attempt at transmitting images of the human reproductive process. She got nothing in reply—or rather, nothing she could interpret. She and the alien apparently diverged so widely here that thought could not carry across the gulf. Only excretion seemed sufficiently similar to be at least referrable to.

At length the alien gave it up, resuming its own veiling and indicating that CP should do likewise.

Then the whole group gathered around her windows and CP was astounded. Abruptly she was assailed by a thought-image that said, as plainly as a shout, "Go away!"

The image was of *Calgary* again taking to the air, and spiraling up and away. The feeling-tone wasn't hostile or threatening, merely practical. If she couldn't live here, she should go elsewhere.

"But I can't!"

Desperately she pointed to the wrecked wing, sent images of the empty fuel reserve.

A counter-image, of *Calgary* being literally lifted off and flung out of atmosphere, came back. Did they propose that the same presumably "mental" force that had slowed her should lift her back to orbit?

"No—no! It wouldn't work!" She sent images of *Calgary*, released in space, falling helplessly back upon them.

But the thought-send persisted. "You-go-away"—and the sequence repeated itself.

Then CP had an idea. But how to indicate time here in this never-changing world? Oh, for an hourglass! Finally she gathered up a handful of crumbs, broken glass, and other small debris of the wreck and let them trickle slowly and deliberately from one hand to the other. She held up her fingers, counting off a dozen or so—and acted out a scene of herself strangling in foul air, collapsing and dying. As an afterthought, she tried to express a feeling of contentment, even joy.

The Senior Tortoise got it first, and seemed to enlighten the others.

She would not be here long alive.

There ensued a brief colloquy among the aliens. Then one after the other came to her window, put up its "hands" to take a look around, and seemed to transmit something grave, and faint. She was not even sure she was receiving. The old tortoise-person came last, its great hands heavy on the glass as it shaded out reflections to look in. From it CP was sure something emanated to her. But she could not name it.

Then they all turned and walked, ambled, or hopped away as they had come, taking the "Watcher" with them. The tree-fellers brought up the rear. CP stared after them, surprised.

They had simply departed, leaving her alone to die.

Well, what more could she have expected?

But it was strange; no curiosity about the stars, for instance, nor whence she had come.

And what had they been trying to impart, there at the last? Of course: "Good-bye."

"Good-bye," CP said through the speaker softly, into the alien air.

Then began an unadmittedly lonely time, waiting to die there in the beauty of the swamp. CP began to wish it wasn't so viewless and closed in. She decided that soon, before the air was all gone, she would go out, and try to climb to some sort of view before she died.

On impulse, she set her Earth-day timer, which had ceased in the crash, to manual-battery operation. She who had fled the world of Earth forever yet had the whim to perish on Earth's time. Only so much of nostalgia persisted. That and her little copybook of poems.

She had long since smoothed out and repaired the captain's damage. Only one page was lost. She occupied herself in reconstructing it from memory:

With delicate mad hands against his sordid bars,
Surely he hath his posies, which they tear and wine—
Those—*something*—wisps of straw that miserably line
His strait caged universe, whereon the dull world stares.
Pedant and pitiful. Oh,—*something—something*—
Know they what dreams divine
Something—like enchanted wine—
And make his melancholy germane to the stars?
Oh lamentable brother, if these pity thee,
Am I not fain of all thy lost eyes promise me?
Half a fool's kingdom, far from—*something*—all their days vanity.
Oh, better than mortal flowers
Thy moon-kissed roses seem:
Better than love or sleep,
The star-crowned solitude of thine oblivious hours!*

Much was muddled, but she had the essential lines. They had kept her company all those years behind her sordid bars. Well, she had had the stars, and now she had the moon-kissed roses, and the fool's kingdom. Presently she would open the port and go out to possess it. . . .

---

* "To One in Bedlam," Ernest Dowson, *ca.* 1875, as all SF readers should know.

It was late on Day Six of the perhaps fifteen left to her that someone else came. She had long ceased to watch the path, but now she felt a tug at her attention. At first there was nothing, and she almost turned away. And then, in the far distance, she made out a single, oddly shaped figure. Quick, the binoculars. It became an alien something like the former Watcher, but ruddy and—yes—carrying or being ridden by a much smaller alien on its back. More—she saw the small alien was legless, with very tiny arms. She had the strong impression of fatigue, of a long-distant goal reached. They had, she thought, come a long, long way.

Then she understood: this world was huge, and she knew nothing of their means of transport, if any. Perhaps those who wished to see *Calgary* must walk so, even from the far side?

She watched, scarcely daring to blink, as these new aliens continued their weary way toward her into naked-eye view. The larger alien raised its head, and must have seen her waiting. She was quite unprepared for the jolt of feeling that shook her—like a shout of welcome and joy.

That she still lived! Had this alien been fearful it was too late, that she would have died before he or she could get here? That must be it.

As the alien came closer yet, she noticed an oddity about the big one's head—where others had had upstanding "ears" or antlerlike antennae, this one had large, triangular velvety flaps that drooped toward its eyes. Where had she seen these before? Oh God—aching half with laughter, half pain, she recognized—the large, folded, triangular earflaps of a pig! And the alien's muzzle was pugged, like hers.

Dear stars, what cosmic joke was this?

The rest of the alien's body was not at all porcine, but seemed worn and gaunt from travel and bearing the weight of its companion. Built more ruggedly than the original Watcher, its pelt was dusty red and it was wearing a thin vest that covered the chest area and tied behind as a knot which its rider clung to. A cloak was also tied around it. Its eyes were not abnormally large, more like pale human eyes without visible whites. Walking quadrupedally, or walk-hopping as it was now, its shoulders were lower than its rump, and the stumpy tail stuck straight out behind, possibly from excitement.

As it approached *Calgary*, its gaze shifted from her to the wrecked ship, and images of the starry night of space filled her head, alternating occasionally with a vision of the lavender cloud ceiling overhead, and the 200-kilometer thickness of cloud that had blanked her view coming down—and then back again to the stars—the stars as she had seen them in a hundred shifting views.

She began to receive a curious new impression.

When the creature—or person—came slowly right to *Calgary*, it sat up as far as it could without spilling its rider, and laid first one hand and then the other on *Calgary*'s broken wing. She became sure.

This was reverence. Here was a longing for the stars that filled its soul, the stars from which it was closed away forever by the implacable, neverending cloud. As plainly as speech, its gesture said, "This—this came from the stars!"

When it raised its gaze to her, its face had changed to a strange openmouthed pursing, like a child trying to pronounce "th"; denoting she knew not what, until she received the image of what must be herself, weirdly exaggerated, among the stars; and understood, from her own experience.

"You—you, an intelligent alien—have come here *from the stars!* Life is out there, beyond our heavy sky!"

It was almost as if it were worshiping *Calgary* and herself—no, it was just that she and it were the most precious, exciting things in life to it. Perhaps, alone of its kind, it had insisted that there was life beyond the sky? And was now proved right? She had met a human astronomer who would have felt this way.

The alien had now clambered up onto the wing stub to peer in, pushing back its beautiful ears to see better. Close up, its muzzle was complex and pleasingly furred. As it alternately inspected the cabin and gazed at her, its small companion clambered off onto the wing, agilely pulling itself by its shrunken arms. She saw that it had a large, thick, apparently partly prehensile tail, which served to boost it along in place of the missing legs. Its bare skin was scurfy and wrinkled; CP understood that it was very old. It seemed to be interested in the length, the width, the sheer size of *Calgary*.

But the larger alien's head kept sagging; it was spent with exhaustion, she saw its eyelids droop, pull open again, and reclose despite itself. It sank down into the uncomfortable corner between the wing stub and the window, not even untying its cloak, looking toward her as long as it could stay conscious. For a moment CP feared it was ill or dying, but received a faint image of it waking up animatedly.

She wished she could at least undo its cloak to cushion its head. A moment later the little old alien dragged itself over and did just that, as if "hearing" her.

Then it turned its bright eyes on her, far less tired than its friend. It seemed to have something to convey: images of herself, her hands as she fought *Calgary* down, came to her. What could this mean?

As if exasperated, the little being pulled itself to the remains of the booster rocket by the wing base; showing an odd combination of the activity of a child with great age. There it patted the booster, pointing first to her and then to itself. This was the first time she'd seen anyone here point manually.

Images of *Calgary* descending came again. She was baffled. Sensing this, the old creature seized a stout twig lying on the wing, raised it high, and dropped it.

The twig fell briskly—then slowed, slowed, halted before touching down —and as she stared, it reversed course and slowly rose upward, back to the alien's hand.

CP's eyes smarted with staring, she had consciously to blink. What had she seen if not movement-by-remote-will—telekinesis!

The act seemed to have tired the alien, but it looked at her intently, holding up one hand. In human gesture-language this would say, "Attend!"

CP "attended." The alien screwed up its small, wrinkled face, closed its eyes.

And *Calgary* rocked. A single startling lurch.

There was no question of some physical shift of weight doing it—the ship took a pull so strong she could hear mud sucking under the crushed hull.

She had to believe.

Incredible as it was, this tiny old being was, or exerted, the force that had slowed *Calgary* and brought her safely in. Somehow it had reached out all those thousands of kilometers, to the heavy, hurtling ship, and slowed it.

Saved her life.

She didn't know how to say thank you, even to show gratitude. She could only point to it and bow her head ignorantly, stammering, "Thank you, oh thank you!" through the speaker. In the end she actually knelt on the tilted deck, but was not satisfied.

The little old being shied away from the speaker, but seemed to understand that she understood. It was panting with fatigue. But after a few moments' rest it did something new. Advancing to the speaker, it pointed to itself and said loudly, "Tadak."

Luckily it spoke loudly enough to reach the mike, too.

"Tadak," it said again with more self-pointing.

Its name, the first one she had known!

"Tadak. Hello, Tadak!" she said eagerly. But it seemed exasperated again. Of course: she pointed to herself. "Cee Pee."

It imitated her roughly, too faint to hear well. She was distracted, but her longing to show her gratitude had produced an idea. It would lose her several liters of air; she reproached herself for even the automatic thought. Too much—in return for her life?

Motioning to Tadak, she laid hold of her most precious human possession, the golden flight emblem pinned to her collar. Tadak watched intently as she demonstrated how to pin and secure it.

Then she crawled under the console, disconnected an old lubricant-intake valve, and rapped loudly on the inside cover to guide its attention. When she heard taps outside, she placed the pin in the opening and recapped it. A considerable struggle to communicate ensued; this world—or Tadak—did not seem familiar with toggles and screw threads. In the end she heard a fearful grinding sound, and guessed that it had used its TK to rip the cap straight off.

Tadak crawled weakly back into view, panting and clutching the shiny trinket with apparent reverence in its old gnarled fingers, first to its chest, then over its upturned face as though marveling. Then its bright eyes went sideways to CP, carrying an impression of both joy and—yes—mischief. The old face puckered hard.

—And *Calgary* jumped again, higher than before. It came down with a jolt that made CP a trifle nervous.

A protesting grunt came from the sleeping alien by her window.

But Tadak was really tired now. It seemed to take all its remaining strength to hump up to where its friend lay and to bed down, too. One tiny hand twitched up at her and slumped. CP was left to watch over the sleep of her new acquaintances.

She felt herself drifting toward sleep, too. This must be a world without the dangers normal to hers; its inhabitants seemed to have no fear of lying vulnerable in the open. With Tadak quiescent, she could see how very old and frail it was.

Her drowsy attention and wonder settled on the head and softly folded "ears" of the larger alien. In all her dream life in the Empire of the Pigs she had never imagined a pig head of such beauty and dignity. There was a shining metallic chain about its neck too, with a medallion of some sort. And its poncho was beautifully embroidered. Evidently her wondrous new visitors weren't paupers, if such things existed here. Still studying them, she fell asleep and dreamed of stars, mixed with her old story of safe arrival home in the Empire.

They were all awakened by more visitors.

By the time she was conscious, the newcomers had filtered into the clearing and quietly surrounded *Calgary*. It was a spoken utterance by the open microphone that awakened her to confront two strange yellow-colored rotund shapes right by the window, squinting in at her. Beyond them she glimpsed pale or dark alien forms on every side.

She reacted with automatic panic, diving under the console. Police? Army? Enemy of some kind?

But a cautious peek out reassured her.

Her two new "friends" were greeting the arrivals calmly, even joyfully. While the flap-eared alien raised its arms to touch palms with one group of newcomers, Tadak clambered onto the carapace of a large turtletype, and was being carried around *Calgary*, to hand-greet other arrivals. She noticed there were different nuances of position and length of contact in the double-palm greeting, like different human handshakes for old friends or new, formal meetings. She saw, too, that most of the newcomers looked travel-worn; only a few seemed fresh. It was difficult to count, but she decided that about thirty strangers had arrived. Here she noticed a novelty —subdued voices were to be heard all around. Evidently many of those new aliens talked in verbal speech. Had she been meeting only mental-projection specialists?

As they saw she was awake, voices rose excitedly and they began to gather around her window and settle down. Clearly these weren't idle tourists. A meeting of some sort impended. Perhaps some ultimatum or scheme to urge her off-planet?

CP splashed her hands and face hurriedly, conserving the water for a second use, and retired to the wastes cubby. When she closed the door on herself, the wave of general disappointment was so strong it reached her. She grinned to herself; maybe, later, she would abandon all her Earth ways. Maybe.

Snatching up a breakfast bar and self-heating kaffy, she came back to the window. Her two new acquaintances had stationed themselves just outside, evidently as her official translators or keepers. All right. Now let's have it.

A truly strange-looking large alien advanced and held up its palms in formal greeting. It was dark ochre-orange and blue, wrinkled, and extravagantly horned, and it squinted. Its body was such a confusing combination of sluglike membranes and legs out behind that she never quite managed to separate it from its complex clothing and equipment. It was one of the road-worn—CP received a subliminal impression that others had waited for it as spokesman or leader.

Evidently it could mind-speak, perhaps assisted by one of the two on the wing. A misty image formed behind her eyes; she closed them to concentrate, and "saw" herself back in *Calgary*. She was—yes—going from port to port, scanning over the whole sky. This was the long, Voiceless last period, after the Empire had faded out, when she was contentedly—but systematically—studying the visible universe. The image turned to her star charts.

On impulse she opened her eyes and pulled the real charts from their locker.

The impression of excited joy that came to her was unmistakable. Unmistakable too, now, was an odd "tone" to the communications, especially those from the antlered one. Familiar!

While Tadak and its large friend helped her explain why she couldn't pass the charts out now, but they'd have them soon, she searched her memory for that "tone," and found it.

Why, it was these aliens to whom she had been "transmitting" all those days after she was on course. They were too weak-voiced to reach her, but she had felt not alone, "all right." Who could they be?

Oh! While she'd been puzzling, a new, very strong phenomenon had emerged: above and around every new head in the clearing came a small halo of stars. Some were weak, barely floating pinpoints of light, others were a full-blown circlet of blackness lit with glory, before all faded.

The astronomers of this world had come to her.

But how could this sealed sunless world, surely without space flight, have "astronomers"? How could they ever have found out the stars at all, unless perhaps the clouds cleared once in a while, like an old story she'd read? Here she was wrong, but she only discovered it later, during one of the most exhausting yet pleasant twenty hours of her life.

They wanted to know everything.

Each had formed its one most vital question, each in turn would walk, hobble, crawl, hop forward to "ask" it. But first the big antlered speaker "asked" a question so comprehensive that it obviated many other planned ones.

An image of a starfield bloomed in her mind, stars of all the types she had unwittingly "shown" them from *Calgary*, each clear and specific before merging into the whole.

This great image was followed by a startlingly strong blankout. Then the stars came back, then the blank, faster to the now familiar flicker-meaning:

"The stars are—what?"

Whew.

She had to explain the universe wordlessly to a race whose concepts and measures—if any—of distance, motion, forces, matter, heat she didn't know.

Afterward, she recalled mostly a mishmash, but she thought she must have given quite a performance. This was, after all, her own beloved study, at an amateur level.

She remembered first trying to convey some notion of energies and distances. She imaged this world's—Auln's—surface from above, then using old tape-teach effects, she "receded" down to a lavender point against the stars, then "pulled" one of the nearer small stars close for comparison, and showed the wild atomic fires of its surface compared with the colder weak processes of Auln. She "built" a star up out of a gas cloud, changed it through its life to red giant and nova, built another, richer one from the debris and condensed its planets. She "started life" on the planet, gave them a glimpse of her own Earth—typical astronomers, they cared little for this—then sent it receding again and built up the Milky Way, and galaxies beyond it, attempted the expanding universe.

It was there she had paused, exhausted.

While she rested and ate, someone sent her the answer to her question: how did they know of the stars?

She received an image of a new sort—framed! Multiply framed, in fact, frame within frame. The image itself was oddly blurred in detail. Sharp, however, was a view of extraordinary metal wreckage, unidentifiable stuff strewn at a deep gash in the ground. Much was splashed with brilliant green, and there was a central ball or cylinder—no, wait, a *head*, not human. Had these aliens actually attempted space flight?

No. The framed image jumped to show a fireball streaking down through the clouds, then back to the green-smeared head. Wrecked as it was, it did seem generically unlike anyone she had seen on Auln. As if to settle her problem, "her" ruddy, flop-eared alien bent and pulled a wrap off its leg, showing a healing cut. Its blood was red, like hers.

So another, a *real* alien had crashed here! And long ago, too. The frames, the blur suggested many transmissions of the scene. But this space alien was obviously dead. How, then—

Into the image came a head like the beaked "aquatics" among her first visitors. Huge-eyed, somehow rather special-seeming. It laid its head against the dead astronaut's. And the image dissolved to faint views of the starry sky from space, an incoming glimpse of Auln, strangeness.

Generations back, then, they had learned of outside space, the stars—by probing a dead brain!

She was so bemused by this that she barely attended to another, clearly contemporary image sequence until a motion like wing beats caught her. She reclosed her eyes in time to "see" a birdlike creature flapping desperately, up—up—it seemed to be driven, or lifted, higher than its wings could sustain it, higher than it could breathe. The image changed. On the ground, a far-"sighted" alien was looking through the dying bird's eyes, seeing weirdly focused images of thinning, darkening cloud. Just before the bird eyes died, a rift opened above it; blackness lit by two bright stars was briefly there.

A living telescope! But the "tone" in which these sequences came through suggested some sadness or disapproval. CP thought that perhaps they used this ruthless technique only rarely and reluctantly. It certainly wasn't sustained enough to be useful, but it sufficed to reassure them that the stars *were* there.

The ensuing hours and hours of sending, trying to understand queries, to invent visual ways to convey the barely communicable, not to omit too much of importance, to share in effect all she knew of the universe, condensed in memory into a great blur, of which she recalled only two things.

The first was rooting out the magnificent star and galaxy color photos poor Don Lamb had collected, and pasting them up inside the ports. This was a sensation; the crowding nearly did tip *Calgary*.

The other was her own graphic warning of all that could happen on Auln if Earthmen or another aggressive species found them.

This changed the mood to a great sobriety, in which she sensed that the thought was not entirely new to all. She sent all she could on human nuclear space bombardment, robot weapons, and air-to-ground attack, which seemed to be attentively received. The idea worried her, but she had done all she could. This telekinetic, mind-probing, perhaps mind-deceiving race might be able to devise adequate defense . . . How she hoped it!

And finally, after more than an Earth-day's wakefulness, they left as abruptly as they'd come, each giving her the two-handed gesture of farewell. Tadak left too, riding on the carapace of a strong young shelled one. But to her relief and pleasure, his larger, flop-eared friend seemed prepared to stay. Indeed, she didn't acknowledge to herself how carefully she had watched for signs of his intentions. It was peculiarly, deeply important to her.

As she watched them struggle up the road, hearing the last of their rather high-pitched, Asiatic converse, it seemed to her that one or two turned into a side path near the ship and disappeared behind a rise. Her attention was drawn to this by seeing the others pause and hand over cloaks, or packets of supplies. Perhaps these were headed another way, by a long route; she forgot it.

When they had all departed and the path was empty, the alien whom she was beginning timidly to think of as a friend came up onto the wing stub at her window. It looked at her, the same look she'd seen at the very first. But now it was looking solely into her eyes, long, deep, searchingly. Peculiar images, apparently just random memories, came to her; the dormitory of her old schooldays, the streets of the Enclave. Her first real desk. And always in them was a figure she reluctantly recognized: herself.

She began to tremble.

These were not . . . memories.

More images of the past. And weaving through them, a gleaming red-gold cap—could that be her hair?

No one but herself knew of all these past scenes.

None but one other.

Could this be—was she at last looking at the one who—was it this alien being who had "spoken" to her all her life? Was this her Voice?

She trembled harder, uncontrollably.

Then her "friend" reared up and placed both thin palms on the window by its head.

Cold struck her to her heart.

She tried to tell herself that this was just to see her better through the port. But that couldn't be, she realized dully; the light was not that bright, the vitrex wasn't that reflective.

This must be—oh please, no, don't let it be like all the others, a final, formal good-bye. Not from the one who held her life, who had been with her lifelong, through all the dark nights, the pain. Who had said, "Come."

The image of herself also holding her hands to the window came urgently to her. She was expected to respond.

Oh please, she pleaded to no one, not good-bye from *you*, too. Not you, my Voice . . . Don't leave me alone. To die. Grief pushed huge tears past all her guards. To distract herself, she thought how rude all the others must have thought her when she failed to respond to them.

This one really wanted her to respond properly. Evidently it had enough personal feeling for her to make this important. Well, she would, in a moment, when she had herself under better control.

A thud shook the wing. Humanlike, but with far more strength, the alien stamped. Perhaps it was impatient to rejoin the others? It stamped again, harder, and slapped both hands on the window, sending a peremptory image of her holding her hands up against the vitrex, matching its own.

All right then. Good-bye.

Blind with unshed tears, she stood up and spread her palms against the window opposite the red-and-cream blurs. The alien made an exasperated sound and moved its hands to cover hers as exactly as possible.

And something—began to flow. It was as if the vitrex grew hot, or not hot but charged. Almost alive. CP shook so hard her hands slid lower; feeling another stamp from outside, she tried to replace them. The "current" flowed again, carrying with it a bloom of feelings, images, wordless knowledge, she didn't know what, all bursting through her from their matched palms.

The alien's eyes caught and held hers, and slowly it brought its hands closer to its head. Hers followed jerkily.

Here the feelings strengthened, became overpowering. She sank to her knees; the alien followed, still holding her palm to palm, through five centimeters of hard vitrex. She couldn't remove her hands if she chose.

But she wouldn't have broken that contact for life itself. She was learning—she was understanding, oh incredulously—that all her life—

Suddenly a strong, rich sound from the audio startled her: The alien's voice.

It had to be repeated before she understood.

"Ca-rol."

Her name. It was known to no one here.

"Ca-rol . . . ehy-ou . . . Iye . . ."

Unmistakable, though strange and jerky here, she recognized her Voice.

There was no need now for the alien to explain that his gesture was not a good-bye, but communion.

But there was more to it than that. Ludicrously, neither of them had her word for it, because it was a word CP had never had occasion to use. It seemed important, for a while, to find it. They went at it the long way round, through her feeling for the stars, and for a rat she had once briefly been allowed to make a pet of. The recognition, the realization scared CP so badly that her teeth rattled. But the alien "held" her, insistently pressed the communication on her, out of its own need. In the end she had to know it fully.

Know that she—Carol-Page-Snotface-CP-Cold Pig—had walked all her days and nights embraced by love. Alien love, at first for a little-alien-among-the-stars, but soon, soon for her alone.

She had never been alone.

She, Carol-Page-Snotface-et-cetera was the Beloved . . . and always had been.

As this rosy, fur-clad, soft-eared, glowing-eyed one was of course hers, though she had never used the word. Her lifelong love.

When two long-parted, unacknowledged lovers meet at last and reveal their love, it is always the same. Even though a wall of vitrex came between them.

Long intervals of speechless communion, absorbing the miracle of You Too Love . . . that You Are Here, that Me + You = One. In other intervals her lover showed her all this world of Auln, about the Viewers, about the early training to become a Star Caller. The alien was still young too, she gathered. It had been on its first Star Search when contact with her occurred. She wanted to be shown everything, she couldn't get enough of images, even trivia of her lover's life. All hers was of course known in detail to her alien Voice.

As the current between them strengthened, she took to thinking of the alien as "he," meaning no more by it than that "it" was insupportable and "she" or "sister" was not quite appropriate in a human sense. Like herself, she found the alien had never borne young. Besides, there were now no other "hes" in CP's universe.

Twice she touched on the violent acts that had brought her here, and each time the current jumped almost to real pain. Strongly, oh how strongly he supported them and her!

Rather wildly, they both sought ways of closer contact, ending whole-body-plastered to the vitrex. Neither could bear to cease contact long enough to eat much. Vaguely she thought that accounted for a slight unnoticed ill feeling.

Then came the day when her timer blatted so insistently that she saw it was past the red mark. The illness she'd ignored was real.

Calgary's air had ended.

It was time to come out—to him. She explained what he already knew, and received grave assent.

When the huge port swung open, the air that rushed upon her was impossibly sweet and fresh—spring air such as CP'd never breathed before. *Calgary*'s foulness made a fog at the port. The first thing she saw through it was his hand, stretched to her. He led her out, to a different end.

Again, when two lovers win to real bodily contact, it is always the same. But these two were still separated, not by a mere wall, but by being prisoned in wholly different bodies with wholly different needs.

Unnecessary to follow all their efforts in those first hours. Sufficient that they learned two things. First, mutual laughter, and second, what all Earthbound lovers find, that *nothing* suffices.

They blamed this on their differences, but they suspected the truth. Where love has been intense and silent and all-consuming, only the impossible, the total merger into one, could slake its fires.

On this world, such a consummation was only a little less impossible than on Earth. In the end, they found the physical palm-to-palm contact deepest and most poignant, and they stayed so.

Outward events were few and slight, but the most important in the universe. While she was still feeling wonderfully well, he led her up a nearby hill to a small glade with a superb view. She saw in reality the glorious self-lit colors of great Auln's cultivated lands, its wildernesses and rivers and, in the distance, a small city or town, the sky overhead reflecting all. Behind them lay the luminous sea, from which blew a gentle breeze, and where she glimpsed strange sea creatures tumbling. Presently her lover lured a few of Auln's "birds" and other strange or charming creatures to them.

At one point she flinched about her nose, and he "told" her in pictures how his own flopped ears were viewed as deplorable. Even on this world where individuals mutated so wildly as scarcely to seem of the same species, by chance all but a few heads bore upright ears or other sensors. His own rounded head was almost the sole feature seen by all as ugly. This revelation caused much time to be occupied by caressing reassurances.

She was weakening fast, but pain seemed absent or muffled for a while. Her exposed pale skin burned and blistered shockingly by the second day, despite the gauzy cover he had made for her by tearing out the lining of his cloak. The burns did not hurt much either. Later, when she saw him wince, she began to suspect why. They had a battle of wills, in which hers was no match for his trained one.

On the third day her beautiful hair was falling out in sheaves. He collected it, strand by strand, smoothed and kept it.

That day she had the whim to cut their names on a stone, and could scarcely bear it when he left her to bring one. Amazed and delighted by the novelty, they realized she had never known his name—Cavaná. She said it, sang it, whispered it a thousand times, built it into all her memories. Finally she did, with help, scratch *Cavaná* and *Carol* onto the stone, and tried to make other lines, but was too weak. He never left her again.

By this time they were lying with their heads on a cushioned log, their hands as if grown together.

One of the last things she noticed was the amusingly fluffed, mossy little vine that made the log so comfortable. He told her its future.

The Fountain had flowed since the Viewers had been here last. Two farmers from Pyenro were now putting in part of their town duty clearing vine from the alien sky-box. They passed on news of two new young ones, and a possible animal-sickness the Viewers should keep track of.

Their task inside the now open sky-box busied the Viewers for some time. Old Andoul, of course, could not enter. While the others were occupied, she communed effortfully by sound with the three sky-obsessed ones who had remained here. They had stayed discreetly out of sight of Cavaná and the alien, but had caught nothing of consequence in that time. However, the open sky-box had given them much of overwhelming interest, including a sheaf of extraordinary, flat, flexible, permanent images, which they called "stars." They asked Andoul and Askelon, a new young Viewer, to view them. This they did. The images were of nothing recognizable, being largely black-spangled, but oddly moving in addition to their fascinating new technique.

The farmers had widened the summit path for Andoul. When all was finished below, the Viewers started up. It was steep. The deformed child Mir-Mir, who was so young it hadn't yet chosen gender, had to clamber up on Andoul's back, tucking up its red veils and complaining aloud, "If you accept any more jewelry, *Saro* Andoul, I'll never find a place to sit. I believe you do it on purpose."

"Speak properly, child," Andoul told it. "And if you eat any more no one will be able to carry you . . . Aah! I View." All halted, and Mir-Mir slid off.

They had arrived at a pretty little glade near the summit. An elongated mound, green-covered by vine, lay with one end on a green-clad log.

Looking more closely, all could see that the form was in fact two, closely apposed and entwined at the log end, where lateral mounding indicated arms.

Xerona and Ekstá advanced to it, squatted, and placed their webbed hands gently on what might be two vine-covered heads pressed tight together.

After a moment both touched one body and Xerona sent them all an image.

"Cavaná," Mir-Mir said aloud. Andoul grunted in disapproval, both of Mir-Mir's vocalizing and what was in its mind. Ferdil, one of the three very silent, hardworking Viewers who resembled Cavaná, was actually Cavaná's cousin.

"See the bigger legs," Mir-Mir said defiantly. "Poor Cavaná, so ugly. But she lived in the sky!"

The two beaked Viewers were indicating the other form, transmitting a rather sketchy image of the orange-maned alien. They were all silent a moment, refining and supplementing the image. Finally Askelon sighed.

"I did ill," he mourned aloud. "It was my responsibility." He sent short images of himself inspecting the nude alien, and himself now, downcast with both hands drooped from the wrists. Shame.

Old Andoul gently corrected that image to raise the hands. "We all must begin," she said in words. "None of us considered it very important. Perhaps it isn't. Although—" She lapsed back to imagery, showed the alien in a framing of color that was short-speed for "Person of perhaps great soul," and then jumped to sketched-in multitudes of other red-headed aliens diving upon them with fantastic sky-boxes and explosions of flame.

The other Viewers sighed, too. Askelon revived slightly. Ferdil and her two friends went over by the feet of the dead ones, and gazed down at the hidden form of Cavaná, locked in death with her alien love. When Ferdil gave the sign of formal last farewell, the others, after a polite interval, did likewise.

Meanwhile Xerona and Ekstá were hard at work, their own heads against first one dead head and then the other. At length they arose, their expressions very sober.

"Nothing . . . of interest or use to others," Ekstá said. "Cavaná . . . took much of the alien's pain."

Xerona was trying to hide weeping, but missed an indigo tear at his throat gills.

"Ah, look!" Askelon, scanning hard to redeem himself, had come upon an odd corner of rock. When he lifted and cleared it, they saw a flat stone with chasings or scratches on it.

"Alien writing!" exclaimed Mir-Mir, hobbling to it. "Ferdil!"

Ferdil and her companions were already Viewing the stone. With a confirmatory transmission to old Andoul, she produced a small container from her belly pack, inserted a straw, and skillfully blew a mist of moss-inhibiting bacteria over the stone. Then she set it on edge beyond the lovers' heads.

Unexpectedly, Ferdil spoke in words.

"I knew Cavaná well, we were deep friends in the early days, before . . . She had only just chosen gender when she made Contact . . . Her love was very severe; changeless, unremitting. Almost a sickness. But she left us much. And one thing more—we know now her communication was real. Many doubted. But the one she Called really heard, answered, and with much effort came."

The others were silent, admitting her right to important verbal speech.

Around them Auln lay in beauty, under the eternal, soft-colored cloud ceiling that was their sky. The plain in view here was vast, bioluminescent to the high horizon. Nothing had ever changed here, nothing would. No light of day, no dark of night, no summer, neither fall nor winter. Only their own works, like the *sumlac* fields, changed the tints reflected in the cloud. People came from great distances to watch the shifts at planting time and harvest, and for their enjoyment the farmers synchronized many crops. Now the sky carried pink bands that came from the simultaneous channeling of water into the *millin* lanes.

Characteristically, it was the child Mir-Mir who broke the silence as they started to descend.

"I am going to change, and become a Star Caller!"

"Oh, child, you don't know what you're saying!" Askelon exclaimed involuntarily. "Look at the life Callers have, they must give up everything to Search and Search—and if they find and focus, they are—well—" He paused, gestured back at the mounds of the dead.

"Doomed!" finished Mir-Mir melodramatically.

Proper transmissions now came from all sides from so many fellow Viewers at once that they blurred. But it understood that this was all discouragement, dismal images of a Star Caller's totally dedicated narrow prison plus Mir-Mir's own flightiness.

"No. I think I really mean this," Mir-Mir said soberly. "I'm not going to become a very good Viewer. And I have this different feeling"—Mir-Mir put its head up to look raptly skyward, stumbled, and almost fell—"not just since this. Before. I didn't say it. I think I . . . I think I'm capable of that love." It had halted them all and was rubbing the hurt, twisted little legs with its frail hands.

Old Andoul spoke, surprising them all.

"I too have felt. Long ago . . . a hint of love. The love of all that is alien. Of the stars. But I believe that with me it was too generalized. Those who Call must focus, and so lose everything to perhaps gain one . . . More, in my youth we were not quite certain even that the stars were there, that it was not delusion. Think hard till you are sure, child. But more Callers are not unnecessary, now . . . and speaking of now we must move along."

"Yes," said Ekstá severely, pushing on at a determined waddle as he sent brisk images of the sessions now beginning at Amberamou, and the urgent matter of the flying herd. As he passed Mir-Mir, he said, not unkindly, "Auln knows, Child, you're loud enough!"

Presently the path was empty; summit and *Calgary*'s hollow lay silent again. Above, more salmon-colored rivers streamed through the clouds, as the great farm channels filled. The pink light touched the stone, on which were scratched human letters, trailing off unfinished:

CAVANÁ + CAROL
OF LOVE & OXYGE

Mir-Mir's intentions held. Sometime later, somewhere a man or alien would turn his gaze up to the stars with ardent longing, would begin to imagine he could hear . . .

BEAM US HOME

Hobie's parents might have seen the first signs if they had been watching about eight-thirty on Friday nights. But Hobie was the youngest of five active bright-normal kids. Who was to notice one more uproar around the TV?

A couple of years later, Hobie's Friday-night battles shifted to 10 P.M. and then his sisters got their own set. Hobie was growing fast then. In public he featured chiefly as a tanned streak on the tennis courts and a ninety-ninth percentile series of math grades. To his parents, Hobie featured as the one without problems. This was hard to avoid in a family that included a diabetic, a girl with an IQ of 185 and another with controllable petit mal, and a would-be ski star who spent most of his time in a cast. Hobie's own IQ was in the fortunate 140s, the range where you're superior enough to lead, but not too superior to be followed. He seemed perfectly satisfied with his communications with his parents, but he didn't use them much.

Not that he was in any way neglected when the need arose. The time he got staph in a corneal scratch, for instance, his parents did a great job of supporting him through the pain bit and the hospital bit and so on. But they couldn't know all the little incidents. Like the night when Hobie called so fiercely for Dr. McCoy that a young intern named McCoy went in and joked for half an hour with the feverish boy in his dark room.

To the end, his parents probably never understood that there was anything to understand about Hobie. And what was to see? His tennis and his model rocket collection made him look almost too normal for the small honors school he went to first.

Then his family moved to an executive bedroom suburb where the school system had a bigger budget than Monaco and a soccer team loaded with National Merit Science finalists. Here Hobie blended right in with the scenery. One more healthy, friendly, polite kid with bright gray eyes under a blond bowl-cut and very fast with any sort of ball game.

The brightest eyes around him were reading *The Double Helix* to find out how to make it in research, or marking up the Dun & Bradstreet flyers. If Hobie stood out at all, it was only that he didn't seem to be worried about making it in research or any other way, particularly. But that fitted in, too. Those days a lot of boys were standing around looking as if they couldn't believe what went on, as if they were waiting for—who knows?— a better world, their glands, something. Hobie's faintly aghast expression was not unique. Events like the installation of an armed patrol around the school enclave were bound to have a disturbing effect on the more sensitive kids.

People got the idea that Hobie *was* sensitive in some indefinite way. His usual manner was open but quiet, tolerant of a put-on that didn't end.

His adviser did fret over his failure to settle on a major field in time for the oncoming threat of college. First his math interest seemed to evaporate after the special calculus course, although he never blew an exam. Then he switched to the precollege anthropology panel the school was trying. Here he made good grades and acted very motivated, until the semester when the visiting research team began pounding on sampling techniques and statistical significance. Hobie had no trouble with things like Chi square, of course. But after making his A in the final he gave them his sweet, unbelieving smile and faded. His adviser found him spending a lot of hours polishing a six-inch telescope lens in the school shop.

So Hobie was tagged as some kind of an underachiever, but nobody knew what kind because of those grades. And something about that smile bothered them; it seemed to stop sound.

The girls liked him, though, and he went through the usual phases rather fast. There was the week he and various birds went to thirty-five drive-in movies. And the month he went around humming "Mrs Robinson" in a meaningful way. And the warm, comfortable summer when he and his then-girl and two other couples went up to Stratford, Ontario, with sleeping bags to see the Czech multimedia thing.

Girls regarded him as different, although he never knew why. "You look at me like it's always good-bye," one of them told him. Actually, he treated girls with an odd detached gentleness, as though he knew a secret that might make them all disappear. Some of them hung around because of his quick brown hands or his really great looks, some because they hoped to share the secret. In this they were disappointed. Hobie talked and he listened carefully, but it wasn't the mutual talk-talk-talk of total catharsis that most couples went through. But how could Hobie know that?

Like most of his peer group, Hobie stayed away from heavies and agreed that pot was preferable to getting juiced. His friends never crowded him too much after the beach party where he spooked everybody by talking excitedly for hours to people who weren't there. They decided he might have a vulnerable ego-structure.

The official high school view was that Hobie had no real problems. In this they were supported by a test battery profile that could have qualified him as the ideal normal control. Certainly there was nothing to get hold of in his routine interviews with the high school psychologist.

Hobie came in after lunch, a time when Dr. Morehouse knew he was not at his most intuitive. They went through the usual openers, Hobie sitting easily, patient and interested, with an air of listening to some sound back of the acoustical ceiling tiles.

"I meet a number of young people involved in discovering who they really are. Searching for their own identities," Morehouse offered. He was idly trueing up a stack of typing headed *Sex Differences in the Adolescent Identity Crisis.*

"Do you?" Hobie asked politely.

Morehouse frowned at himself and belched disarmingly.

"Sometimes I wonder who *I* am," he smiled.

"Do you?" inquired Hobie.

"Don't you?"

"No," said Hobie.

Morehouse reached for the hostility that should have been there, found it wasn't. Not passive aggression. What? His intuition awoke briefly. He looked into Hobie's light hazel eyes and suddenly found himself slipping toward some very large uninhabited dimension. A real pubescent preschiz, he wondered hopefully? No again, he decided, and found himself thinking, What if a person is sure of his identity but it isn't his identity? He often wondered that; perhaps it could be worked up into a creative insight.

"Maybe it's the other way around," Hobie was saying before the pause grew awkward.

"How do you mean?"

"Well, maybe you're all wondering who you are," Hobie's lips quirked; it was clear he was just making conversation.

"I asked for that," Morehouse chuckled. They chatted about sibling rivalry and psychological statistics and wound up in plenty of time for Morehouse's next boy, who turned out to be a satisfying High Anx. Morehouse forgot about the empty place he had slid into. He often did that too.

It was a girl who got part of it out of Hobie, at three in the morning. "Dog" she was called then, although her name was Jane. A tender, bouncy little bird who cocked her head to listen up at him in a way Hobie liked.

Dog would listen with the same soft intensity to the supermarket clerk and the pediatrician later on, but neither of them knew that.

They had been talking about the state of the world, which was then quite prosperous and peaceful. That is to say, about seventy million people were starving to death, a number of advanced nations were maintaining themselves on police terror tactics, four or five borders were being fought over, Hobie's family's maid had just been cut up by the suburban peacekeeper squad, and the school had added a charged wire and two dogs to its patrol. But none of the big nations were waving fissionables, and the U.S.-Sino-Soviet détente was a twenty-year reality.

Dog was holding Hobie's head over the side of her car because he had been the one who found the maid crawling on her handbones among the azaleas.

"If you feel like that, why don't you do something?" Dog asked him between spasms. "Do you want some Slurp? It's all we've got."

"Do what?" Hobie quavered.

"Politics?" guessed Dog. She really didn't know. The Protest Decade was long over, along with the New Politics and Ralph Nader. There was a school legend about a senior who had come back from Miami with a busted collarbone. Sometime after that the kids had discovered that flowers weren't really very powerful, and that movement organizers had their own bag. Why go on the street when you could really do more in one of the good jobs available Inside? So Dog could offer only a vague image of Hobie running for something, a sincere face on TV.

"You could join the Young Statesmen."

"Not to interfere," gasped Hobie. He wiped his mouth. Then he pulled himself together and tried some of the Slurp. In the dashlight his seventeen-year-old sideburns struck Dog as tremendously mature and beautiful.

"Oh, it's not so bad," said Hobie. "I mean, it's not *unusually* bad. It's just a stage. This world is going through a primitive stage. There's a lot of stages. It takes a long time. They're just very very backward, that's all."

"They," said Dog, listening to every word.

"I mean," he said.

"You're alienated," she told him. "Rinse your mouth out with that. You don't relate to people."

"I think you're people," he said, rinsing. He'd heard this before. "I relate to you," he said. He leaned out to spit. Then he twisted his head to look up at the sky and stayed that way a while, like an animal's head sticking out of a crate. Dog could feel him trembling the car.

"Are you going to barf again?" she asked.

"No."

But then suddenly he did, roaringly. She clutched at his shoulders while he heaved. After a while he sagged down, his head lolling limply out at one arm.

"It's such a mess," she heard him whispering. "It's such a s—ting miserable mess mess mess MESS MESS—"

He was pounding his hand on the car side.

"I'll hose it," said Dog, but then she saw he didn't mean the car.

"Why does it have to go on and on?" he croaked. "Why don't they just *stop* it? I can't bear it much longer, please, please, I can't—"

Dog was scared now.

"Honey, it's not that bad. Hobie honey, it's not that bad," she told him, patting at him, pressing her soft front against his back.

Suddenly he came back into the car on top of her, spent.

"It's unbearable," he muttered.

"What's unbearable?" she snapped, mad at him for scaring her. "What's unbearable for you and not for me? I mean, I know it's a mess, but why is it so bad for *you?* I have to live here too."

"It's your world," he told her absently, lost in some private desolation. Dog yawned.

"I better drive you home now," she said.

He had nothing more to say and sat quietly. When Dog glanced at his profile, she decided he looked calm. Almost stupid, in fact; his mouth hung open a little. She didn't recognize the expression, because she had never seen people looking out of cattle cars.

Hobie's class graduated that June. His grades were well up, and everybody understood that he was acting a little unrelated because of the traumatic business with the maid. He got a lot of sympathy.

It was after the graduation exercises that Hobie surprised his parents for the first and last time. They had been congratulating themselves on having steered their fifth offspring safely through the college crisis and into a high-status Eastern. Hobie announced that he had applied for the United States Air Force Academy.

This was a bomb, because Hobie had never shown the slightest interest in things military. Just the opposite, really. Hobie's parents took it for granted that the educated classes viewed the military with tolerant distaste. Why did their son want this? Was it another of his unstable motivational orientations?

But Hobie persisted. He didn't have any reasons, he had just thought carefully and felt that this was for him. Finally they recalled that early model rocket collection; his father decided he was serious, and began sorting out the generals his research firm did business with. In September Hobie disappeared into Colorado Springs. He reappeared for Christmas in the form of an exotically hairless, erect and polite stranger in uniform.

During the next four years, Hobie the person became effectively invisible behind a growing pile of excellent evaluation reports. There seemed to be no doubt that he was working very hard, and his motivation gave no sign of flagging. Like any cadet, he bitched about many of the Academy's little ways and told some funny stories. But he never seemed discouraged. When he elected to spend his summers in special aviation skills training, his parents realized that Hobie had found himself.

Enlightenment—of a sort—came in his senior year when he told them he had applied for and been accepted into the new astronaut training program. The U.S. space program was just then starting up again after the revulsion caused by the tragic loss of the manned satellite lab ten years before.

"I bet that's what he had in mind all along," Hobie's father chuckled. "He didn't want to say so before he made it." They were all relieved. A son in the space program was a lot easier to live with, statuswise.

When she heard the news, Dog, who was now married and called herself Jane, sent him a card with a picture of the Man in the Moon. Another girl, more percipient, sent him a card showing some stars.

But Hobie never made it to the space program.

It was the summer when several not-very-serious events happened all together. The British devalued their wobbly pound again, just when it was found that far too many dollars were going out of the States. North and South Korea moved a step closer to reunion, which generated a call for strengthening the U.S. contribution to the remains of SEATO. Next there was an expensive, though luckily nonlethal, fire at Kennedy, and the Egyptians announced a new Soviet aid pact. And in August it was discovered that the Guévarrista rebels in Venezuela were getting some very unpleasant-looking hardware from their Arab allies.

Contrary to the old saying that nations never learn from history, the U.S. showed that it had learned from its long agony in Vietnam. What it had learned was not to waste time messing around with popular elections and military advisory and training programs, but to ball right in. Hard.

When the dust cleared, the space program and astronaut training were dead on the pad and a third of Hobie's graduating class was staging through Caracas. Technically, he had volunteered.

He found this out from the task force medico.

"Look at it this way, lieutenant. By entering the Academy, you volunteered for the Air Force, right?"

"Yes. But I opted for the astronaut program. The Air Force is the only way you can get in. And I've been accepted."

"But the astronaut program has been suspended. Temporarily, of course. Meanwhile the Air Force—for which you volunteered—has an active requirement for your training. You can't expect them just to let you sit around until the program resumes, can you? Moreover you have been given the very best option available. Good God, man, the Volunteer Airpeace Corps is considered a superelite. You should see the fugal depressions we have to cope with among men who have been rejected for the VAC."

"Mercenaries," said Hobie. "Regressive."

"Try 'professional,' it's a better word. Now—about those headaches."

The headaches eased up some when Hobie was assigned to long-range sensor recon support. He enjoyed the work of flying, and the long, calm, lonely sensor missions were soothing. They were also quite safe. The Guévarristas had no air strength to waste on recon planes and the U.A.R. SAM sites were not yet operational. Hobie flew the pattern, and waited zombielike for the weather, and flew again. Mostly he waited, because the fighting was developing in a steamy jungle province where clear sensing was a sometimes thing. It was poorly mapped. The ground troops could never be sure about the little brown square men who gave them so much trouble; on one side of an unknown line they were Guévarristas who should be obliterated, and on the other side they were legitimate national troops warning the blancos away. Hobie's recon tapes were urgently needed, and for several weeks he was left alone.

Then he began to get pulled up to a forward strip for one-day chopper duty when their tactical duty roster was disrupted by gee-gee. But this was relatively peaceful too, being mostly defoliant spray missions. Hobie, in fact, put in several months without seeing, hearing, smelling, or feeling the war at all. He would have been grateful for this if he had realized it. As it was he seemed to be trying not to realize anything much. He spoke very little, did his work, and moved like a man whose head might fall off if he jostled anything.

Naturally he was one of the last to hear the rumors about gee-gee when they filtered back to the coastal base, where Hobie was quartered with the long-range stuff. Gee-gee's proper name was Guairas Grippe. It was developing into a severe problem in the combat zone. More and more replacements and relief crews were being called forward for temporary tactical duty. On Hobie's next trip in, he couldn't help but notice that people were acting pretty haggard, and the roster was all scrawled up with changes. When they were on course, he asked about it.

"Are you kidding?" his gunner grunted.

"No. What is it?"

"B.W."

"What?"

"Bacteriological weapon, skyhead. They keep promising us vaccines. Stuck in their zippers—look out, there's a ground burst."

They held Hobie up front for another mission, and another after that, and then they told him that a sector quarantine was now in force.

The official notice said that movement of personnel between sectors would be reduced to a minimum as a temporary measure to control the spread of respiratory ailments. Translation: you could go from the support zone to the front, but you couldn't go back.

Hobie was moved into a crowded billet and assigned to Casualty and Supply. Shortly he discovered that there was a translation for respiratory ailments too. Gee-gee turned out to be a multiform misery of groin rash, sore throat, fever, and unending trots. It didn't seem to become really acute; it just cycled along. Hobie was one of those who were only lightly affected, which was lucky because the hospital beds were full. So were the hospital aisles. Evacuation of all casualties had been temporarily suspended until a controlled corridor could be arranged.

The Gués did not, it seemed, get gee-gee. The ground troops were definitely sure of that. Nobody knew how it was spread. Rumor said it was bats one week, and then the next week they were putting stuff in the water. Poisoned arrows, roaches, women, disintegrating canisters, all had their advocates. However it was done, it was clear that the U.A.R. technological aid had included more than hardware. The official notice about a forthcoming vaccine yellowed on the board.

Ground fighting was veering closer to Hobie's strip. He heard mortars now and then, and one night the Gués ran in a rocket launcher and nearly got the fuel dump before they were chased back.

"All they got to do is wait," said the gunner. "We're dead."

"Geegee doesn't kill you," said C/S control. "You just wish it did."

"They say."

The strip was extended, and three attack bombers came in. Hobie looked them over. He had trained on AX92's all one summer; he could fly them in his sleep. It would be nice to be alone.

He was pushing the C/S chopper most of the daylight hours now. He had gotten used to being shot at and to being sick. Everybody was sick, except a couple of replacement crews who were sent in two weeks apart, looking startlingly healthy. They said they had been immunized with a new antitoxin. Their big news was that gee-gee could be cured outside the zone.

"We're getting reinfected," the gunner said. "That figures. They want us out of here."

That week there was a big drive on bats, but it didn't help. The next week the first batch of replacements were running fevers. Their shots hadn't worked and neither did the stuff they gave the second batch.

After that, no more men came in except a couple of volunteer medicos. The billets and the planes and the mess were beginning to stink. That dysentery couldn't be controlled after you got weak.

What they did get was supplies. Every day or so another ton of stuff would drift down. Most of it was dragged to one side and left to rot. They were swimming in food. The staggering cooks pushed steak and lobster at men who shivered and went out to retch. The hospital even had ample space now, because it turned out that gee-gee really did kill you in the end. By that time, you were glad to go. A cemetery developed at the far side of the strip, among the skeletons of the defoliated trees.

On the last morning Hobie was sent out to pick up a forward scout team. He was one of the few left with enough stamina for long missions. The three-man team was far into Gué territory, but Hobie didn't care. All he was thinking about was his bowels. So far he had not fouled himself or his plane. When he was down by their signal, he bolted out to squat under the chopper's tail. The grunts climbed in, yelling at him.

They had a prisoner with them. The Gué was naked and astonishingly broad. He walked springily; his arms were lashed with wire and a shirt was tied over his head. This was the first Gué Hobie had been close to. As he got in he saw how the Gué's firm brown flesh glistened and bulged around the wire. He wished he could see his face. The gunner said the Gué was a Sirionó, and this was important because the Sirionós were not known to be with the Gué's. They were a very primitive nomadic tribe.

When Hobie began to fly home, he realized he was getting sicker. It became a fight to hold onto consciousness and keep on course. Luckily nobody shot at them. At one point he became aware of a lot of screaming going on behind him, but couldn't pay attention. Finally he came over the strip and horsed the chopper down. He let his head down on his arms.

"You okay?" asked the gunner.

"Yeah," said Hobie, hearing them getting out. They were moving something heavy. Finally he got up and followed them. The floor was wet. That wasn't unusual. He got down and stood staring in, the floor a foot under his nose. The wet stuff was blood. It was sprayed around, with one big puddle. In the puddle was something soft and fleshy-looking.

Hobie turned his head. The ladder was wet. He held up one hand and looked at the red. His other hand too. Holding them out stiffly, he turned and began to walk away across the strip.

Control, who still hoped to get an evening flight out of him, saw him fall and called the hospital. The two replacement parameds were still in pretty good shape. They came out and picked him up.

When Hobie came to, one of the parameds was tying his hands down to the bed so he couldn't tear the IV out again.

"We're going to die here," Hobie told him.

The paramed looked noncommittal. He was a thin dark boy with a big Adam's apple.

" 'But I shall dine at journey's end with Landor and with Donne,' " said Hobie. His voice was light and facile.

"Yeats," said the paramed. "Want some water?"

Hobie's eyes flickered. The paramed gave him some water.

"I really believed it, you know," Hobie said chattily. "I had it all figured out." He smiled, something he hadn't done for a long time.

"Landor and Donne?" asked the medic. He unhooked the empty IV bottle and hung up a new one.

"Oh, it was pathetic, I guess," Hobie said. "It started out . . . I believed they were real, you know? Kirk, Spock, McCoy, all of them. And the ship. To this day, I swear . . . one of them talked to me once; I mean, he really did . . . I had it all figured out; they had me left behind as an observer." Hobie giggled.

"They were coming back for me. It was secret. All I had to do was sort of fit in and observe. Like a report. One day they would come back and haul me up in that beam thing; maybe you know about that? And there I'd be back in real time where human beings were, where they were human. I wasn't really stuck here in the past. On a backward planet."

The paramed nodded.

"Oh, I mean, I didn't really *believe* it; I knew it was just a show. But I did believe it, too. It was like *there*, in the background, underneath, no matter what was going on. They were coming for me. All I had to do was observe. And not to interfere. You know? Prime directive . . . Of course after I grew up, I realized they weren't; I mean, I realized consciously. So I was going to go to them. Somehow, somewhere. Out there . . . Now I know. It really isn't so. None of it. Never. There's nothing . . . Now I know I'll die here."

"Oh now," said the paramed. He got up and started to take things away. His fingers were shaky.

"It's clean there," said Hobie in a petulant voice. "None of this shit. Clean and friendly. They don't torture people," he explained, thrashing his head. "They don't kill—" He slept. The paramed went away.

Somebody started to yell monotonously.

Hobie opened his eyes. He was burning up.

The yelling went on, became screaming. It was dusk. Footsteps went by, headed for the screaming. Hobie saw they had put him in a bed by the door.

Without his doing much about it, the screaming seemed to be lifting him out of the bed, propelling him through the door. Air. He kept getting close-ups of his hands clutching things. Bushes, shadows. Something scratched him.

After a while the screaming was a long way behind him. Maybe it was only in his ears. He shook his head, felt himself go down onto boards. He thought he was in the cemetery.

"No," he said. "Please. Please no." He got himself up, balanced, blundered on, seeking coolness.

The side of the plane felt cool. He plastered his hot body against it, patting it affectionately. It seemed to be quite dark now. Why was he inside with no lights? He tried the panel, the lights worked perfectly. Vaguely he noticed some yelling starting outside again. It ignited the screaming in his head. The screaming got very loud—loud—LOUD—and appeared to be moving him, which was good.

He came to above the overcast and climbing. The oxy-support tube was hitting him in the nose. He grabbed for the mask, but it wasn't there. Automatically, he had leveled off. Now he rolled and looked around.

Below him was a great lilac sea of cloud, with two mountains sticking through it, their western tips on fire. As he looked, they dimmed. He shivered, found he was wearing only sodden shorts. How had he got here? Somebody had screamed intolerably and he had run.

He flew along calmly, checking his board. No trouble except the fuel. Nobody serviced the AX92's any more. Without thinking about it, he began to climb again. His hands were a yard away and he was shivering but he felt clear. He reached up and found his headphones were in place; he must have put them on along with the rest of the drill. He clicked on.

Voices rattled and roared at him. He switched off. Then he took off the headpiece and dropped it on the floor.

He looked around: 18,000, heading 88–05. He was over the Atlantic. In front of him the sky was darkening fast. A pinpoint glimmer ten o'clock high. Sirius, probably.

He thought about Sirius, trying to recall his charts. Then he thought about turning and going back down. Without paying much attention, he noticed he was crying with his mouth open.

Carefully he began feeding his torches and swinging the nose of his pod around and up. He brought it neatly to a point on Sirius. Up. Up. Behind him a great pale swing of contrail fell away above the lilac shadow, growing, towering to the tiny plane that climbed at its tip. Up. Up. The contrail cut off as the plane burst into the high cold dry.

As it did so, Hobie's ears skewered and he screamed wildly. The pain quit; his drums had burst. Up! Now he was gasping for air, strangling. The great torches drove him up, up, over the curve of the world. He was hanging on the star. Up! The fuel gauges were knocking. Any second they would quit and he and the bird would be a falling stone. "Beam us up, Scotty!" he howled at Sirius, laughing, coughing—coughing to death, as the torches faltered—

—And was still coughing as he sprawled on the shining resiliency under the arcing grids. He gagged, rolled, finally focused on a personage leaning toward him out of a complex chair. The personage had round eyes, a slitted nose, and the start of a quizzical smile.

Hobie's head swiveled slowly. It was not the bridge of the *Enterprise*. There were no viewscreens, only a View. And Lieutenant Uhura would have had trouble with the freeform flashing objects suspended in front of what appeared to be a girl wearing spots. The spots, Hobie made out, were fur.

Somebody who was not Bones McCoy was doing something to Hobie's stomach. Hobie got up a hand and touched the man's gleaming back. Under the mesh it was firm and warm. The man looked up, grinned; Hobie looked back at the captain.

"Do not have fear," a voice was saying. It seemed to be coming out of a globe by the captain's console. "We will tell you where you are."

"I know where I am," Hobie whispered. He drew a deep, sobbing breath.

"I'm HOME!" he yelled. Then he passed out.

LOVE IS THE PLAN
THE PLAN IS DEATH

Remembering—

Do you hear, my little red? Hold me softly. The cold grows.

I remember:

—I am hugely black and hopeful, I bounce on six legs along the mountains in the new warm! . . . *Sing the changer, Sing the stranger! Will the changes change forever?* . . . All my hums have words now. Another change!

Eagerly I bound on sunward following the tiny thrill in the air. The forests have been shrinking again. Then I see. It is me! Me-Myself, MOG-GADEET—I have grown bigger more in the winter cold! I astonish myself, Moggadeet-the-small!

Excitement, enticement shrilling from the sun-side of the world. I come! . . . The sun is changing again, too. *Sun is walking in the night! Sun is walking back to Summer in the warming of the light!* . . . Warm is MeMoggadeet Myself. Forget the bad-time winter.

Memory quakes me.

The Old One.

I stop, pluck up a tree. So much I wanted to ask the Old One. No time. Cold. Tree goes end over end downcliff, I watch the fatclimbers tumble out. Not hungry.

The Old One warned me of the cold—I didn't believe him. I move on, grieving. . . . *Old One told you, The cold, the cold will hold you. Chill cold! Kill cold! In the cold I killed you.*

But it's warm now, all different. I'm Moggadeet again.

I bound over a hill and see my brother Frim.

At first I don't know him. A big black old one! I think. And in the warm, we can speak!

I surge toward him bashing trees. The big black is crouched over a ravine, peering down. Black back has shiny ripples like—It IS Frim! Frim-

I-hunted-for, Frim-run-away! But he's so big now! Giant Frim! *A stranger, a changer—*

"Frim!"

He doesn't hear me; all his eye-turrets are under the trees. His end is sticking up oddlike, all atremble. What's he hunting?

"Frim! It's me, Moggadeet!"

But he only quivers his legs; I see his spurs pushing out. What a fool, Frim! I remind myself how timid he is, I try to move gently. When I get closer, I'm astonished again. I'm bigger than he is now! *Changes!* I can see right over his shoulder into the ravine.

Hot yellow-green in there. A little glade all lit with sun. I bend my eyes to see what Frim is after, and all astonishments blow up the world.

I see you.

I saw you.

I will always see you. Dancing in the green fire, my tiny red star! So bright! So small! So perfect! So fierce! I knew you—Oh yes, I knew you in that first instant, my dawnberry, my scarlet minikin. *Red!* A tiny baby red one, smaller than my smallest eye. And so brave!

The Old One said it. Red is the color of love.

I see you swat at a hopper twice your size, my eyes bulge as you leap after it and go rolling, shrilling *Lililee! Lilileee-ee!* in baby wrath. Oh my mighty hunter, you don't know someone is looking right into your tender little love-fur! Oh yes! Palest pink it is, just brushed with rose. My jaws spurt, the world flashes and reels.

And then Frim, poor fool, feels me behind him and rears up.

But what a Frim! His throat-sacs are ballooning purple-black, his plates are engorged like the Mother of the storm-clouds! Glittering, rattling his spurs! His tail booms! "It's mine!" he bellows—I can hardly understand him. He jumps straight at me!

"Stop, Frim, stop!" I cry, dodging away bewildered. It's warm—how can Frim be wild, kill-wild?

"Brother Frim!" I call gently, soothingly. But something is badly wrong! My voice is bellowing too! Yes, in the warm and I want only to calm him, I am full of love—but the kill-roar is rushing through me, I too am swelling, rattling, booming! Invincible! To crush—to rend—

Oh, I am shamed.

I came to myself in the wreckage of Frim, Frim-pieces everywhere, myself is sodden with Frim. But I did not eat him! I did not! Should I take joy in that? Did I defy the Plan? But my throat was closed. Not because it was Frim but because of darling you. *You!* Where are you? The glade is empty! Oh fearful fear, I have frightened you, you are run away! I forget Frim. I forget everything but you, my heartmeat, my precious tiny red.

I smash trees, I uproot rocks, I tear the ravine open! Oh, where are you hiding? Suddenly I have a new fear: has my wild search harmed you? I force myself calm. I begin questing, circling, ever wider over the trees, moving cloud-silent, thrusting my eyes and ears down into every glade. A new humming fills my throat. *Oooo, Oo-oo, Rum-a-looly-loo,* I moan. Hunting, hunting for you.

Once I glimpse a black bigness far away and I am suddenly up at my full height, roaring. Attack the black! Was it another brother? I would slay him, but the stranger is already vanishing. I roar again. No—*it roars me,* the new power of black. Yet deep inside, Myself-Moggadeet is watching, fearing. Attack the black—even in the warm? Is there no safety, are we truly like the fatclimbers? But at the same time it feels—Oh, right! Oh, good! Sweet is the Plan. I give myself up to seeking you, my new song longing *Oo-loo* and *Looly rum-a-loo-oo-loo.*

And you answered! You!

So tiny you, hidden under a leaf! Shrilling *Li! Li! Lililee!* Trilling, thrilling—half-mocking, already imperious. Oh, how I whirl, crash, try to look under all my feet, stop frozen in horror of squashing the *Lilili! Lee!* Rocking, longing, moaning Moggadeet.

And you came out, you did.

My adorable firemite, threatening ME!

When I see your littlest hunting claws upraised, my whole gut melts, it floods me. I am all tender jelly. *Tender!* Oh, tender-fierce like a Mother, I think! Isn't that how a Mother feels? My jaws are sluicing juice that isn't hunger-juice—I am choking, with fear of frighting you or bruising your tininess—I ache to grip and knead you, to eat you in one gulp, in a thousand nibbles—

Oh the power of *red*—the Old One said it! Now I feel my special hands, my tender hands I always carry hidden—now they come swelling out, come pushing toward my head! What? What?

My secret hands begin to knead and roll the stuff that's dripping from my jaws.

Ah, that arouses, you, too, my redling, doesn't it?

Yes, yes, I feel—torment—I feel your shy excitement! How your body remembers even now our love-dawn, our very first moments of Moggadeet-Leely. Before I knew You-Yourself, before you knew Me. It began then, my heartlet, our love-knowing began in that very first instant when your Moggadeet stared down at you like a monster bursting. I saw how new you were, how helpless!

Yes, even while I loomed over you marveling—even while my secret hands drew and spun your fate—even then it came to me in pity that long ago, last year when I was a child, I saw other little red ones among my brothers, before our Mother drove them away. I was only a foolish baby then; I didn't understand. I thought they'd grown strange and silly in their redness and Mother did well to turn them out. Oh stupid Moggadeet!

But now I saw *you*, my flamelet—I understood! You were only that day cast out by your Mother. Never had you felt the terrors of a night alone in the world; you couldn't imagine that such a monster as Frim was hunting you. Oh my ruby nestling, my baby red! Never, I vowed it, never would I leave you—and have I not kept that vow? Never! I, Moggadeet, *I would be your Mother.*

Great is the Plan, but I was greater!

All I learned of hunting in my lonely year, to drift like the air, to leap, to grip so delicately—all these learnings became for you! Not to bruise the smallest portion of your bright body. Oh, yes! I captured you whole in all your tiny perfection, though you sizzled and spat and fought me like the sunspark you are. And then—

And then—

I began to—Oh, terror! Delight-shame! How can I speak such a beautiful secret?—the Plan took me as a Mother guides her child and with my special hands I began to—

I began to bind you up!

Oh yes! Oh yes! My special hands that had no use, now all unfurled and engorged and alive, never stopping the working in the strong juice of my jaws—they began to *bind* you, passing over and around and beneath you, every moment piercing me with fear and joy. I wound among your darling little limbs, into your inmost delicate recesses, gently swathing and soothing you, winding and binding until you became a shining jewel. Mine!

—But you responded. I know that now. We know! Oh yes, in your fierce struggles, shyly you helped me, always at the end each strand fell sweetly into place . . . *Winding you, binding you, loving Leelyloo!* . . . How our bodies moved in our first weaving song! I feel it even now, I melt with excitement! How I wove the silk about you, tying each tiny limb, making you perfectly helpless. How fearlessly you gazed up at me, your terrifying captor! You! You were never frightened, as I'm not frightened now. Isn't it strange, my loveling? This sweetness that floods our bodies when we yield to the Plan. Great is the Plan! Fear it, fight it—but hold the sweetness yet.

Sweetly began our lovetime, when first I became your new true Mother, never to cast you out. How I fed you and caressed and tended and fondled you! What a responsibility it is to be a Mother. Anxiously I carried you furled in my secret arms, savagely I drove off all intruders, even the harmless banlings in the grass, in fear every moment that you were stifled or crushed!

And all the warm nights long, how I cared for your helpless little body, carefully releasing each infant limb, flexing and stretching it, cleaning every scarlet morsel of you with my giant tongue, nibbling your baby claws with my terrible teeth, reveling in your baby hum, pretending to devour you while you shrieked with glee, *Li! Lilili! Love-lili, Leelylee!* But the greatest joy of all—

We spoke!

We spoke together, we two! We communed, we shared, we poured ourselves one into the other. Love, how we stammered and stumbled at the first, you in your strange Mother-tongue and I in mine! How we blended our singing wordlessly and then with words, until more and more we came to see with each other's eyes, to hear, to taste, to feel the world of each other, until I became Leelyloo and you became Moggadeet, until finally we became together a new thing, Moggadeet-Leely, Lilliloo-Mogga, Lili-Moggalooly-deet!

Oh love, are we the first? Have others loved with their whole selves? Oh sad thinking, that lovers before us have left no trace. Remember us! Will you remember, my adored, though Moggadeet has spoiled everything and the cold grows? If only I could hear you speak once more, my red, my innocent one. You are remembering, your body tells me you remember even now. Softly, hold me softly yet. Hear your Moggadeet!

You told me how it was being you, yourself, tiny-redling-Lilliloo. Of your Mother, your dreams, your baby joys and fears. And I told you mine, and all my learnings in the world since the day when my own Mother—

Hear me, my heartmate! Time runs away.

—On the last day of my childhood my Mother called us all under her. "Sons! S-son-n-nss!" Why did her dear voice creak so?

My brothers came in slowly, fearfully from the summer green. But I, small Moggadeet, I climb eagerly up under the great arch of her body, seeking the golden Mother-fur. Right into her warm cave I come, where her Mother-eyes are glowing, the cave that sheltered us so strongly all our lives, as I shelter you, my dawn-flower.

I long to touch her, to hear her speak and sing to us again. Her Mother-fur troubles me, it is tattered and drab. Shyly I press against one of her huge food-glands. It feels dry, but a glow sparks deep in her Mother-eye.

"Mother," I whisper. "It's me, Moggadeet!"

"SONNNNNS!" Her voice rumbles through her armor. My big brothers huddle by her legs, peering back at the sunlight. They look so funny, shedding, half gold, half black.

"I'm afraid!" whimpers my brother Frim nearby. Like me, Frim still has his gold baby fur. Mother is speaking again but her voice booms so I can hardly understand.

"WINNN-TER! WINTER, I SAY! AFTER THE WARM COMES THE COLD WINTER. THE COLD WINTER BEFORE THE WARM COMES AGAIN, COMES . . ."

Frim whimpers louder, I cuff him. What's wrong, why is her loving voice so hoarse and strange now? She always hummed us so tenderly, we nestled in her warm Mother-fur sucking the lovely Mother-juices, rocking to her steady walking-song. *Ee-mooly-mooly, Ee-mooly-mooly,* while far below the earth rolled by. Oh, yes, and how we held our breaths and squealed when she began her mighty hunting-hum! *Tann! Tann! Dir! Dir! Dir Hataan! HATONN!* How we clung in the thrilling climax when she plunged upon her prey and we heard the crunching, the tearing, the gurgling in her body that meant soon her food-glands would be richly full.

Suddenly I see a black streak down below—a big brother is running away! Mother's booming voice breaks off. Her great body tenses, her plates clash. Mother roars!

Running, screaming down below! I burrow up into her fur, am flung about as she leaps.

"OUT! GO OUT!" she bellows. Her terrible hunting-limbs crash down, she roars without words, shuddering, jolting. When I dare to peek out, I see the others all have fled. All except one!

A black body is lying under Mother's claws. It's my brother Sesso—yes! But Mother is tearing him, is eating him! I watch in horror—Sesso she cared for so proudly, so tenderly! I sob, bury my head in her fur. But the beautiful fur is coming loose in my hands, her golden Mother-fur is dying! I cling desperately, trying not to hear the crunches, the gulps and gurgling. The world is ending, all is terrible, terrible.

And yet, my fireberry, even then I almost understood. Great is the Plan!

Presently Mother stops feeding and begins to move. The rocky ground jolts by far below. Her stride is not smooth but jerks me, even her deep hum is strange. *On! On! Alone! Ever alone. And on!* The rumbling ceases. Silence. Mother is resting.

"Mother!" I whisper. "Mother, it's Moggadeet. I'm here!"

Her stomach-plates contract, a belch reverberates in her vaults.

"Go," she groans. "Go. Too late. Mother no more."

"I don't want to leave you. Why must I go? Mother!" I wail, "Speak to me!" I keen my baby hum, *Deet! Deet! Tikki-takka! Deet!* hoping Mother will answer, crooning deep, *Brum! Brrumm! Brumaloo-brum!* Now I see one huge Mother-eye glow faintly, but she only makes a grating sound.

"Too late. No more. . . . The winter, I say. I did speak. . . . Before the winter, go. Go."

"Tell me about Outside, Mother," I plead.

Another groan or cough nearly shakes me from my perch. But when she speaks again her voice sounds gentler.

"Talk?" she grumbles, "Talk, talk, talk. You are a strange son. Talk, like your Father."

"What's that, Mother? What's a Father?"

She belches again. "Always talk. The winters grow, he said. Oh, yes. Tell them the winters grow. So I did. Late. Winter, I spoke you. Cold!" Her voice booms. "No more! Too late." Outside I hear her armor rattle and clank.

"Mother, speak to me!"

"Go. Go-o-o!"

Her belly-plates clash around me. I jump for another nest of fur but it comes loose in my grip. Wailing, I save myself by hanging to one of her great walking limbs. It is rigid, thrumming like rock.

"GO!" she roars.

Her Mother-eyes are shriveling, dead! I panic, scramble down, everything is vibrating, resonating around me. Mother is holding back a storm of rage!

I leap for the ground, I rush diving into a crevice, I wiggle and burrow under the fearful bellowing and clanging that rains on me from above. Into the rocks I go with the hunting claws of Mother crashing behind me.

Oh my redling, my little tenderling! Never have you known such a night. Those dreadful hours hiding from the monster that had been my loving Mother!

I saw her once more, yes. When dawn came, I clambered up a ledge and peered through the mist. It was warm then, the mists were warm. I knew what Mothers looked like; we had glimpses of huge horned dark shapes before our own Mother hooted us under her. Oh yes, and then would come Mother's earth-shaking challenge and the strange Mother's answering roar, and we'd cling tight, feeling her surge of kill-fury, buffeted, deafened, battered while our Mother charged and struck. And once while our Mother fed, I peeped out and saw a strange baby squealing in the remnants on the ground below.

But now it was my own dear Mother I saw lurching away through the mists, that great rusty-gray hulk so horned and bossed that only her hunting-eyes showed above her armor, swiveling mindlessly, questing for anything that moved. She crashed her way across the mountains, and as she went, she thrummed a new harsh song. *Cold! Cold! Ice and Lone. Ice! And cold! And end.* I never saw her again.

When the sun rose, I saw that the gold fur was peeling from my shiny black. All by itself my hunting-limb flashed out and knocked a hopper right into my jaws.

You see, my berry, how much larger and stronger I was than you when Mother sent us away? That also is the Plan. For you were not yet born! I had to live on while the warm turned to cold and while the winter passed to warm again before you would be waiting. I had to grow and learn. To *learn*, my Lilliloo! That is important. Only we black ones have a time to learn—the Old One said it.

Such small learnings at first! To drink the flat water-stuff without choking, to catch the shiny flying things that bite and to watch the storm-clouds and the moving of the sun. And the nights, and the soft things that moved on the trees. And the bushes that kept shrinking, shrinking—only it was me, Moggadeet, growing larger! Oh yes! And the day when I could knock down a fatclimber from its vine!

But all these learnings were easy—the Plan in my body guided me. It guides me now, Lililoo, even now it would give me peace and joy if I yielded to it. But I will not! I will remember to the end, I will speak to the end!

I will speak the big learnings. How I saw—though I was so busy catching and eating more, more, always more—I saw all things were changing, changing. *Changers!* The bushes changed their buds to berries, the fatclimbers changed their colors, even the sun changed, and the hills. And I saw all things were together with others of their kind but only me, Moggadeet. I was alone. Oh, so alone!

I went marching through the valleys in my shiny new black, humming my new song *Turra-tarra! Tarra Tan!* Once I glimpsed my brother Frim and I called him, but he ran like the wind. Away, alone! And when I went to the next valley I found the trees all mashed down. And in the distance I saw a black one like me—only many times as big! Huge! Almost as big as a Mother, sleek and glossy-new. I would have called but he reared up and saw me and roared so terribly that I too fled like the wind to empty mountains. Alone.

And so I learned, my redling, how we are alone even though my heart was full of love. And I wandered, puzzling and eating ever more and more. I saw the Trails; they meant nothing to me then. But I began to learn the important thing.

The cold.

You know it, my little red. How in the warm days I am me, Myself-Moggadeet. Ever-growing, ever-learning. In the warm we think, we speak. We love! We make our own Plan, Oh, did we not, my lovemate?

But in the cold, in the night—for the nights were growing colder—in the cold night I was—what?—Not Moggadeet. Not Moggadeet-thinking. Not Me-Myself. Only Something-that-lives, acts without thought. Help-less-Moggadeet. In the cold is only the Plan. I almost thought it.

And then one day the night-chill lingered and lingered, and the sun was hidden in the mists. And I found myself going up the Trails.

The Trails are a part of the Plan too, my redling.

The Trails are of winter. There we must go, all of us, we blacks. When the cold grows stronger, the Plan calls us upward, upward, we begin to drift up the Trails, up along the ridges to the cold, the night-side of the mountains. Up beyond the forests where the trees grow scant and turn to stony deadwood.

So the Plan drew me and I followed, only half-aware. Sometimes I came into warmer sunlight where I could stop and feed and try to think, but the cold fogs rose again and I went on, on and up. I began to catch sight of others like me far along the mountain-flank, moving steadily up. They didn't rear or roar when they saw me. I didn't call to them. Each one alone we climbed on toward the Caves, unthinking, blind. And so I would have gone too.

But then the great thing happened.

—Oh no, my Lililoo! Not the *greatest.* The greatest of all is you, will always be you. My precious sunmite, my red lovebaby! Don't be angry, no, no, my sharing one. Hold me softly. I must say our big learning. Hear your Moggadeet, hear and remember!

In the sun's last warm I found him, the Old One. A terrible sight! So maimed and damaged, parts rotting and gone. I stared, thinking him dead. Suddenly his head rolled feebly and a croak came out.

"Young . . . one?" An eye opened in his festering head, a flier pecked at it. "Young one . . . wait!"

And I understood him! Oh, with love—

No, no, my redling! Gently! Gently hear your Moggadeet. We *spoke*, the Old One and I! Old to young, we shared. I think it cannot happen.

"No old ones," he creaked. "Never to speak . . . we blacks. Never. It is not . . . the Plan. Only me . . . I wait . . ."

"Plan," I ask, half-knowing. "What is the Plan?"

"A beauty," he whispers. "In the warm, a beauty in the air . . . I followed . . . but another black one saw me and we fought . . . and I was damaged, but still the Plan made me follow until I was crushed and torn and dead. . . . But I lived! And the Plan let me go and I crawled here . . . to wait . . . to share . . . but—"

His head sags. Quickly I snatch a flier from the air and push it to his torn jaws.

"Old One! What is the Plan?"

He swallows painfully, his one eye holding mine.

"In us," he says thickly, stronger now. "In us, moving us in all things necessary for the life. You have seen. When the baby is golden the Mother cherishes it all winter long. But when it turns red or black she drives it away. Was it not so?"

"Yes, but—"

"That's the Plan! Always the Plan. Gold is the color of Mother-care but black is the color of rage. Attack the black! Black is to kill. Even a Mother, even her own baby, she cannot defy the Plan. Hear me, young one!"

"I hear. I have seen," I answer. "But what is red?"

"Red!" He groans. "Red is the color of love."

"No!" I say, stupid Moggadeet! "I know love. Love is gold."

The Old One's eyes turns from me. "Love," he sighs. "When the beauty comes in the air, you will see . . ." He falls silent. I fear he's dying. What can I do? We stay silent there together in the last misty sunwarm. Dimly on the slopes I can see other black ones like myself drifting steadily upward on their own Trails among the stone-tree heaps, into the icy mists.

"Old One! Where do we go?"

"You go to the Caves of Winter. That is the Plan."

"Winter, yes. The cold. Mother told us. And after the cold winter comes the warm. I remember. The winter will pass, won't it? Why did she say, the winters grow? Teach me, Old One. What is a Father?"

"Fa-ther? A word I don't know. But wait—" His mangled head turns to me. *"The winters grow?* Your mother said this? Oh cold! Oh, lonely," he groans. "A big learning she gave you. This learning I fear to think."

His eye rolls, glaring. I am frightened inside.

"Look around, young one. These stony deadwoods. Dead shells of trees that grow in the warm valleys. Why are they here? The cold has killed them. No living tree grows here now. Think, young one!"

I look, and true! It is a warm forest killed to stone.

"Once it was warm here. Once it was like the valleys. But the cold has grown stronger. The winter grows. Do you see? *And the warm grows less and less.*"

"But the warm is life! The warm is Me-Myself!"

"Yes. In the warm we think, we learn. In the cold is only the Plan. In the cold we are blind . . . Waiting here, I thought, was there a time when it was warm here once? Did we come here, we blacks, in the warm to speak, to share? Oh young one, a fearful thinking. Does our time of learning grow shorter, shorter? Where will it end? Will the winters grow until we can learn nothing but only live blindly in the Plan, like the silly fatclimbers who sing but do not speak?"

His words fill me with cold fear. Such a terrible learning! I feel anger.

"No! We will not! We must—we must hold the warm!"

"Hold the warm?" He twists painfully to stare at me. "Hold the warm. . . . A great thinking. Yes. But how? How? Soon it will be too cold to think, even here!"

"The warm will come again," I tell him. "Then we must learn a way to hold it, you and I!"

His head lolls.

"No. . . . When the warm comes I will not be here . . . and you will be too busy for thinking, young one."

"I will help you! I will carry you to the Caves!"

"In the Caves," he gasps, "In each Cave there are two black ones like yourself. One is living, waiting mindless for the winter to pass. . . . And while he waits, he eats. He eats the other, that is how he lives. That is the Plan. As you will eat me, my youngling."

"No!" I cry in horror. "I will never harm you!"

"When the cold comes you will see," he whispers. "Great is the Plan!"

"No! You are wrong! I will break the Plan," I shout. A cold wind is blowing from the summit; the sun dies.

"Never will I harm you," I bellow. "You are wrong to say so!"

My scaleplates are rising, my tail begins to pound. Through the mists I hear his gasps.

I recall dragging a heavy black thing to my Cave.

Chill cold, kill cold. . . . In the cold I killed you.

Leelyloo. He did not resist.

Great is the Plan. He accepted all, perhaps he even felt a strange joy, as

I feel it now. In the Plan is joy. But if the Plan is wrong? *The winters grow.*
Do the fatclimbers have their Plan too?

Oh, a hard thinking! How we tried, my redling, my joy. All the long
warm days I explained it to you, over and over. How the winter would
come and change us if we did not hold the warm. You understood! You
share, you understand me now, my precious flame—though you can't
speak I feel your sharing love. Softly . . .

Oh, yes, we made our preparations, our own Plan. Even in the highest
heat we made our Plan against the cold. Have other lovers done so? How I
searched, carrying you, my cherry bud, I crossed whole mountain ranges,
following the sun until we found this warmest of warm valleys on the
sunward side. Surely the cold would be weak here, I thought. How could
they reach us here, the cold fogs, the icy winds that froze my inner Me and
drew me up the Trails into the dead Caves of Winter?

This time I would defy!

This time I have *you.*

"Don't take me there, my Moggadeet!" you begged, fearful of the
strangeness. "Don't take me to the cold!"

"Never, my Leeliloo! Never, I vow it. Am I not your Mother, little
redness?"

"But you will change! The cold will make you forget. Is it not the
Plan?"

"We will break the Plan, Lili. See, you are growing larger, heavier, my
fireberry—and always more beautiful! Soon I will not be able to carry you
so easily, I could never carry you to the cold Trails. And I will never leave
you!"

"But you are so big, Moggadeet! When the change comes you will
forget and drag me to the cold."

"Never! Your Moggadeet has a deeper Plan! When the mists start I will
take you to the farthest, warmest cranny of this cave, and there I will spin
a wall so you can never never be pulled out. And I will never never leave
you. Even the Plan cannot draw Moggadeet from Leelyloo!"

"But you will have to go hunting for food and the cold will take you
then! You will forget me and follow the cold love of winter and leave me
there to die! Perhaps that is the Plan!"

"Oh, no, my precious, my redling! Don't grieve, don't cry! Hear your
Moggadeet's Plan! From now on I'll hunt twice as hard. I'll fill this cave to
the top, my fat little blushbud, I will fill it with food now so I can stay by
you all the winter through!"

And so I did, didn't I my Lilli? Silly Moggadeet, how I hunted, how I brought lizards, hoppers, fatclimbers and banlings by the score. What a fool! For of course they rotted, there in the heat, and the heaps turned green and slimy—but still tasting good, eh, my berry?—so that we had to eat them then, gorging ourselves like babies. And how you grew!

Oh, beautiful you became, my jewel of redness! So bursting fat and shiny-full, but still my tiny one, my sunspark. Each night after I fed you, I would part the silk, fondling your head, your eyes, your tender ears, trembling with excitement for the delicious moment when I would release your first scarlet limb to caress and exercise it and press it to my pulsing throatsacs. Sometimes I would unbind two together for the sheer joy of seeing you move. And each night it took longer, each morning I had to make more silk to bind you up. How proud I was, my Leely, Lilliloo!

That was when my greatest thinking came.

As I was weaving you so tenderly into your shining cocoon, my joyberry, I thought, why not bind up living fatclimbers? Pen them alive so their flesh will stay sweet and they will serve us through the winter!

That was a great thinking, Lilliloo, and I did this, and it was good. Fatclimbers in plenty I walled in a little tunnel, and many, many other things as well, while the sun walked back toward winter and the shadows grew and grew. Fatclimbers and banlings and all tasty creatures and even— Oh, clever Moggadeet!—all manner of leaves and bark and stuffs for them to eat! Oh, we had broken the Plan for sure now!

"We have broken the Plan for sure, my Lilli-red. The fatclimbers are eating the twigs and bark, the banlings are eating juice from the wood, the great runners are munching grass, and we will eat them all!"

"Oh, Moggadeet, you are brave! Do you think we can really break the Plan? I am frightened! Give me a banling, I think it grows cold."

"You have eaten fifteen banlings, my minikin!" I teased you. "How fat you grow! Let me look at you again, yes, you must let your Moggadeet caress you while you eat. Ah, how adorable you are!"

And of course—Oh, you remember how it began then, our deepest love. For when I uncovered you one night with the first hint of cold in the air, I saw that you had changed.

Shall I say it? Your secret fur. Your *Mother-fur*.

Always I had cleaned you there tenderly, but without difficulty to restrain myself. But on this night when I parted the silk strands with my huge hunting claws, what new delights met my eyes! No longer pink and pale but fiery red! *Red!* Scarlet blaze like the reddest sunrise, gold-tipped! And swollen, curling, dewy—Oh! Commanding me to expose you, all of you. Oh, how your tender eyes melted me and your breath musky-sweet and your limbs warm and heavy in my grasp!

Wildly I ripped away the last strands, dazed with bliss as you slowly stretched your whole blazing redness before my eyes. I knew then—*we* knew!—that the love we felt before was only a beginning. My hunting-limbs fell at my sides and my special hands, my weaving hands grew, filled with new, almost painful life. I could not speak, my throat-sacs filling, filling! And my love-hands rose up by themselves, pressing ecstatically, while my eyes bent closer, closer to your glorious *red!*

But suddenly the Me-Myself, Moggadeet awoke! I jumped back!

"Lilli! What's happening to us?"

"Oh, Moggadeet, I love you! Don't go away!"

"What is it, Leelyloo? Is it the Plan?"

"I don't care! Moggadeet, don't you love me?"

"I fear! I fear to harm you! You are so tiny. I am your Mother."

"No Moggadeet, look! I am as big as you are. Don't be afraid." I drew back—Oh, hard, hard!—and tried to look calmly.

"True, my redling, you have grown. But your limbs are so new, so tender. Oh, I can't look!"

Averting my eyes, I began to spin a screen of silk, to shut away your maddening redness.

"We must wait, Lilliloo. We must go on as before. I don't know what this strange urging means; I fear it will bring you harm."

"Yes, Moggadeet. We will wait."

And so we waited. Oh yes. Each night it grew more hard. We tried to be as before, to be happy, Leely-Moggadeet. Each night as I caressed your glowing limbs that seemed to offer themselves to me as I swathed and unswathed them in turn, the urge rose in me hotter, more strong. To unveil you wholly! To look again upon your whole body!

Oh yes, my darling, I feel—unbearable—how you remember with me those last days of our simple love.

Colder . . . colder. Mornings when I went to harvest the fatclimbers, there was a whiteness on their fur and the banlings ceased to move. The sun sank every lower, paler, and the cold mists hung above us, reaching down. Soon I dared not leave the cave. I stayed all day by your silken wall, humming Motherlike, *Brum-a-loo, Mooly-mooly, Lilliloo, Love Leely.* Strong Moggadeet!

"We'll wait, fireling. We will not yield to the Plan! Aren't we happier than all others, here with our love in our warm cave?"

"Oh, yes, Moggadeet."

"I'm Myself now. I am strong. I'll make my own Plan. I will not look at you until . . . until the warm, until the Sun comes back."

"Yes, Moggadeet . . . Moggadeet? My limbs are cramped."

"Oh, my precious, wait—see, I am opening the silk very carefully, I will not look—I won't—"

"Moggadeet, don't you love me?"

"Leelyloo! Oh, my glorious one! I fear, I fear—"

"Look, Moggadeet! See how big I am, how strong!"

"Oh, redling, my hands—my hands—what are they doing to you?"

For with my special hands I was pressing, pressing the hot juices from my throat-sacs and tenderly, tenderly parting your sweet Mother-fur and *placing my gift within your secret places.* And as I did this, our eyes entwined and our limbs made a wreath.

"My darling, do I hurt you?"

"Oh, no, Moggadeet! Oh, no!"

Oh, my adored one, those last days of our love!

Outside the world grew colder yet, and the fatclimbers ceased to eat and the banlings lay still and began to stink. But still we held the warmth deep in our cave and still I fed my beloved on the last of our food. And every night our new ritual of love became more free, richer, though I compelled myself to hide all but a portion of your sweet body. But each dawn it grew hard and harder for me to replace the silken bonds around your limbs.

"Moggadeet! Why do you not bind me! I am afraid!"

"A moment, Lilli, a moment. I must caress you just once more."

"I'm afraid, Moggadeet! Cease now and bind me!"

"By why, my lovekin? Why must I hide you? Is this not some foolish part of the Plan?"

"I don't know, I feel so strange. Moggadeet, I—I'm changing."

"You grow more glorious every moment, my Lilli, my own. Let me look at you! It is wrong to bind you away!"

"No, Moggadeet! No!"

But I would not listen, would I? Oh foolish Moggadeet-who-thought-to-be-your-Mother. Great is the Plan!

I did not listen, I did not bind you up. No! I ripped them away, the strong silk strands. Mad with love I slashed them all at once, rushing from each limb to the next until all your glorious body lay exposed. At last—I saw you whole!

Oh, Lilliloo, greatest of Mothers.

It was not I who was your Mother. You were mine.

Shining and bossed you lay, your armor newly grown, your mighty hunting limbs thicker than my head! What I had created. You! A Supermother, a Mother such as none have ever seen!

Stupefied with delight, I gazed.

And your huge hunting limb came out and seized me.

Great is the Plan. I felt only joy as your jaws took me.

As I feel it now.

And so we end, my Lilliloo, my redling, for your babies are swelling through your Mother-fur and your Moggadeet can speak no longer. I am nearly devoured. The cold grows, it grows, and your Mother-eyes are growing, glowing. Soon you will be alone with our children and the warm will come again.

Will you remember, my heartmate? Will you remember and tell them?

Tell them of the cold, Leelyloo. Tell them of our love.

Tell them . . . *the winters grow.*

THE MAN WHO
WALKED HOME

—Transgression! Terror! And he thrust and lost there, punched into impossibility, abandoned, never to be known how, the wrong man in the most wrong of all wrong places in that unimaginable collapse of never-to-be-reimagined mechanism, he stranded, undone, his lifeline severed, he in that nanosecond knowing his only tether parting, going away, the longest line to life withdrawing, winking out, disappearing forever beyond his grasp, telescoping away from him into the closing vortex beyond which lay his home, his life, his only possibility of being; seeing it sucked back into the deepest maw, melting, leaving him orphaned on what never-to-be-known shore of total wrongness—of beauty beyond joy, perhaps? Of horror? Of nothingness? Of profound otherness only, it may be—whatever it was, that place into which he transgressed, certainly it could not support his life there, his violent and violating aberrance; and he, fierce, brave, crazy—clenched into one fist of protest, one body-fist of utter repudiation of himself there in that place, forsaken there—what did he do? He rejected, exiled, hungering homeward more desperate than any lost beast driving for its unreachable home, his home, his home—and no way, no transport, no vehicle, means, machinery, no force but his intolerable resolve aimed homeward along that vanishing vector, that last and only lifeline—he did, what?

He walked.

Home.

Precisely what hashed up in the work of the major industrial lessee of the Bonneville Particle Acceleration Facility was never known. Or rather, all those who might have been able to diagnose the original malfunction were themselves obliterated almost at once in the greater catastrophe which followed.

The nature of this second cataclysm was not at first understood either. All that was ever certain was that at 1153.6 of May 2, 1989 Old Style, the Bonneville laboratories and all their personnel were transformed into an intimately disrupted form of matter resembling a high-energy plasma, which became rapidly airborne to the accompaniment of radiating seismic and atmospheric events.

The disturbed area unfortunately included an operational MIRV Watchdog bomb.

In the confusions of the next hours the earth's population was substantially reduced, the biosphere was altered, and the earth itself was marked with numbers of more conventional craters. For some years thereafter the survivors were preoccupied with other concerns and the peculiar dust-bowl at Bonneville was left to weather by itself in the changing climatic cycles.

It was not a large crater; just over a kilometer in width and lacking the usual displacement lip. Its surface was covered with a finely divided substance which dried into dust. Before the rains began, it was almost perfectly flat. Only in certain lights had anyone been there to inspect it; a small surface marking or abraded place could be detected almost exactly at the center.

A decade after the disaster a party of short brown people appeared from the south, together with a flock of somewhat atypical sheep. The crater at this time appeared as a wide shallow basin in which the grass did not grow well, doubtless from the almost complete lack of soil microorganisms. However, neither this nor the surrounding vigorous grass was found to harm the sheep. A few crude hogans went up at the southern edge, and a faint path began to be traced across the crater itself, passing by the central bare spot.

One spring morning two children who had been driving sheep across the crater came screaming back to camp. A monster had burst out of the ground before them, a huge flat animal making a dreadful roar. It vanished in a flash and a shaking of the earth, leaving an evil smell. The sheep had run away.

Since this last was visibly true, some elders investigated. Finding no sign of the monster and no place in which it could hide, they settled for beating the children, who settled for making a detour around the monster-spot, and nothing more occurred for a while.

The following spring the episode was repeated. This time an older girl was present but she could add only that the monster seemed to be rushing flat out along the ground without moving at all. And there was a scraped place in the dirt. Again nothing was found; an evil-ward in a cleft stick was placed at the spot.

When the same thing happened for the third time a year later, the detour was extended and other charm-wands were added. But since no harm seemed to come of it and the brown people had seen far worse, sheep-tending resumed as before. A few more instantaneous apparitions of the monster were noted, each time in the spring.

In the second decade of the new era a tall man limped down the hills from the north, pushing his pack upon a bicycle wheel. He camped on the far side of the crater, and soon found the monster-site. He attempted to question people about it, but no one understood him, so he traded a knife for some meat. Although he was obviously feeble, something about him dissuaded them from killing him, and this proved wise because he later assisted the women to treat several sick children.

He spent much time around the place of the apparition and was nearby when it made its next appearance. This excited him very much, and he did several inexplicable but apparently harmless things, including moving his camp into the crater by the trail. He stayed on for a full year watching the site and was close by for its next manifestation. After this he spent a few days making a new charm for the spot and then left, hobbling, as he had come.

More decades passed. The crater eroded and a rain-gully became an intermittent streamlet across one edge of the basin. The brown people and their sheep were attacked by a band of grizzled men, after which the survivors went away eastward. The winters were now frost-free; aspen and eucalyptus sprouted in the moist plain. Still the crater remained treeless, visible as a flat bowl of grass, and the bare place at the center remained. The skies cleared somewhat.

After another three decades a larger band of black people with ox-drawn carts appeared and stayed for a time, but left again when they too saw the thunderclap-monster. A few other vagrants straggled by.

Five decades later a small permanent settlement had grown up on the nearest range of hills, from which men riding on small ponies with dark stripes down their spines herded humped cattle near the crater. A herdsman's hut was built by the streamlet, which in time became the habitation of an olive-skinned, red-haired family. In due course one of this clan again observed the monster-flash, but these people did not depart. The object the tall man had placed was noted and left undisturbed.

The homestead at the crater's edge grew into a group of three and was joined by others, and the trail across it became a cartroad with a log bridge over the stream. At the center of the still faintly discernible crater the cartroad made a bend, leaving a grassy place which bore on its center about a square meter of curiously impacted bare earth and a deeply etched sandstone rock.

The apparition of the monster was now known to occur regularly each spring on a certain morning in this place, and the children of the community dared each other to approach the spot. It was referred to in a phrase that could be translated as "the Old Dragon." The Old Dragon's appearance was always the same: a brief, violent thunderburst which began and cut off abruptly, in the midst of which a dragonlike creature was seen apparently in furious motion on the earth although it never actually moved. Afterward there was a bad smell and the earth smoked. People who saw it from close by spoke of a shivering sensation.

Early in the second century two young men rode into town from the north. Their ponies were shaggier than the local breed, and the equipment they carried included two boxlike objects, which the young men set up at the monster site. They stayed in the area a full year, observing two materializations of the Old Dragon, and they provided much news and maps of roads and trading-towns in the cooler regions to the north. They built a windmill, which was accepted by the community, and offered to build a lighting machine, which was refused. Then they departed with their boxes after unsuccessfully attempting to persuade a local boy to learn to operate one.

In the course of the next decades other travelers stopped to marvel at the monster, and there was sporadic fighting over the mountains to the south. One of the armed bands made a cattle-raid into the crater hamlet. It was repulsed, but the raiders left a spotted sickness which killed many. For all this time the bare place at the crater's center remained, and the monster made his regular appearances, observed or not.

The hill-town grew and changed and the crater hamlet grew to be a town. Roads widened and linked into networks. There were gray-green conifers in the hills now, spreading down into the plain, and chirruping lizards lived in their branches.

At century's end a shabby band of skin-clad squatters with stunted milkbeasts erupted out of the west and were eventually killed or driven away, but not before the local herds had contracted a vicious parasite. Veterinaries were fetched from the market-city up north, but little could be done. The families near the crater moved to the hill-town. Decades later still, cattle of a new strain reappeared in the plain and the deserted crater hamlet was reoccupied. Still the bare center continued annually to manifest the monster, and he became an accepted phenomenon of the area. On several occasions parties came from the distant Northwest Authority to observe it.

The crater hamlet flourished and grew into the fields where cattle had grazed, and part of the old crater became the town park. A small seasonal tourist industry based on the monster-site developed. The townspeople rented rooms for the appearances, and many more-or-less authentic monster-relics were on display in the local taverns.

Several cults had grown up around the monster. One persistent belief was that it was a devil or damned soul forced to appear on earth in torment to expiate the catastrophe of two centuries back. Others believed that it, or he, was some kind of messenger whose roar portended either doom or hope according to the believer. One very vocal sect taught that the apparition registered the moral conduct of the townspeople over the past year, and scrutinized the annual apparition for changes which could be interpreted for good or ill. It was considered lucky, or dangerous, to be touched by some of the dust raised by the monster. In every generation at least one small boy would try to touch the monster with a stick, usually acquiring a broken arm and a lifelong tavern tale. Pelting the monster with stones or other objects was a popular sport, and for some years people systematically flung prayers and flowers at it. Once a party tried to net it and were left with strings and vapor. The area itself had long since been fenced off at the center of the park.

Through all this the monster made his violently enigmatic annual appearance, sprawled furiously motionless, unreachably roaring.

Only as the third century of the new era went by was it apparent that the monster had been changing slightly. He was now no longer on the earth but had an arm and a leg thrust upward in a kicking or flailing gesture. As the years passed, he began to change more quickly until at the end of the third century he had risen to a contorted crouching pose, arms outflung as if frozen in gyration. His roar, too, seemed somewhat differently pitched and the earth after him smoked more and more.

It was then widely felt that the man-monster was about to do something, to make some definitive manifestation, and a series of natural disasters and marvels gave support to a vigorous cult teaching this doctrine. Several religious leaders journeyed to the town to observe the apparitions.

However, the decades passed and the man-monster did nothing more than turn slowly in place, so that he now appeared to be in the act of sliding or staggering while pushing himself backward like a creature blown before a gale. No wind, of course, could be felt, and presently the general climate quieted and nothing came of it all.

Early in the fifth century New Calendar, three survey parties from the North Central Authority came through the area and stopped to observe the monster. A permanent recording device was set up at the site, after assurances to the townfolk that no hardscience was involved. A local boy was trained to operate it; he quit when his girl left him but another volunteered. At this time nearly everyone believed that the apparition was a man, or the ghost of one. The record-machine boy and a few others such as the school mechanics teacher referred to him as The Man John. In the next decades the roads were greatly improved; and all forms of travel increased and there was talk of building a canal to what had been the Snake River.

One May morning at the end of Century Five, a young couple in a smart green mule-trap came jogging up the highroad from the Sandreas Rift Range to the southwest. The girl was golden-skinned and chatted with her young husband in a language unlike that ever heard by the Man John either at the end or the beginning of his life. What she said to him has, however, been heard in every age and tongue.

"Oh Serli, I'm so glad we're taking this trip now! Next summer I'll be too busy with Baby."

To which Serli replied as young husbands often have, and so they trotted up to the town's inn. Here they left trap and bags and went in search of her uncle, who was expecting them there. The morrow was the day of the Man John's annual appearance, and her Uncle Laban had come from the MacKenzie History Museum to observe it and to make certain arrangements.

They found him with the town school instructor of mechanics, who was also the recorder at the monster-site. Presently, Uncle Laban took them all with him to the town mayor's office to meet with various religious personages. The mayor was not unaware of the tourist value of the "monster," but he took Uncle Laban's part in securing the cultists' grudging assent to the MacKenzie authorities' secular interpretation, which was made easier by the fact that they disagreed among themselves. Then, seeing how pretty the niece was, the mayor took them all home to dinner.

When they returned to the inn for the night, it was abrawl with holiday makers.

"Whew," said Uncle Laban. "I've talked myself dry, sister's daughter. What a weight of holy nonsense is that Resurrection female! Serli, my lad, I know you have questions. Let me hand you this to read, it's the guide book we're giving 'em to sell. Tomorrow I'll answer for it all." And he disappeared into the crowded tavern.

So Serli and his bride took the pamphlet upstairs to bed with them, but it was not until the next morning at breakfast that they found time to read it.

" 'All that is known of John Delgano,' " read Serli with his mouth full, " 'comes from two documents left by his brother Carl Delgano in the archives of the MacKenzie Group in the early years after the holocaust.' Put some honey on this cake, Mira my dove. 'Verbatim transcript follows, this is Carl Delgano speaking:

" 'I'm not an engineer or an astronaut like John, I ran an electronics repair shop in Salt Lake City. John was only trained as a spaceman; the slump wiped all that out. So he tied up with this commercial group who were leasing part of Bonneville. They wanted a man for some kind of hard vacuum tests, that's all I knew about it. John and his wife moved to Bonneville, but we all got together several times a year, our wives got on real good. John had two kids, Clara and Paul.

" 'The tests were all supposed to be secret, but John told me confidentially they were trying for an anti-gravity chamber. I don't know if it ever worked. That was the year before.

" 'Then that winter they came down for Christmas and John said they had something new. He was all lit up. A temporal displacement, he called it; some kind of time effect. He said the chief honcho, the boss man was like a real mad scientist. Big ideas. He kept adding more angles every time some other project would quit and leave equipment he could lease. No, I don't know who the top company was—maybe an insurance conglomerate, they had all the cash, didn't they? And I guess they'd pay to catch a look at the future, that figures. Anyway, John was all gung-ho and Katharine was scared, that's natural. She pictured him like, you know, H. G. Wells— walking around in some future world. John told her it wasn't like that at all. All they'd get would be this kind of flicker, like a second or two. All kinds of complications'—Yes, yes, my greedy piglet, some brew for me too. This is thirsty work!

"So . . . 'I remember I asked him, what about the earth moving? I mean, you could come back in a different place, right? He said they had that all figured. A spatial trajectory. Katharine was so scared we shut up. John told her, don't worry, I'll come home. But he didn't. Not that it makes any difference, of course, everything was wiped out. Salt Lake too. The only reason I'm here is that I went up by Calgary to see Mom, April twenty-ninth. May second it all blew. I didn't find you folks at MacKenzie until July. I guess I may as well stay. That's all I know about John, except that he was an all-right guy. If that accident started all this it wasn't his fault.

" 'The second document'—In the name of love, little mother, do I have to read all this! Oh very well; a kiss, please, Madam. Must you look so ineffable? . . . 'The second document. Dated in the year eighteen, New Style, written by Carl'—see the old handwriting, my plump pigeon. Oh, very well, very well. 'Written at Bonneville Crater.

" 'I have seen my brother John Delgano. When I knew I had the rad sickness I came down here to look around. Salt Lake's still hot. So I came over here by Bonneville. You can see the crater where the labs were, it's grassed over. It's different, it's not radioactive. My film's ok. There's a bare place in the middle. Some Indios here told me a monster shows up here every year in the spring. I saw it myself a couple of days after I got here but I was too far away to see much, except I'm sure it's a man. In a vacuum suit. There was a lot of noise and dust, took me by surprise. It was all over in a second. I figure it's pretty close to the day, I mean, May second, old.

" 'So I hung around a year and he showed up again yesterday. I was on the face side and I could see his face through the faceplate. It's John all right. He's hurt. I saw blood on his mouth and his suit is frayed some. He's lying on the ground. He didn't move while I could see him but the dust boiled up, like a man sliding onto base without moving. His eyes are open like he was looking. I don't understand it any way, but I know it's John, not a ghost. He was in exactly the same position each time and there's a loud crack like thunder and another sound like a siren, very fast. And an ozone smell, and smoke. I felt a kind of shudder.

" 'I know it's John there and I think he's alive. I have to leave here now to take this back while I can still walk. I think somebody should come here and see. Maybe you can help John. Signed, Carl Delgano.

" 'These records were kept by the MacKenzie Group but it was not for several years—' Etcetera, first light-print, etcetera, archives, analysts, etcetera—very good! Now it is time to meet your uncle, my edible one, after we go upstairs for just a moment."

"No, Serli, I will wait for you downstairs," said Mira prudently.

When they came into the town park, Uncle Laban was directing the installation of a large durite slab in front of the enclosure around the Man John's appearance-spot. The slab was wrapped in a curtain to await the official unveiling. Townspeople and tourists and children thronged the walks and a Resurrection choir was singing in the bandshell. The morning was warming up fast. Vendors hawked ices and straw toys of the monster and flowers and good-luck confetti to throw at him. Another religious group stood by in dark robes; they belonged to the Repentance church beyond the park. Their pastor was directing somber glares at the crowd in general and Mira's uncle in particular.

Three official-looking strangers who had been at the inn came up and introduced themselves to Uncle Laban as observers from Alberta Central. They went on into the tent which had been erected over the enclosure, carrying with them several pieces of equipment which the town-folk eyed suspiciously.

The mechanics teacher finished organizing a squad of students to protect the slab's curtain, and Mira and Serli and Laban went on into the tent. It was much hotter inside. There were rings of benches around a railed enclosure about twenty feet in diameter. Inside the railing the earth was bare and scuffed. Several bunches of flowers and blooming poinciana branches leaned against the rail. The only thing inside the rail was a rough sandstone rock with markings etched on it.

Just as they came in, a small boy raced across the open center and was yelled at by everybody. The officials from Alberta were busy at one side of the rail, where the light-print box was mounted.

"Oh no," muttered Mira's uncle, as one of the officials leaned over to set up a tripod stand inside the rails. He adjusted it, and a huge horse-tail of fine feathery filaments blossomed out and eddied through the center of the space.

"Oh *no*," Laban said again. "Why can't they let it be?"

"They're trying to pick up dust from his suit, is that right?" Serli asked.

"Yes, insane. Did you get time to read?"

"Oh yes," said Serli.

"Sort of," added Mira.

"Then you know. He's falling. Trying to check his—well, call it velocity. Trying to slow down. He must have slipped or stumbled. We're getting pretty close to when he lost his footing and started to fall. What did it? Did somebody trip him?" Laban looked from Mira to Serli, dead serious now. "How would you like to be the one who made John Delgano fall?"

"Ooh," said Mira in quick sympathy. Then she said, "Oh."

"You mean." asked Serli, "Whoever made him fall caused all the, caused—"

"Possible," said Laban.

"Wait a minute." Serli frowned. "He did fall. So somebody had to do it —I mean, he has to trip or whatever. If he doesn't fall, the past would all be changed, wouldn't it? No war, no—"

"Possible," Laban repeated. "God knows. All *I* know is that John Delgano and the space around him is the most unstable, improbable, highly charged area ever known on earth and I'm damned if I think anybody should go poking sticks in it."

"Oh come now, Laban!" One of the Alberta men joined them, smiling. "Our dust-mop couldn't trip a gnat. It's just vitreous monofilaments."

"Dust from the future," grumbled Laban. "What's it going to tell you? That the future has dust in it?"

"If we could only get a trace from that thing in his hand."

"In his hand?" asked Mira. Serli started leafing hurriedly through the pamphlet.

"We've had a recording analyzer aimed at it." The Albertan lowered his voice, glancing around. "A spectroscope. We know there's something there, or was. Can't get a decent reading. It's severely deteriorated."

"People poking at him, grabbing at him," Laban muttered. "You—"

"Ten minutes!" shouted a man with a megaphone. "Take your places, friends and strangers."

The Repentance people were filing in at one side, intoning in chorus, "Mer-cy, Mer-cy."

The atmosphere suddenly took on tension. It was now very close and hot in the big tent. A boy from the Mayor's office wiggled through the crowd, beckoning Laban's party to come and sit in the guest chairs on the second level on the "face" side. In front of them at the rail, one of the Repentance ministers was arguing with an Albertan official over his right to occupy the space taken by a recorder, it being his special duty to look into the Man John's eyes.

"Can he really see us?" Mira asked her uncle.

"Blink your eyes," Laban told her. "A new scene every blink, that's what he sees. A phantasmagoria. Blink-blink-blink—for god knows how long."

"Mer-cy, Mer-er-cy!" intoned the Repentancites. "May the red of sin pa-aa-ass from us!" neighed a woman's voice.

"They believe his oxygen tab went red because of the state of their souls," Laban chuckled. "Their souls are going to have to stay damned awhile; John Delgano has been on oxygen reserve for five centuries—or rather, he *will be* low for five centuries more. At a half-second per year his time, that's fifteen minutes. We know from the audio trace he's still breathing more or less normally and the reserve was good for twenty minutes. So they should have their salvation about the year seven hundred, if they last that long."

"Five minutes! Take your seats, folks. Please sit down so everyone can see. Sit down, folks."

"It says we'll hear his voice through his suit speaker," Serli whispered. "Do you know what he's saying?"

"You get mostly a twenty-cycle howl," Laban hissed back. "The recorders have spliced up something like '*ayt*,' part of an old word. Take centuries to get enough to translate."

"Is it a message?"

"Who knows? Could be his word for 'date' or 'hate.' 'Too late,' maybe. Anything."

The tent was quieting. A fat child by the railing started to cry and was pulled back onto a lap. There was a subdued mumble of praying. The Resurrection faction on the far side rustled their flowers.

"Why don't we set our clocks by him?"

"It's changing. He's on sidereal time."

"*One minute.*"

In the hush the praying voices rose slightly. From outside, a chicken cackled. The bare center space looked absolutely ordinary. Over it the recorder's silvery filaments eddied gently in the breath from a hundred lungs. Another recorder could be heard ticking faintly.

For long seconds nothing happened.

The air developed a tiny hum. At the same moment, Mira caught a movement at the railing on her left.

The hum developed a beat and vanished into a peculiar silence and suddenly everything happened at once.

Sound burst on them, raced shockingly up the audible scale. The air cracked as something rolled and tumbled in the space. There was a grinding, wailing roar and—

He was there.

Solid, huge—a huge man in a monster suit, his head only a dull bronze transparent globe. Behind it a human face, dark smear of open mouth. His position was impossible, legs strained forward thrusting himself back, his arms frozen in a whirlwind swing. Although he seemed to be in frantic forward motion, nothing moved; only one of his legs buckled or sagged slightly—

—And then he was gone, utterly and completely gone in a thunderclap, leaving only the incredible afterimage in a hundred pairs of staring eyes. Air boomed, shuddering; dust roiled out mixed with smoke.

"Oh, oh my God," gasped Mira, unheard, clinging to Serli. Voices were crying out, choking. "He saw me, he saw me!" a woman shrieked. A few people dazedly threw their confetti into the empty dust-cloud; most had failed to throw at all. Children began to howl. "He *saw* me!" the woman screamed hysterically. "Red, Oh Lord have mercy!" a deep male voice intoned.

Mira heard Laban swearing furiously and looked again into the space. As the dust settled, she could see that the recorder's tripod had tipped over into the center. There was a dusty mound lying against it—flowers. Most of the end of the stand seemed to have disappeared or been melted. Of the filaments nothing could be seen.

"Some damn fool pitched flowers into it. Come on, let's get out."

"Was it under, did it trip him?" asked Mira, squeezed in the crowd.

"It was still red, his oxygen thing," Serli said over her head. "No mercy this trip, eh, Laban?"

"Shsh!" Mira caught the Repentance pastor's dark glance. They jostled through the enclosure gate and were out in the sunlit park, voices exclaiming, chattering loudly in excitement and relief.

"It was terrible," Mira cried softly. "Oh, I never thought it was a real live man. There he is, he's *there*. Why can't we help him? Did we trip him?"

"I don't know, I don't think so," her uncle grunted. They sat down near the new monument, fanning themselves. The curtain was still in place.

"Did we change the past?" Serli laughed, looked lovingly at his little wife, wondering for a moment why she was wearing such odd earrings. Then he remembered he had given them to her at that Indian pueblo they'd passed.

"But it wasn't just those Alberta people," said Mira. She seemed obsessed with the idea. "It was the flowers really." She wiped at her forehead.

"Mechanics or superstition," chuckled Serli. "Which is the culprit, love or science?"

"Shsh," said Mira again. "The flowers were love, I guess . . . I feel so strange. It's hot. Oh, thank you." Uncle Laban had succeeded in attracting the attention of the iced-drink vendor.

People were chatting normally now and the choir struck into a cheerful song. At one side of the park a line of people were waiting to sign their names in the visitors' book. The mayor appeared at the park gate, leading a party up the bougainvillea alley for the unveiling of the monument.

"What did it say on that stone?" Mira asked. Serli showed her the guidebook picture of Carl's rock with the inscription translated below: WELCOME HOME JOHN.

"I wonder if he can see it."

The mayor was about to begin his speech.

Much later when the crowd had gone away, the monument stood alone in the dark, displaying to the moon the inscription in the language of that time and place:

> ON THIS SPOT THERE APPEARS ANNUALLY THE FORM OF MAJOR JOHN DELGANO, THE FIRST AND ONLY MAN TO TRAVEL IN TIME.
>
> MAJOR DELGANO WAS SENT INTO THE FUTURE SOME HOURS BEFORE THE HOLOCAUST OF DAY ZERO. ALL KNOWLEDGE OF THE MEANS BY WHICH HE WAS SENT IS LOST, PERHAPS FOREVER. IT IS BELIEVED THAT AN ACCIDENT OCCURRED WHICH SENT HIM MUCH FARTHER THAN WAS INTENDED. SOME ANALYSTS SPECULATE THAT HE MAY HAVE GONE AS FAR AS FIFTY THOUSAND YEARS. HAVING REACHED THIS UNKNOWN POINT MAJOR DELGANO APPARENTLY WAS RECALLED, OR ATTEMPTED TO RETURN, ALONG THE COURSE IN SPACE AND TIME THROUGH WHICH HE WAS SENT. HIS TRAJECTORY IS THOUGHT TO START AT THE POINT WHICH OUR SOLAR SYSTEM WILL OCCUPY AT A FUTURE TIME AND IS TANGENT TO THE COMPLEX HELIX WHICH OUR EARTH DESCRIBES AROUND THE SUN.
>
> HE APPEARS ON THIS SPOT IN THE ANNUAL INSTANTS IN WHICH HIS COURSE INTERSECTS OUR PLANET'S ORBIT AND HE IS APPARENTLY ABLE TO TOUCH THE GROUND IN THOSE INSTANTS. SINCE NO TRACE OF HIS PASSAGE INTO THE FUTURE HAS BEEN MANIFESTED, IT IS BELIEVED THAT HE IS RETURNING BY A DIFFERENT MEANS THAN HE WENT FORWARD. HE IS ALIVE IN OUR PRESENT. OUR PAST IS HIS FUTURE AND OUR FUTURE IS HIS PAST. THE TIME OF HIS APPEARANCES IS SHIFTING GRADUALLY IN SOLAR TIME TO CONVERGE ON THE MOMENT OF 1153.6, THE SECOND OF MAY 1989 OLD STYLE, OR DAY ZERO. THE EXPLOSION WHICH ACCOMPANIED HIS RETURN TO HIS OWN TIME AND PLACE MAY HAVE OCCURRED WHEN SOME ELEMENTS OF THE PAST INSTANTS OF HIS COURSE WERE CARRIED WITH HIM INTO THEIR OWN PRIOR EXISTENCE. IT IS CERTAIN THAT THIS EXPLOSION PRECIPITATED THE HOLOCAUST WHICH ENDED FOREVER THE AGE OF HARDSCIENCE.

—He was falling, losing control, failing in his fight against the terrible momentum he had gained, fighting with his human legs shaking in the inhuman stiffness of his armor, his soles charred, not gripping well now, not enough traction to brake, battling, thrusting as the flashes came, the punishing alternation of light, dark, light, dark, which he had borne so long, the claps of air thickening and thinning against his armor as he skidded through space which was time, desperately braking as the flickers of earth hammered against his feet—only his feet mattered now, only to slow and stay on course —and the course, the beam was getting slacker; as he came near home, it

was fanning out, hard to stay centered; he was becoming, he supposed, more probable; the wound he had punched was healing itself. In the beginning it had been so tight, a single ray, a beacon in a closing tunnel—he had hurled himself after it like an electron flying to the anode, aimed surely along that exquisitely complex single vector of possibility of life, shot and been shot like a squeezed pip into the last chink in that rejecting and rejected nowhere through which he, John Delgano, could conceivably continue to exist, the hole leading to home—had pounded down it across time, across space, pumping with his human legs as the real earth of that unreal time came under him, his course as certain as the twisting dash of an animal down its burrow, he a cosmic mouse on an interstellar, intertemporal race for his nest with the wrongness of everything closing round the rightness of that one course, the atoms of his heart, his blood, his every cell crying Home— Home!—as he drove himself after that fading breath-hole, each step faster, surer, stronger, until he raced with invincible momentum upon the rolling flickers of earth as a man might race a rolling log in a torrent. Only the stars stayed constant around him from flash to flash, he looking down past his feet at a million strobes of Crux, of Triangulum; once at the height of his stride he had risked a century's glance upward and seen the Bears weirdly strung out from Polaris—But a Polaris not the Pole Star now, he realized, jerking his eyes back to his racing feet, thinking, I am walking home to Polaris, home! to the strobing beat. He had ceased to remember where he had been, the beings, people or aliens or things he had glimpsed in the impossible moment of being where he could not be; had ceased to see the flashes of worlds around him, each flash different, the jumble of walls, faces, plains, forests, colors—some lasting a breath, some changing pell-mell—the faces, forms, things poking at him; the nights he had pounded through, dark or lit by strangeness, roofed or unroofed; the days of jumbled sunlight, stormclouds, indoors, outdoors, wet spray, dust, into night again, strobe after strobe, to day; he was in day now. I am getting closer at last, he thought, the feel is changing—but he had to slow down, to check; and that stone near his feet, it had stayed there some time now; he wanted to risk a look but he did not dare, he was so tired, and he was sliding, was going out of control, fighting to kill the merciless velocity that would not let him slow down; he was hurt, too, something had hit him back there, they had done something, he didn't know what back somewhere in the kaleidoscope of faces, arms, hooks, beams, centuries of creatures grabbing at him—and his oxygen was going, never mind, it would last—it had to last, he was going home, home! And he had forgotten now the message he had tried to shout, hoping it could be picked up somehow, the important thing he had repeated; and the thing he had carried, it was gone now, his camera was gone too, something had torn it away—but he was coming home! Home! If only he could kill this momentum, could stay on the failing course, could slip, scramble, slide, somehow ride this avalanche down to home, to home—and his throat said Home!—said Kate, Kate! And his heart shouted, his lungs almost gone now, as his legs fought, fought and failed, as his feet gripped and skidded and held and slid, as he pitched, flailed, pushed, strove in the gale of timerush across space, across time, at the end of the longest path ever: the path of John Delgano, coming home.

YOUR FACES, O MY SISTERS!
YOUR FACES FILLED
OF LIGHT!

Hot summer night, big raindrops falling faster now as she swings along the concrete expressway, high over the old dead city. Lightning is sizzling and cracking over the lake behind her. Beautiful! The flashes jump the roofs of the city to life below her, miles of cube-buildings gray and sharp-edged in the glare. People lived here once, all the way to the horizons. Smiling, she thinks of all those walls and windows full of people, living in turbulence and terror. Incredible.

She's passing a great billboard-thing dangling and banging in the wind. Part of a big grinning face: W-O-N-D-E-R-B-R-E-A, whatever that was, bright as day. She strides along, enjoying the cool rain on her bare head. No need to pull up her parka for a few minutes yet; the freshness is so great. All headaches completely gone. The sisters were wrong; she's perfectly fine. There was no reason to wait any longer, with the messages in her pack and Des Moines out there ahead. They didn't realize how walking rests you.

Sandals just getting wet, she notes. It feels good, but she mustn't let them get wet through; they'll chafe and start a blister. Couriers have to think of things like that. In a few minutes she'll climb down one of the ramps and take shelter.

There's ramps along here every half-mile or so, over the old city. Chicago or She-cago, which was it. She should find out; she's been this way several times now. Courier to the West. The lake behind her is Michigam, Michi-gami, the shining Big Sea Water. Satisfied, she figures she has come nearly seventy miles already since she left the hostel yesterday, and only one hitch. I'm not even tired. That beautiful old sister, she thinks. I'd have liked to talk with her more. Like the wise old Nokomis. That's the trouble, I always want to stop and explore the beautiful places and people, and I always want to get on too, get to the next. Couriers see so much. Someday she'll come back here and have a good swim in the lake, loaf and ramble around the old city. So much to see; no danger except from falling walls; she's expert at watching that. Some sisters say there are dog-packs here; she doesn't believe it. And even if there are, they wouldn't be dangerous. Animals aren't dangerous if you know what to do. No dangers left at all, in the whole free wide world!

She shakes the rain out of her face, smiling up at the blowing night. To be a courier, what a great life! Rambling woman, on the road. Heyo, sister! Any mail, any messages for Des Moines and points west? Travel, travel on. But she is traveling in really heavy downpour now, she sees. She squeezes past a heap of old wrecked "cars" and splash! one foot goes in ankle-deep. The rain is drumming little fountains all over the old roadway. Time to get under; she reaches back and pulls the parka hood up from under her pack, thinking how alive the highway looks in the flashing lightning and rain. This road must have been full of the "cars" once, all of them shiny new, roaring along probably quite close together, belching gases, shining their lights, using all this space. She can almost hear them, poor crazy creatures. *Rrrr-oom!* A blazing bolt slaps down quite near her, strobes on and off. Whew! That was close. She chuckles, feeling briefly dizzy in the ozone. Ah, here's a ramp right by her, it looks okay.

Followed by a strange whirling light-shaft, some trick of the storm, she ducks aside and runs lightly down from the Stevenson Expressway into the Thirty-fifth Street underpass.

"Gone." Patrolman Lugioni cuts the flasher, lets the siren growl diminuendo. The cruiser accelerates in the curb lane, broadcasting its need of a ring job. "S—tass kids out hitching on a night like this." He shakes his head.

Al, the driver, feels under his leg for the pack of smokes. "I thought it was a girl."

"Who can tell," Lugioni grunts. Lightning is cracking all around them; it's a cloudburst. On every side of them the Saturday night madhouse tears on, every car towing a big bustle of dirty water in the lights of the car behind.

—Dry under the overpass, but it's really dark in here between the lightning flashes. She pushes back her parka, walks on, carefully avoiding wrecks and debris. With all that flashing, her night-vision won't develop. Too bad, she has keen night-vision. Takes forty-five minutes to come up fully; she knows a lot of stuff like that.

She's under a long elevated roadway down the center of an old street; it seems to go on for miles straight ahead. Almost straight West, good. Outside on both sides the open street is jumping with rain, splashing up white like plaster grass as the lightning cracks. *Boom! Barooomm-m-m!* The Midwest has great storms. She loves the wild uproar; she loves footing through a storm. All for her! How she'd like to strip and run out into it. Get a good bath, clean off all the dust and sweat. Her stuff would keep dry in here. Hey, shall I? . . . Almost she does, but she isn't really that dirty yet and she should get on; she lost so much time at that hostel. Couriers have to act responsible. She makes herself pad soberly along dodging junk in the dark, thinking, Now here's the kind of place a horse would be no good.

She has always this perennial debate with herself about getting a horse. Some of the couriers like to ride. It probably *is* faster, she thinks. But not much, not much. Most people have no idea how fast walking goes; I'm up and moving while they're still fussing with the horse. And so much trouble, feeding them, worrying about their feet. You can carry more, of course. But the real point is how isolated it makes you. No more hitching, no more fun of getting to know all kinds of sisters. Like that wise motherly sister back there who picked her up coming into the city. Sort of a strange dialect, but I could understand her, and the love showed through. A mother. . . . Maybe I'll be a mother someday, she thinks. But not yet. Or I'll be the good old Nokomis. *The wrinkled old Nokomis, many things Nokomis taught her.* . . . And those horses she had, I never saw horses go like that. Must be some tremendous farms around here. Tomorrow when she's out of the city, she'll get up on a high place where she can really look over the country. If I see a good horse-farm, I'll remember. A horse would be useful if I take the next route, the route going all the way West, across the Rockies. But Des Moines is far enough now. Des Moines is just right, on my own good legs.

"She was one of *them*, one of those bra-burners," Mrs. Olmsted says pursily, sliding gingerly out of her plastic raincoat. She undoes her plastic Rainflower bonnet. "Oh god, my set."

"You don't usually pick up hitchers, Mom." Bee is sitting in the dinette, doing her nails with Plum Love.

"It was starting to storm," the mother says defensively, hustling into the genuine Birdseye kitchen area. "She had a big knapsack on her back. Oh, to tell you the truth, I thought it was a Boy Scout. That's why I stopped."

"Ha ha ha."

"I dropped her right at Stony Island. That's as far as we go, I said. She kept talking crazy about my face."

"Probably stoned. She'll get murdered out there."

"Bee, I told you, I wish you wouldn't use that word. I don't want to know about it, I have no sympathy at all. She's made her bed, I say. Now, where's the Fricolator lid?"

"In the bathroom. What about your face?"

"What's it doing in the bathroom?"

"I used it to soak my fluffbrush, it's the only thing the right shape. What'd she say about your face?"

"Oh, Bee, your father would murder you. That's no way to do, we eat out of that." Her voice fades and rises, still protesting, as she comes back with the lid.

"My hair isn't poison, Mom. Besides, the heat will fix it. You know my hair is pure hell when it rains, I have to look good at the office."

"I wish you wouldn't swear, either."

"What did she say about your face, Mom?"

"Oh, my face. Well! 'Your face has wisdom,' she says in this crazy way. 'Mother-lines full of wisdom and light.' *Lines.* Talk about rude! She called me the wrinkled old somebody. I told her what I thought about girls hitchhiking, believe me I told her. Here, help me clear this off, your father will be home any minute. You know what she said?"

"What did she say? Here, hand me that."

"She asked, did I mean dogs? *Dogs!* 'There is no fear,' she says, 'there is no fear on the whole wide earth.' And she kept asking me where did I get the horses. I guess that's some word they have, she meant the Buick."

"Stoned, I told you. Poor kid."

"Bee, *please.* What I say is, a girl like that is asking for it. Just asking for whatever she gets. I don't care what you say, there are certain rules. I have no sympathy, no sympathy at all."

"You can say that again."

—Her sandals are damp but okay. Good leather, she sewed and oiled them herself. When she's real old, she'll have a little cabin by the road somewhere, make sandals and stuff for the sisters going by. How would I get the leather, she thinks. She could probably deal with one of the peddler sisters. Or can she tan it herself? It isn't so hard. Have to look that up some time.

The rain is still coming down hard; it's nice and cool now. She notices she has been scuffling through drifts of old paper, making it sail away into the gusty wind. All kinds of trash, here and everywhere. How they must have lived. The flashing outside is lighting up a solid wall of ruined buildings. Big black empty windows, some kind of factory. A piece of paper blows up and sticks on her neck. She peels it off, looks at it as she walks. In the lightning she can see it's a picture. Two sisters hugging. Neat. They're dressed in funny old clothes. And the small sister has such a weird look, all painted up and strange. Like she was pretending to smile. A picture from the troubles, obviously.

As she tucks it in her pocket, she sees there's a light, right ahead between the pillars of the overpass. A hand-lantern, it moves. Somebody in here too, taking shelter. How great! Maybe they even live here, will have tales to tell! She hastens toward the light, calling the courier's cry:

"Heyo, Sister! Any mail, any messages? Des Moines and going West!"

Yes—she sees there are two of them, wrapped up in raingear, leaning on one of the old "cars." Probably travelers too. She calls again.

"Hello?" one of them replies hesitantly. They must be worried by the storm. Some sisters are. She'll reassure them, nothing to be afraid of, nothing at all. How she loves to meet new sisters; that's the beautiest part of a courier's life. Eagerly she strides through papers and puddles and comes into the circle of their light.

"But who can we report it *to*, Don? You aren't even known here, city police wouldn't pay any attention."

He shrugs regretfully, knowing his wife is right.

"*One more unfortunate, weary of breath, rashly importunate, gone to her death.*"

"What's that from?"

"Oh, Hood. Thomas Hood. When the Thames used to be full of ruined women."

"Wandering around in this district at night, it's suicide. We're not so safe here ourselves, you know. Do you think that AAA tow truck will really come?"

"They said they would. They have quite a few calls ahead of us. Nobody's moving out there, she'll probably be safe as long as this downpour lasts, anyway. We'll get inside when it eases up."

"Yes. . . . I wish we could have done something, Don. She seemed so, I don't know, not just a tramp."

"We couldn't very well hit her over the head and take her in, you know. Besides, she was a fairly strong-looking little piece, if you noticed."

"Yes. . . . Don, she *was* crazy, wasn't she? She didn't hear one thing you said. Calling you Sister. And that ad she showed us, she said it was two women. That's sick, isn't it—I mean, seriously disturbed? Not just drugs?"

He laughs ruefully. "Questions I'd love to be able to answer. These things interact, it's tough to unscramble. But yes, for what it's worth, my intuition says it was functional. Of course my intuition got some help, you heard her say she'd been in a hospital or hostel somewhere. . . . If I had to bet, Pam, I'd say post-ECS. That placid waxy cast to the face. Capillary patches. A lot of rapid eye movement. Typical."

"You mean, she's had electric shock."

"My guess."

"And we just let her walk away. . . . You know, I don't think that truck is coming at all. I think they just say yes and forget it. I've heard the triple-A is a terrible fraud."

"Got to give them time on a night like this."

"Ummm . . . I wonder where she is now."

"Hey, look, the rain's letting up. We better hop inside and lock the doors."

"Right, sister."

"Don't you start that, I warn you. Lock that back window, too."

"Don . . ."

"Yeah, what?"

"Don, she seemed so, I don't know. Happy and free. She—she was *fun.*"

"That's the sick part, honey."

—The rain is letting up now, she sees. How convenient, because the sheltering ramp is now veering away to the North. She follows the median strip of the old avenue out into the open, not bothering to put the parka up. It's a wrecked part of the city, everything knocked down flat for a few blocks, but the street is okay. In the new quiet she can hear the lake waves smacking the shore, miles behind. Really have to stop and camp here awhile some trip, she thinks, skirting a wreck or two on the center strip. By the Shining Big Sea Waters.

Was it Michi-Gami or Gitche-Gumee? No matter; she loves the whole idea of Hiawatha. In fact she always felt she *was* the sister Hiawatha somehow; it's one of the few pieces from the old days that makes any sense to her. Growing up learning all the ways of the beautiful things, the names of the wild creatures, learning lovingly all the richness, learning how. There are words for it, some of the sisters talk so beautifully. But that's not her way, words; she just knows what's the way that feels right. The good way, and herself rambling through the wonderful world. Maybe she's a little superficial, but it takes all kinds. I'm the *working* kind, she thinks proudly. Responsible, too, a courier. Speaking of which, she's at a Y; better make sure she's still headed West. These old streets can twist you.

She stops and opens her belt compass, watches the dim green needle steady. There! Right that way. And what luck. In the last flickers of lightning she can see trees a couple of blocks ahead. Maybe a park!

How fast these storms go. She dodges across a wreck-filled intersection, and starts trotting for the sheer joy of strength and health down the open median toward the park. Yes, it looks like a long strip of greenery, heading due West for quite a ways. She'll have nice walking. Somewhere ahead she'll hit another of the old freeways, the Kennedy or the Dan Ryan, that'll take her out of the city. Bound to be traffic on them too, in the morning. She'll get a hitch from a grain-cart maybe, or maybe a peddler. Or maybe something she's never seen before, one more of the surprises of the happy world.

Jogging, feeling her feet fall fast and free, she thinks with respect of the two sisters she met back there under the ramp. The big one was some kind of healer, from down South. So loving together, making jokes. But I'm not going to get sick anymore, I'm really well. Proud of the vitality in her, she strides swiftly across the last intersection and spots a path meandering into the overgrown strip of park. Maybe I can go barefoot in there, no glass, she thinks. The last lightning-flash helps her as she heads in under the dripping trees.

The biker cuts off his spotlight fast, accelerates past the park entrance. She looked okay, little and running. Scared. But something about her bothers him. Not quite right. Maybe she's meeting somebody in there?

He's running alone tonight, the rain freaked them all out. Alone isn't so good. But maybe she's alone, too? Small and alone. . . .

Gunning up Archer Avenue, he decides to cut back once through the park cross-over, check it out. The main thing is not to get the bike scratched up.

—Beautiful cool clean breeze on her face, and clouds are breaking up. Old moon is trying to shine out! The path is deep in leaves here; okay to get the sandals off and dry them awhile.

She balances one-legged, unbuckling. The left one is soaked, all right. She hangs them over her pack and steps out barefoot. Great.

Out beyond the trees the buildings are reared up high on both sides now, old cubes and towers sticking up at the racing clouds, glints of moonlight where the glass windows are still in. Fantastic. She casts a loving thought back toward the long-dead ones who had built all this. The Men, the city-builders. So complex and weird, so different from the good natural way. Too bad they never lived to know the beautiful peaceful free world. But they wouldn't have liked it, probably. They were sick, poor things. But maybe they could have been different; they were people too, she muses.

Suddenly she is startled by the passage of something crashing across the path ahead, and without thinking springs nimbly into a big bush. Lightning, growling noises—in a minute it fades away. A deer, maybe, she wonders, rubbing her head. But what was the noise? One of those dogs, maybe? Could it be a dog-pack?

H'mmm. She rubs harder, frowning because the headache seems to have come back. Like a knife-blade in her temple. Ouch! It's really bad again; it's making her dizzy. She blinks, sees the buildings beyond the park blaze up brightly—squares of yellow light everywhere like a million windows. Oh no, not the bad hallucinations again. No, she's well now!

But yes, it is—and great lights seem to be suddenly everywhere; a roar of noise breaks out all around her in the dead streets; things are rushing and clanging. Maybe she isn't quite as well as she thought.

Grunting softly with pain, she strips a bunch of cool wet leaves, presses it against her forehead, the veins in her neck. Pressure. That's what it is; the air-pressure must have changed fast in the storm. She'll be all right in a few minutes. . . . Even the memory of the deer seems strange, as if she'd glimpsed some kind of crazy machine with a sister riding on it. Crazy! The uproar around her has voices in it, too, a ghostly whistle blows. . . . Go away, dreams. . . .

She stands quietly, pressing the coolness to her temples, willing the noisy hallucination to leave. Slowly it does; subsides, fades, vanishes. Leaving her in peace back in the normal, happy world. She's okay; that was nothing at all!

She tosses the leaves down and strikes out on the path, remembering— whew!—how bad it had been when she was back there at the hostel. All because of that funny flu or whatever that made her gut swell up so. Bad dreams all the time, real horrible hallucinations. Admit it; couriers do catch things. But it's worth it.

The sisters had been so scared. How they kept questioning her. Are you dreaming now? Do you see it now, dear? Making her describe it, like she was a historical play. They must read too much history, she thinks, splashing through a puddle, scaring up some little night-thing. A frog, probably, out in the rain like me. And all that talk about babies. Babies. . . . Well, a baby might be nice, someday. Not till after a lot more trips, though. Right now she's a walking sister, traveling on, heading for Des Moines and points West!

Left-right, left-right, her slim strong legs carry her Indian style, every bit of her feeling good now in the rain-fresh night. Not a scrap weary; she loves her tough enduring wiry body. To be a courier, surely that's the best life of all. To be young and night-walking in the great free moonlit world. Heyo, sisters! She grins to herself, padding light-foot. Any messages, any mail?

"Of course she's not dangerous, Officer," the doctor says authoritatively. The doctor is a heavy, jolly-looking woman with a big Vuitton carry-all parked on the desk. The haggard young man slumped in a lounger over at the side stares tiredly, says nothing.

"Jeans, green parka, knapsack, sandals. May have credit cards," the detective repeats, writing in his notebook. "Hair?"

"Short. Just growing out, in fact, it was shaved during treatment. I realize that isn't much to go on."

The policeman juts his lip out noncommittally, writing. Why can't they keep track of their patients, a big place like this? One medium-height, medium-looking girl in jeans and a parka. . . .

"You see, she is quite, quite helpless," the heavy woman says seriously, fingering her desk calendar. "The delusional system has expanded."

"You were supposed to break that up," the young man says suddenly, not looking up. "My wife was, I mean, when I brought her here . . ."

His voice is stale with exhausted anger; this has all been said before. The psychiatrist sighs briefly, says nothing.

"The delusion, is it dangerous? Is she hostile?" the detective asks hopefully.

"No. I told you. It takes the form of a belief that she's living in another world where everybody is her friend. She's completely trusting, you'll have no difficulty."

"Oh." He puts the notebook away with finality, getting up. The psychiatrist goes with him to the door. Out of earshot of the husband she says quietly, "I'll be at my office number when you've checked the morgue."

"Yeah."

He leaves, and she walks back to the desk, where the young man is now staring unseeingly at a drift of Polaroid snaps. The one on top shows a young brown-haired woman in a yellow dress in a garden somewhere.

—Moon riding high now in the summer night, cutting through a race of little silver clouds, making shafts of light wheel over the still city. She can see where the park is ending up ahead; there's a wreck-strewn traffic circle. She swings along strongly, feeling now just the first satisfying edge of tiredness, just enough to make her enjoy her own nimble endurance. Right-and-a-left-and-a-right-and-a-left, toes-in Indian style, that trains the tendons. She can go on forever.

Now here's the traffic circle; better watch out for metal and glass underfoot. She waits for a bright patch of moonlight and trots across to the center, hearing one faint hallucinatory screech or roar somewhere. No, no more of *that.* She grins at herself firmly, making her way around the pieces of an old statue toppled here. *That is but the owl and owlet, talking in their native language,* something *Hiawatha's Sisters.* I'd like to talk with them in their native language, she thinks—and speaking of which, she sees to her delight there's a human figure on the far side of the circle. What, another sister out night-walking too!

"Heyo, sister!"

"Hi," the other replies. It's a Midwest person, she can tell. She must live here, can tell about the old city!

Eagerly she darts between the heaps in the roadway, joyfully comes to the beautiful sister, her face so filled in light.

"Where heading? Out to ramble? I'm a courier," she explains, taking the sister's arm. So much joy, a world of friends. "Any messages, any mail?" she laughs.

And they stride on together, free-swinging down the median strip of the old avenue to keep away from falling stuff in the peaceful old ruins. Over to one side is a bent sign saying *To Dan Ryan Expressway. O'Hare Airport.* On the heading for Des Moines and points West!

"I don't remember," the girl, or woman, repeats hoarsely, frowning. "I really don't remember, it was all strange. My head was really fucked up, I mean, all I wanted was to get back and sack out, the last john was a bummer. I mean, I didn't know the area. You know? I asked her could she give me some change."

"What did she say? Did she have money with her?" the older man asks with deadly patience. His wife is sitting on the leather sofa, her mouth trembling a little.

"I don't remember, really. I mean, she was talking but she wasn't listening, I could see she was behind some heavy stuff. She offered me some chocolate. Oh shit, she was gone. Excuse me. She was really gone. I thought she was—well, she kept saying, y'know. Then she gave me all her cards."

The man looks down at them silently, lying on the coffee table. His daughter's married name embossed on the brown Saks plastic.

"So when I saw the paper, I thought I should, well, you know." She gets up, smoothing her white Levis. "It wasn't just the reward. She. . . . Thanks anyway."

"Yes," he says automatically. "We do thank you, Miss Jackson, was it."

"Yes," his wife echoes shakily.

Miss Jackson, or whatever, looks around at the woman, the man, the elegantly lived-in library; hitches her white shoulderbag.

"I tried to tell her," she says vaguely. "She said, about going West. She wouldn't. . . . I'm sorry."

"Yes, thank you." He's ushering her to the door. "I'm afraid there wasn't anything anyone could do."

"She wasn't in this world."

"No."

When the door closes behind her, the older woman makes an uncertain noise and then says heavily, "Why?"

Her husband shakes his head, performs a non-act of straightening the credit cards, putting them on another table.

"We'll have to call Henry, when he gets back from . . ."

"*Why?*" the wife repeats as if angry. "*Why* did she? What did she want? Always running away. Freedom. Doesn't she know you can't have freedom? Why isn't this world good enough for her? She had everything. If I can take it, why can't she?"

He has nothing to say, only moves near her and briefly touches her shoulder.

"Why didn't Doctor Albers *do* something? All those drugs, those shocks, it just made her worse. Henry never should have taken her there, it's all his fault—"

"I guess Henry was desperate," her husband says in a gray tone.

"She was all right when she was with us."

"Maria. Maria, please. She was out of her head. He had to do something. She wouldn't even recognize her own baby."

His wife nods, trembling harder. "My little girl, my little girl . . ."

—Glorious how bright it is now; she pads along still barefoot on the concrete median, tipping her head back to watch the moon racing above the flying clouds, imparting life and motion to the silent street, almost as if it was alive again. Now watch it, she cautions herself cheerfully—and watch the footing too; no telling what kind of sharp stuff is lying out here. No more dreaming about the old days; that was what gave her the fever-nightmares. Dreaming she was stuck back in history like a caged-up animal. An "affluent young suburban matron," whatever that was. All those weird people, telling her, Don't go outside, don't do this, don't do that, don't open the door, don't breathe. Danger everywhere.

How did they *live*, she wonders, seeing the concrete good and clean underfoot. Those poor old sisters, never being free, never even being able to go walking! Well, those dreams really made history live and breathe for her, that was sure. So vivid—whew! Maybe some poor old sister's soul has touched hers, maybe something mystical like that. She frowns faintly, feeling a stab of pressure in her forehead.

Now really, watch it! she scolds herself, hoisting up the pack-straps, flapping the drying parka. All secure. She breaks into a slow, light-footed jog, just because she feels so good. Cities are so full of history. Time to forget all that, just appreciate being alive. Hello, moon! Hello, sky! She trots on carefully, tickled by it all, seeing a moon's-eye view of herself: one small purposeful dot resolutely moving West. Courier to Des Moines. All alone in the big friendly night-world, greeting the occasional night-bird sisters. One traveling woman, going on through.

She notes a bad scatter of debris ahead and slows to pick her way with care through the "cars," not wanting to put her sandals back on yet. It's so bright—and Hello! The sky really is brightening in the East behind her. Sunrise in another hour or so.

She's been on the road about twenty hours but she isn't really weary at all; she could go on all day if it didn't get so hot. She peers ahead, looking for signs of the Ryan Freeway that'll carry her West. What she'll do is stop and have a snack in the sunrise, maybe boil up some tea. And then go on awhile until it heats up, time to find a nice cool ruin and hole up for the day. Hey, maybe she can make O'Hare! She stayed there once before; it's neat.

She had enough rations in her pack to go at least two days easy, she figures. But she's short on chocolate now; have to get some at the next settlement if they have it. Sweet stuff is good for calories when you're exercising. She pads on, musing about the sister she shared her chocolate with while they walked together after the park. Such a free sweet face, all the sisters are so great but this one was especially interesting, living here studying the old days. She knew so much, all those stories, whew! Imagine when people had to sell their sex organs to the Men just to eat!

It's too much for her, she thinks, grinning. Leave that to the students. I'm an action-person, yes. A courier, a traveler, moving along looking at it all, the wonderfilled world. Sampling, enjoying, footing it over the miles. Right-and-a-left-and-a-right-and-a-left on the old roadways. A courier's feet are tough and brown as oak. *Of all beasts she learned the language, learned their names and all their secrets. Talked with them whene'er she met them* —a great rhythm for hiking, with a fresh breeze behind her and the moon setting ahead!

The breeze is making the old buildings on both sides creak and clank, too, she notices. Better stay out here in the middle, even if it's getting narrow. The houses are really crowded in along here, all sagging and trashy. "Slums," probably. Where the crazy people lived on top of each other. What a mess it must have been; interesting to her but rotten for them. Well, they're gone now, she thinks, dodging around a heap of broken junk in the intersection, starting down the center-strip of the next long block.

But something isn't gone, she notices; footsteps that have been pad-padding along after her for a while are still there. An animal, one of the poor dogs, she thinks. Following her. Oh well, they must do all right in here, with rats and such.

She whirls around a couple of times, but sees nothing. It must be scared. What's its native language, she wonders, and forgets about it as she sees ahead, unmistakable, the misty silhouette of a freeway overpass. Hey, is that the Ryan already?

She casts a glance up at the floating-down moon, sees the sky is paling fast. And the left side of the street is passing an empty cleared place, the going looks all right there. She decides to cross over.

Yes, it's good walking, and she settles into her easy barefoot swing, letting one last loving thought go back to the poor maddened people who once strove here, who somehow out of their anguish managed to send their genes down to her, to give her happy life: courier going West! With the dawn wind in her hair and the sun coming up to light the whole free world!

"A routine surveillance assignment," the young policewoman, O'Hara, says carefully.

"A stake-out." The bald reporter nods.

"Well, yes. We were assigned to surveil the subject building entrance. Officer Alioto and myself were seated in the parked car."

"So you saw the assault."

"No," she says stiffly. "We did not observe anything unusual. Naturally we observed the pedestrians, I mean the female subject and the alleged alleged assailants, they were moving West at the time."

"You saw four punks following her."

"Well, it could look that way."

"You saw them going after her and you just sat there."

"We carried out our *orders*," she tells him. "We were assigned to surveil the building. We did not observe any alleged attack, nobody was running."

"You see the four of them jump this girl and you don't call that an attack?"

"We did not observe it. We were two blocks away."

"You could have seen if you wanted to," he says tiredly. "You could have cruised one block, you could have tapped the horn."

"I told you we were on a covert detail. You can't expect an officer to destroy his cover every time some little tramp runs down the street."

"You're a woman," he says wonderingly. "You'd sit there and let a girl get it."

"I'm not a nursemaid," she protests angrily. "I don't care if she was crazy. A spoiled brat if you ask me, all those women lib freaks. I work. Who does she think she is, running on the street at night? She thinks the police have nothing more important to do than that?"

—Sunrise coming on sure enough though it's still dark down here. The magic hour. And that stupid dog or dogs are still coming on too, she notes. Pad-pad-pad, they've crossed over to the sidewalk behind her. Well, dogs don't attack people, it's just like those of false wolf-scares. *Learn of every beast its nature. Learn their names and all their secrets.* They're just lonesome and curious, it's their nature to follow people. Tag along and veer off if I say Boo.

She strides along, debating whether she should put her wet sandals on or whether it's going to stay this clean. If so, she can make it barefoot up to the expressway ramp—and it *is* the Ryan; she can see the big sign now. Great, that'll be the perfect place to make her breakfast, just about sunrise. Better remember to pick up a couple of dry sticks and some paper under the ramp, not much to burn on those skyways.

Ignoring the footfalls pattering behind, she lets her mind go back pleasurably to the great breakfasts she's had. All the sunrise views, how she loves that. Like the morning on the old Ohio Turnpike, when all the owls hooted at once, and the mists turned pink and rose up and there was the shining river all spread out below her. Beautiful. Even with the mosquitoes. If you're going to appreciate life, you can't let little things like mosquitoes bother you. . . . That was before her peculiar sickness, when she was at the hostel. So many good hostels she's stopped at, all the interesting different settlements and farms, all the great sister-people. Someday she'll do the whole West route, know people everywhere. . . . Pad-pad-pad; she hears them again momentarily, rubs away a tiny ache in her temple. *Boo,* she chuckles to herself, feeling her bare feet falling sturdy and swift, left-and-a-right-and-a-left, carrying her over the miles, across the free beautiful friendly Earth. O my sisters, living in light!

Pictures flit through her head, all the places she wants to visit. The Western mountains, the real big ones. And the great real Sea. Maybe she'll visit the grave of the Last Man when she's out there, too. That would be interesting. See the park where he lived, hear the tapes of his voice and all. Of course he probably wasn't the actually last Man, just the one they knew about. It would be really something to hear such a different person's voice.

Pad-pad-pad—louder, closer than before. They're going to be a nuisance if they follow her up the ramp and hang around her breakfast.

"Boo!" she shouts, laughing, swinging around at them. They scatter so fast she can barely glimpse dark shapes vanishing into the old walls. Good. "Boo!" she shouts again, sorry to have to drive them away, and swings back on course, satisfied.

The buildings are beside her now, but they're pretty intact, no glass she can see underfoot. In fact, the glass is still in the old store windows here. She glances in curiously as she passes, heaps of moldy stuff and faded pictures and printing. "Ads." Lots of sisters' faces, all looking so weird and fake-grinning. One window has nothing but dummy heads in it, all with strange-looking imitation hair or something on them. Fantastic.

—But here they come again behind her, pad-pad-pad, and she really ought to discourage them before they decide to stick with her up the freeway.

"Boo, boo! No—" Just as she's turning on them, something fast and dark springs and strikes or snaps at her arm. And before she can react, she sees they are suddenly all around her, ahead of her—rearing up weirdly, just like people!

"Get *out!*" she shouts, feeling a rush of something unknown—anger?—sending heat through her. This is almost like one of the dreams! But hardness strikes her neck, staggers her, with roaring in her ears.

She hits out awkwardly, feels herself slammed down on concrete—pain—her head is hurt. And she is striking, trying to fend them off, realizing unbelieving that the brutes are tugging at her, terribly strong, pulling her legs and arms apart, spread-eagling her.

"Sisters!" she shouts, really being hurt now, struggling strongly. "*Sisters! Help!*" But something gags her so that she can only choke, while she feels them tearing at her clothes, her belly. *No, no*—she understands with horror that they really are going to bite her, to eat her flesh, and remembers from somewhere that wild dogs tear out the victim's guts first.

A great wave of anger convulses her against their fangs, she knows this is a stupid accident, a mistake—but her blood is fountaining everywhere, and the pain, the *pain!* All in a moment she is being killed; she knows now she is going to die here.

—But as a truly terrible agony cuts into her crotch and entrails, she sees or thinks she sees—yes!—in the light, in the patches of sky between the terrible bodies of her attackers, she can see them coming—see far off but clear the beautiful faces of her sisters speeding to save her, to avenge her! O my sisters, yes—it will be all right now, she knows, choking in her blood. They will finish these animals. And my knapsack, my messages—somewhere inside the pain and the dying she knows it is all right, it will be all fixed when they get here; the beloved sisters will save her, this is just an accident—and soon she, or someone like her, will be going on again, will be footing over the wide free Earth, courier to Des Moines and points west—

THE PEACEFULNESS OF VIVYAN

The newsman had come a long way, studied by small spaceburned men who wore their lasers against naked callus. And he in turn had stared at his first sealmen, the natives of McCarthy's World. The newsman had been careful not to call it McCarthy's World now, but Sawewe. *Sawewe* meaning of course *Freedom*.

For another long wait all the newsman had seen of Sawewe was the dilapidation of the old Terran Enclave: a perfectly flat view of sea on one side and tropical scrub on the other. The surface of Sawewe was a limestone plain pitted with sinkholes which led—some of them—to the continent-wide cavern system in which the sealmen lived. Worthless, except that those gray-green spikes stretched unharvested to the horizon were silweed. The newsman, whose name was Keller, blew out his lips when he saw it. Back in the Empire a gram bag of silweed was worth half his payvoucher. He knew now why the planet-burners had been held off.

Finally because Keller was patient and tough and his credentials were good, there came the long trip in the sealed floater, and the blindfold, and the longer hours of stumbling down and down. Sawewe was not trusting toward Terrans. Keller tripped, heard a faint splash echo. Sealmen hooted; a scanner clicked. He trudged on, hoping he would not have to swim.

At last a hard woman's voice said, "Leave him here. You can take that off now."

He blinked into an enormous green dimness, a maze of terraces crumbling into water, low walls, incongruous wires, a plastic console in a carved niche. Folds of rock hung from the sky. This was a very old place.

"He will be here in an hour," said the woman, watching him. "He is on the reef."

Her hair was gray. She wore a wetsuit but no weapons, and her nose had been slit and crudely repaired. An Empire prisoner, one of the Terran traitors who had worked for Sawewe.

"Did they tell you about the contamination?"

Keller nodded.

"The Empire had no need to do that. We never had weapons there. If he talks to you, will you tell lies like the others?"

"No."

"Maybe."

"Did I lie about Atlixco?"

Her shrug conceded nothing. Keller could see that her face had once been very different.

"That's why he decided to see you."

"I'm very grateful, Mamsen."

"No titles. My name is Kut." She hesitated. "His wife Nantli was my sister."

She went away and Keller settled on a stone bench beside an ancient stalagmite frieze. Through the fins of a fish-god he could see two sealmen wearing headsets: a communications center. The pavement in front of him ended in a natural pool which shimmered away into gloom, lit here and there by yellow light-shafts from the stone sky. Water chuckled; a generator keened.

Suddenly Keller was aware that a man was squatting quietly by the poolside, looking at him. When their eyes met, the man smiled. Keller was immediately struck by the peaceful openness of the stranger's face. His smile was framed in a curly black beard. A gentle pirate, Keller thought, or a minstrel. A very tall man hunkered down like a boy, holding something.

Keller rose and sauntered over. It was a curious shell.

"The carapace has two openings," the man told him, turning the shell. "The animal inside is bimorphic, sometimes a single organism, sometimes two. The natives call it *Noshingra*, the come-and-go animal." He smiled up at Keller, his eyes very clear and defenseless. "What's your name?"

"Keller, Outplanet News. What's yours?"

The man's eyes softened as though Keller had made him a present, and he continued to gaze at Keller in a way so receptive and innocent that the newsman, who was very tired, found himself speaking of his journey and his hopes for the coming interview. The tall man listened peacefully, touching the shell with his hands as if it were a talisman that could protect them both from war and power and pain.

Presently the woman Kut came back with a mug of maté, and the man unfolded himself and drifted quietly away.

"Biologist?" Keller asked. "I didn't catch his name."

The woman's face went bleaker.

"Vivyan."

The newsman's memory hunted, jarred.

"*Vivyan?* But—"

She sighed. Then she jerked her head, motioning Keller to follow her. They went along behind a wall which became an open fretwork. Looking through, Keller could see the tall figure ambling toward them across a little bridge, still holding his shell.

"Watch," the woman told him.

The boy Vivyan had noticed the brown man first around the ski-fires of the snowy planet Horl. Vivyan noticed him particularly because he did not come to talk as most people did. Better so, Vivyan felt obscurely. He did not even learn the brown man's name then but simply saw him among the flame-lit faces, a stocky gray-brown man textured all over except for two white owl-rings around his eyes, which meant he wore goggles a lot.

Vivyan smiled at him as he did at everyone and when the singing was over he skied out across the moonlight to the ice-forests, pausing often to touch and examine lovingly the life of this mountain world. It was not long before certain snow-creatures trusted him, and the even shyer floating animals who were Horl's birds. The girl who had been with the brown man came to him too. Girls usually did. Vivyan found this delightful but not remarkable. People and animals always came to him and his body knew the friendly and joyful ways to touch each kind.

People, of course, seemed to need also to talk and talk which was a pity because their talk was mostly without meaning. Vivyan himself talked only to his special friend on Horl, the man who knew the names and hidden lives of the snow world and accepted all that Vivyan had observed. Thus should a man live, Vivyan knew, questing and learning and loving. He always remembered everything he encountered; his memory was perfect, like his eyes and ears. Why not? It pained him to see how other humans lived in dimness and distraction and he tried to help.

"See," he said tenderly to the brown man's girl, "Each branchlet has one drop of sap frozen on the tip of the bud. That makes a warming lens. It is called photothermal sap; without it the tree cannot grow."

The brown man's girl looked, but she turned out to be a strange tense girl preoccupied with hurtful things. She became preoccupied also with Vivyan's body and he did all he could for her, very enjoyably. And then when she and some of the others weren't around any more it was time to move on.

He didn't expect to see the brown man again. But some while later in the cantinas of McCarthy's World he did. McCarthy's World was the best yet—its long bright beaches with hidden marvels of its reefs by day and unending welcome in its nights. He had a special friend here too, a marine zoologist who lived up the coast beyond the Terran Enclave. Vivyan never went into the Enclave. His life was in the combers or drifting through the redolent cantinas, flowing with the music and the good vibrations. Young people from countless Terran worlds came to McCarthy's beaches and many short, excitable spacers on leave from the Terran base and even a few real aliens.

As always, arms and lips opened to him and he smiled patiently at the voices without hearing the words that his memory could not help recording. It was while he was being harangued by one of the spacers that Vivyan saw the white owl-eyes watching from the shadows. It was the brown man. A new girl was with him now.

The spacer pulled at him, obscurely and drunkenly outraged. Something about the natives of McCarthy's World. Vivyan had never seen one. He longed to. His friend had told him they were very shy. And there was something negative connected with them about which he did not inquire. It was tied in some way with a large badness—the lost third planet whose name Vivyan did not know. Once, he knew, all these three worlds, Horl and McCarthy's and the nameless one, had been all together and all friendly until the wrong thing had occurred. Terrans were hurt. A pity. Vivyan did not probe into negative, angry things. He smiled and nodded gently at the spacer, longing to share with him the reality of sunlight on the reef, quietness in the wind, love. The brown man was as before, remote. Not in need. Vivyan smiled and let arms pull him out to fly firekites on the murmuring beaches.

On another evening they were all linked in a circle singing one of the aliens' songs when the brown man's girl began to sing to him with slow intensity across the shadows. Vivyan saw she was a delicate cool girl like the firelace on the reefs and hoped she would come to him soon. When she sought him out next day he learned that her name was Nantli. To his delight she spoke very little. Her eyes, and her red-gold body made him feel enveloped in sun-foam.

"Beautiful Vivyan." Her hands traced him shyly. He smiled his innocent pirate's smile. People always said that; it seemed to be their way of making him feel good. They didn't understand that he always felt good. It was part of his way to be, natural that his long olive body was strong and that his beard curled joyfully. Why did other people hurt themselves so?

"Come to the reefs." It was fine how eagerly she came and let him teach her to quest down among the firelace to the hidden caverns below. Mc-

Carthy's fish circled and danced above their nests, rolling horrified eyes, so tame and ludicrous that the humans spluttered and had to surface to laugh.

Nantli dived and laughed and dived again until Vivyan became concerned and hauled her out on the rocks. And later in the breast of the moonlit dunes, it was very good. When she had left him, he stretched and set out up the beach to the home of his friend, bearing many things of which he wished to be told the names.

McCarthy's sun was a ghost flower rising on the misty sea when he walked back. Beautiful how it fitted, Vivyan thought, the total serenity he always felt after his long talk in the lamplit room.

When he looked back at the beach ahead, there was a gray-brown figure by the line of sea-wrack. Jarring. He could think of nothing to do but walk on forward.

The brown man was turning a sea-feather with his foot. He didn't look up, only said quietly, "Strange pattern. What's it called?"

Reassured, Vivyan squatted down to trace the sea-feather's veins. "It's a gorgonia, I think. A colony of animals in a common tissue, a coenchyme. This one came from somewhere else, a spore from the ships maybe."

"Another pattern." The brown man frowned, looking out to sea. "I'm interested in patterns. Like on Horl you were doing birds then, wasn't it? With that xenoecologist wallah around the mountain. And my girl went with you, on Horl. And you checked in with your friendly ecologist and my girl and a couple of our group turned up missing. Somebody came for them. Only it wasn't anybody we know and nobody's heard of them since."

He looked at Vivyan.

"And here you're into marine biology. And there's this marine-life wallah down the line you have long sessions with. And Nantli's got interested in you. A pattern. How does the pattern go, Vivyan? Does Nantli disappear too? I wouldn't like that. Not Nantli."

Vivyan kept turning the sea-feather, waiting for the sea-wind to carry away the harshness in the brown man's voice. After a moment he looked up and smiled. "What's your name?"

Their eyes met really close then, and something began happening inside Vivyan. The brown man's face was changing too, as if they were both under water.

"Vivyan," the brown man said fearful with intensity, *"Vivyan?"*

He pronounced it wrong, like *Feefyane.* Their eyes locked together and a hurt started lunging behind Vivyan's eyes.

"Vivyan!" the brown man insisted in a horrible tearing voice. "Oh, no. You—" And then everything was perfectly still until he whispered, "I think . . . I've been looking for you . . . Vivyan."

Vivyan's whole head was jerking; he tore his eyes down from the white-ringed glare. "Who are you?" he stammered. "What's your name?"

The brown man put two hard fingers under Vivyan's jaw and turned his face up.

"Look at me. Think of Zilpan, Vivyan, Tlaara, Tlaara-tzunca . . . little Vivyan, *don't you know my name?*"

Vivyan gave a raw cry and lunged clumsily at this small dangerous man. Then he was running into the sea, hurling himself across the shallows to the green depths where no one could follow. He stroked with all his strength, not looking back until he was in the thunders of the reef.

When the anger and hurtfulness had been cleaned away, he made for a coralhead far out, where he rested and dived and ate a conch and some sweet wet seahares and drowsed in the foam. He saw many calming things, and when the sun set, he went back to shore. It was in his mind that he should go again to visit his friend, but warm voices called him and he let himself be drawn to where huge arthrostraca were being roasted in seaweed. He had never seen the brown man in this place, and soon he began to grin again and eat vastly of the tender shellfish in the silvery silweed smoke.

But there was an undercurrent here too, a strainedness. People were restless, talking quick and low-voiced, looking past each other's shoulders. Was something unpleasant building, cramping the air?

Vivyan recalled sadly that he had noticed such feelings before. Certainly he must go soon to visit his friend. He hoped it was not becoming time to move on from this place too. He wolfed the delicious clams, soothing himself with the names of peaceful things, *Tethys, Alcyonaria, Coniatities, Coccolobis, Nantli.*

But Nantli was not a sea-creature; she was the brown man's girl, and suddenly she was here in the silsmoke by herself, coming to him smiling and still. All at once he felt better. Maybe the badness had gone now, he thought, stroking her hair. They went out together.

When they reached their place in the dune, he felt the tension under her stillness.

"You wouldn't hurt us, would you, Vivyan?" She held his sides, peering at his face. The stress inside her was disgusting to feel. He tried to help her, to let his calm flow into her. Her talking was like claws. Something about his friend. Patiently he recounted to her some of his new knowledge of the reef world.

"But about us," she persisted. "You didn't talk with him about us, about Cox?"

He stroked her breast, automatically registering the news that the brown man's name was *Cox*. Wrongness. He concentrated on the beautiful flow of his palms on her body. Nantli, Nantli. If only he could ease this frenzy that was eating at her. His body guided him and presently she quieted and let him mold them together, let the life rhythm rise in peace. When it had crested and spent itself, he stood up into the moonlight, pointing his beard at the sea.

"No, you go," she smiled. "I'm sleepy."

He touched her gratefully and went down to the silver water. As he dived, he heard her call.

Beyond the surf, he turned and began to swim along the coast. It was better this way; no one could bother him here as they had on the beach. His friend lived in a small cove, beyond the far point; to swim would mean only taking more time and the tide was running with him toward the setting moon. It drew him strongly, but not more strongly than his desire for the peace that only the long quiet talk would bring.

In the rhythm of his swimming he mused. Always there had been a friend for him, as the brown man—*Cox?*—had said. But that was good; that was necessary. How else could he understand a new place? On Horl there had been his friend on the mountain, and before that in another part of Horl where the mines were he had known a man who told him about the folding of mountains and the alien relics at which so many people came to wonder. That had been interesting but somehow troubled; he had not stayed long. And before that on the stations there had been the friends who taught him the names of stars and the large ways of suns. And before that, on the ships . . . so many lives to learn, such a universe of marvels to remember. His arms rose and thrust tirelessly, carried on the moon tide. He was just feeling the long swells off the point when the strange heads rose around him.

At first Vivyan thought they were McCarthy's seals, or a kind of dugong. Then a streaming crest came up alongside, and he saw moonlight on intelligent eyes and knew at once what they were: the natives of McCarthy's World.

He wasn't in the least frightened, only intensely curious. The moon was so bright he could see wet mottlings on the stranger's pelt, like a seal pup. It touched his arm with webbed fingers, pointing to the reef. They wanted him to go there. But he couldn't. Not now. He shook his head regretfully, trying to tell them he would come back when he had talked with his friend.

The sealman pointed again, and the others came closer. Then he saw they had weapons. A kind of spring-load spear. As they closed in, Vivyan shot downward with all his power. It would have carried him far from any Terran but the sealmen were easily before him in the glimmering darkness, herding him back.

It was not in his nature to fight. He surfaced and swam with them, debating what to do. Was it possible that it was intended for him to bring this too to his friend? But that did not seem fair, when he was already so burdened.

He swam mechanically, watching the stranger's eyes film and clear. They seemed to have transparent inner lids like certain fish which could focus either in water or air. Their eyes were huge, too; undoubtedly they were nocturnal.

"N'ko, n'ko!" the leader hooted, the first sound they had made. They were motioning him to dive. He did so and found himself being pulled under the reef. Just as his lungs began to knot, he saw, incredibly, a bright light ahead. They burst up into a cavern booming with sea-sound. He gulped air, staring with delight at a lantern on a ledge. All doubts vanished; he was glad he had come.

The webbed ones were scrambling out around him. Bipeds no taller than his waist, with lobed and crested heads. When they tugged his arms he bent and let them blindfold him before they led him into a tunnel. What an adventure to tell his friend!

The tunnel was dripping and musty, and the way was hard to his feet. Coral. Presently he had to go under water again, still blindfolded. When they came out, the air was dry and warmer, and when he stumbled, he felt crumbling limestone shelves. His sealmen hooted, were answered. Suddenly he was jostled and turned, and they were taking his blindfold off, in a crowded place where several passageways met.

Before him stood three much larger sealmen. To Vivyan's intense surprise they were holding weapons of a type which he knew was forbidden. He was just looking at these when the scent of the girl Nantli pulled his head around. How could she be here? He smiled uncertainly and then he saw the white eyes of the man Cox. The adventure was going bad.

"All right." Cox spoke to the sealmen who had brought him and they pulled at Vivyan.

"Strip down."

Wondering, he did so and felt an instrument sliding on the base of his spine.

"See," said Nantli's voice. "A scar, I told you."

The brown man made a grunt like a sob and came and grasped Vivyan by the shoulders.

"Vivyan," he said thickly in the strange way. "Where are you from?"

"Alpha Centauri Four," Vivyan told him, automatically remembering the garden city, his parents. The memory felt queer, thin. He saw the big sealmen gazing expressionlessly, cradling their weapons.

"No, before that." Cox's grasp tightened. "Think, Vivyan. Where were you born?"

Vivyan's head began to hurt unpardonably. He squinted down through the pain, wondering how he could get away.

"They've done something to him, I told you," Nantli said.

"In God's name, try." Cox shook him. "Your real home! Your home, Vivyan. Remember Zilpan mountain? Remember—remember your black pony? Remember *Tlaara?* Have you forgotten your mother Tlaara, who sent you away when the revolt started, to keep you safe?"

The pain was terrible now. "Alpha Centauri Four," he whimpered.

"Stop, Cox," Nantli cried.

"Not Alpha!" Cox shook him savagely, his white eyes glaring. "Atlixco! Can a prince of Atlixco forget so easily?"

"Please stop it, please." Nantli begged. But Vivyan had realized he must listen very carefully in spite of the pain. Atlixco was the bad place, the world he didn't think about ordinarily. This was not ordinary. His friend would want him to listen.

"The scar." Cox breathed through his teeth, made a kind of dreadful chuckle. "I have one too. They've tried to make you look like an ordinary Terran. Don't you remember that little deformity you were so proud of, Vivyan? Alpha Centauri! You're twenty generations of inbred Atlixco, Vivyan, born with a curly, hairy tail. *Remember?"*

Vivyan cringed helplessly under the angry voice. Nantli pushed forward.

"What did they tell you about Atlixco, Vivyan?" she asked gently.

A painful shutter seemed to grate in Vivyan's head.

"Butchers . . . murderers . . . All dead," he whispered.

Nantli pried at the brown man's hands. "Alpha Centauri, he grew up believing it all. A good Terran upbringing. Let him be, there isn't time."

"All dead?" Cox demanded. "Look at me, Vivyan. *You know me.* Who am I?"

"Cox," Vivyan gasped. "I must tell—"

A hard hand slashed across his face; he went down on one knee.

"Tell!" Cox roared. "You traitorous crotchlouse! Little Prince Vivyan, the Empire spy. You're the bloody answer to what happened to us on Horl, aren't you? And if we hadn't caught you tonight—"

A kick sent him sprawling at the sealmen's feet. They hooted and stamped. Everyone was yelling, Nantli screaming, "Cox! It's not his fault, they've messed up his mind, you can see that—" until Cox's bellow cut them all off.

He walked over to Vivyan and took him by the hair, scowling down into his face. It never occurred to Vivyan to use his strength against the terrifying little man.

"I should kill you," Cox said quietly. "Maybe I will. But maybe first we have a use for little Vivyan." He straightened up, releasing Vivyan. "If I can bear the sight. All those years," he said in a harsh hurting voice. *"Thank God at least the kid is safe. . . .* Terran filth. Take him to Doc."

He went out abruptly with the three big sealmen.

The pain in Vivyan's head quieted as he followed Nantli through green flaking tunnels to a large dim place. Seal people were lying everywhere, on ledges and piles of seaweed. Vivyan saw a small face bubbling at him over its mother's side. He smiled eagerly and then he noticed that there was something wrong with it. With all of them.

"Their skins," he said. An old Terran stood up.

"Hull-scrapers from the Enclave," the man said. "Poisons 'em."

"This is Vivyan, Doc," said Nantli. "He doesn't know who he is or anything."

"Who does?" grunted the doctor. Vivyan studied him, wondering if this could possibly be his new friend. He felt horribly shaken. Maybe this man was to prepare him to go on to a new place?

"Lie down," the doctor told him. Vivyan felt the flash of an injector. Suddenly he was very frightened. There was a danger he'd been warned against, a thing that was not allowed. If this man was not a friend, he had done something very wrong. How had this happened? He was trapped. Bad.

But then he remembered that there was some way to be all right, something his friends had fixed in case of trouble. He must relax. Peacefulness was the key. He lay quietly breathing the wet cave air, not looking or listening. But it was hard to be peaceful here. Sealmen were coming through, hooting at the sick ones on the seaweed, who roused themselves and hooted back. Shouting, stamping, more hooting.

Something seemed to be happening. A sealman shook a laser at the doctor, laughing in a wild yowling way. The doctor grunted, doing things to the seal-baby. Vivyan felt dizzy and unclean. In a moment he would leave this place.

But white-ringed eyes were over him. Cox.

"Now. Talk. How much have you passed your contact here?"

Vivyan could only stare; the words meant nothing. Nantli's face appeared, saying gently, "Don't be frightened, Vivyan. Just tell us. You did talk to your friend about me, didn't you?"

The shutter-thing in Vivyan's brain seemed to be sliding, melting.

"Oh yes." His lips felt floppy.

"That's right. And Captain Palcay, did you talk about him?"

"Pal, Palcay?" Vivyan mumbled. The brown man made an angry noise.

"The spacer you were with at Flor's, Vivyan, the one who got so drunk. Did you tell your friend about that?"

Vivyan could not follow her clearly, but at the words "tell your friend" he nodded his head, yes. Cox snarled.

"And have you told him you've seen Cox here?"

Vivyan felt a sudden jar inside him as though he had missed a step. The brown man—had he ever? This was very peculiar. Frightening. He turned his head to meet the pale ringed eyes.

"Cox?"

"Not Cox!" the brown man said furiously. "Cancoxtlan. *Cancoxtlan!* Remember yourself, Vivyan of Atlixco, son of Tlaara."

"My mother was raped and butchered by the rebels," Vivyan heard his voice saying in a weird flat tone. The words meant only pain. "They burned my father alive and all my family. The shrikes ate their bodies. My pony too." He began to sob. "Butchers. Traitors. You're hurting me, it hurts—"

The brown face watched him, suddenly still. Then Cox said heavily, "Yes. Princes get killed. Even good kind princes too. . . . I couldn't make them see, Vivyan. At the end I couldn't even get to them in time."

"We were so happy." Vivyan wept. "We were peaceful and beautiful."

"You were five years old," said Cox. "Didn't anybody ever tell you what we'd done to the Atlixcans? The real Atlixcans? Two centuries of happiness for Terran princes, two centuries of slavery—the debt got paid, Vivyan."

A sealman ran up uttering barking cries. Cox turned to him.

"Oh, God, they're going ahead," Nantli exclaimed. "Cox—"

"All the way," Cox said. He turned back and gripped Vivyan's head. "They lied to you, can you understand? *We* were wrong. *We* were the butchers. The Empire, us. We're fighting it now, Vivyan. You've got to come with us. You must. You owe it, Prince of Atlixco. We can use you in place, in their spy net—"

One of the big sealmen had come up and grabbed Cox's shoulder. Vivyan heard Nantli saying something and suddenly the white eyes had left him; they were all gone. Other sealmen and Terrans ran through, but no one bothered him.

He lay with his head whirling and hurting, wondering if it had been all right. His lips seemed to have spoken by themselves, as they did when he was with his friend. Was it all right? He must get out of here as soon as he could stand up.

He drowsed a little and then more sealmen were all around him, hooting, groaning, smelling of burned flesh and blood. A body bumped him. It was a Terran in a wetsuit, oozing blood. The man slumped down, yelling, "Hey Doc, you gloomy sod, we got the goddamn transmitters! You bloody pervert, Doc!" he shouted. "The 'Tlixcan ships are coming in. How about that, you gutless mother?"

"They'll burn the planet," the doctor told him. "Cut that off so you can fry clean."

He hauled the man away. Vivyan saw that the passage was now clear. Next minute he was out and running back the way he had come.

His memory was perfect, although he felt a little ill. All he had to do was let his feet carry him while his eyes and ears kept watch. Twice he ducked into side tunnels while sealmen went by with their wounded. Then he was at the place where many tunnels met, where they had removed his blindfold trusting to the maze.

Vivyan simply closed his eyes and let his body guide him back. Turn, rough place to the left, bend his head, cool air on his right side; the natural mechanism within him unspooled its perfect tape. He only had to hide once more. These passages seemed to be unused.

Presently he was through the inner pool and into the last dark tunnel undersea. This was easier yet; he could hear the water churning under the reef, and he ran stooped in the darkness, longing to be out in the clean, away from this peaceless place. Surely they would take him away now to a new place, after he had given all these things to his friend?

He reached the cavern. No lantern now. That didn't matter; Vivyan knew exactly where to dive, how to come up under the reef. He kicked powerfully down into blackness, thinking he must be sure to remember everything. This must be a secret way to the caves; it would be a wonderful surprise.

In a moment he had surfaced and marked the horizon and the stars. There seemed to be fires on the shore. He began to swim eagerly, feeling marvelous now. This would be his best yet. If only the name *Cancoxtlan* didn't trouble his head . . . but he would forget about that, he felt sure. Peace flooded him as he saw the far light of his friend's house by the cove.

"No one noticed he had gone," the woman told the newsman. "The fight for the Enclave had started and Cancoxtlan was there. When the Terrans broke in through the reef tunnel, we managed to blow the section between the hospital and the armory. They got the wounded, of course, and Doctor Vose. And Nantli. But it had no effect." Her scarred face was impassive. "Cox wouldn't surrender to save Nantli, she wouldn't have wanted that. The raid diverted one of their core units."

They watched Vivyan's tall figure moving aimlessly along the terrace, glancing in the water. Seen from behind he looked older, stooped, under the striking black hair.

"The spacers were with us, did you know that?" The woman was suddenly animated. "Oh yes, even the officers. When the cruiser from Atlixco showed up, they all came in." She grimaced. "We intercepted a Space Command signal about indoctrination to combat, quotes, *apathy*. . . . Empires grow old and foolish, even the revolt on Horl didn't wake them up. We'll have Horl next."

She checked herself then. They saw Vivyan glance round quickly and turn toward the wall.

"We found him wandering, afterward," the woman went on quietly. "Cancoxtlan's brother, after all. . . . He never understood what he'd done. We think now he was basically retarded, in addition to the conditioning they'd put him through. Nothing reached. You've heard of idiot savants? He's very gentle and that smile, one doesn't realize."

The newsman remembered his own gut response to the gentle stranger and shuddered. Exquisite tool of empire. A deadly child.

Vivyan had halted before a peculiar carving in an alcove. The newsman frowned. A Terran eagle, here? The boy-man seemed to be whispering to it.

"He carved it himself. Cox let him keep it. What does it matter now?" The woman bowed her bleak head. "Listen."

By a trick in the wall structure the newsman could hear perfectly what Vivyan was whispering.

". . . he says his name is Keller of Outplanet News. He didn't tell his first name. He says he came from Aldebaran Sector on the *Komarov* to interview the traitor Prince Cancoxtlan. He is about one meter eighty, medium build, gray hair and eyes. He has a scar on his right earlobe and his timer is forty-five units ahead of planet time . . ."

EXCURSION FARE

Several curious events were in the news that year, but young Dag and Philippa had been too busy to notice. And right now they were overwhelmed beyond thought of all else.

They were dying, or about to die, all alone in the reaches of the northern Atlantic Ocean.

"Letting up," Philippa gasped through crusted lips.

Feebly, she began to bail again. She was wedged into the rope-holds of the swamped, inflated raft that had been the passenger-pod of their balloon. In the gray-churned sea around her writhed bright tatters, all that was left of *Sky-Walker*.

They had been driven down into the ocean fifty screaming hours ago.

"No," Dag croaked from the other end of the pod, his voice startlingly loud in the sudden quiet. The wind-shriek had dropped, and the hail of spume upon them was subsiding. "It's only the eye. We're in the eye. Look up."

She looked and saw, above the great storm-walls curving away on either side, a strange gray-yellow patch of clear sky. It seemed to be evening, far away up there. But she could see, too, that the clear patch ended; dimly in the distance, the terrible storm-walls joined again. Beneath them would be raving, driving mountains of sea, air that was smashed and flying brine. The North side, too—worse even than what they'd miraculously lived through. Now the miracles were over.

"We can't—possibly—"

"No. Oh, god, f—k it," Dag groaned for the hundredth time. "This wasn't supposed to be here. 'Degenerated into a low'—aaagh!" He gave a bitter bark, and in the increasing calm, pried loose their last canteen and crawled over to her with it.

"Might as well finish this."

As they drank, pale sunlight touched them. "Good-bye, sun," Philippa whispered very low. They grasped each other in numb arms and kissed deeply.

"I got you into this. I got you into this," Dag said into her neck.

"It's all right, darling." Her lips were too cracked for her to speak clearly.

A big brownish flap of something dead slithered over the swamped side, washed away again. She shivered harder. "Do you think . . . I'd want you to be alone in this?"

There was clearly no hope, but he pulled away and crouched up to wrench loose and jettison the remains of the heater-struts that were weighing down one side of the raft. Their transceiver had doubtless long since ceased bleating out its SOS. He started to send it over too.

"No," Philippa protested weakly.

He tried to grin at her—a salt-crusted, sodden, red-eyed specter—and let it be, even straining over to straighten the antenna and give the emergency generator a few more cranks. Then he collapsed down in the water before her, grasping her cold legs with water-wrinkled hands. She dropped her futile bailer and clumsily caressed his head and shoulders, pulling him up into her lap. The sun-gleam had gone; they were both shivering uncontrollably now.

Over his head she could see the oncoming wind-wall, the end of the eye: great yellow-black spume-walls, racing from right to left.

"Let's . . . let's hold together now."

"No," he said unclearly. "Better chance if we balance it."

She nodded. They both knew there was no chance; he made no move to leave her. A burst of rain hissed onto them, mingled with a last light-ray. The roaring, howling mountains of death loomed louder, nearer. Already their raft was starting to move with it. As they waited for the end, Dag mumbled incomprehensibly: she caught the repeated word *prove* and held him tighter. He was affirming for the last time the deep dream, the drive that had powered their attempt: that lone human beings were still free to achieve high adventure, free to master fate, and defy the edicts of an overorganized world. . . .

Their pathetic little raft was already tossing in the first great chop before the roaring, racing mountains took them. Dag had forced himself away from Philippa when the raft was almost doubled end-over-end, but she had made her frozen fingers tie a rope from his waist to hers, and he had stretched his numb legs to clamp his feet around her ankles.

Darkness was all but on them now. The roaring grew. The tossing and spinning became more violent. Soon the first torrent of water broached over them. As they surfaced again, each struggled simultaneously to breathe and to see if the other lived.

Suddenly he heard her cry out so loudly that it pierced the storm. A terrible fear for her took him—and then he heard it too: through the howl and slamming came the pound of a powerful engine.

An instant later a blinding light poured on them through the spume, lost them, and came back from windward.

The two young people had only a momentary glimpse of something huge and white rising and falling alongside a few yards away, when a cable shot over their heads and their pod lurched, tilted, folded in on them and physically flew, struck something that might have been a plunging gunwale, and tumbled them out half smothered and drowned, onto a solid floor.

Quick hands cut them loose, a white-capped bronzed face with the name *Charon* in gold on the visor looked briefly down at them, then vanished. Great sobs were racking them both. They tried to say "thank you" through the spasms at half-seen grayish faces in the gray light as they felt themselves piled onto a bunk. Presently they realized the bunk was sodden, and more green water suddenly poured into what they saw was a cockpit.

The strange craft had seemed utter safety, steady as a rock, after the helpless raft, but they now could feel that she was pitching wildly. They were in fact far from safe yet; they were only in a lifeboat, with a hurricane still upon them. But they could feel no more fear, only trust in the tall white-clad man at the helm, and in his quick, silent crew.

"Okay, let's get out of here," the tall man said now. "Give 'em masks."

Scubalike masks were pressed over their faces. Philippa's head was gently pulled away from Dag's neck. She offered no resistance, but only reached for Dag's arm just as his hand found and gripped hers.

"Breathe. Breathe," ordered an accented voice.

The mask-air was fresh and sweet. The last thing they remembered was a swiftly increasing motor-roar, and a heave as if the lifeboat were planing up on foils as she drove into the gray-lit gale.

They came to in the beds of a pleasant room; only a calm, almost imperceptible engine-throb, and the slight swaying of the sunlight on the window-curtains, told them they were still at sea.

Dag twisted and groggily scanned a discreet panel displaying dials, lights, an outlet marked Oxygen, and then located Philippa in the next bed. Her dark eyes were on him, glowing and merry with love.

"I've been waiting for you to wake up. Watch it, you're hooked to a zillion IVs. The thing is—uh, oh!—" She retched noisily into a yellow basin she was holding.

"Are you okay? Hey, Phil!"

"The problem *is*," she continued with great dignity as the spasm waned, "you have to throw up a lot of salt water. Your basin's on the stand there. Maybe nausea won't hit you."

But it did; he grabbed his blue basin just in time, discovering in the process that his ribs on one side were bandaged and so was one knee.

When he could look up again, a red-haired nurse was in the room.

"You kids both with us again? I'm Anna Boyd." She wasn't pretty, but she had a great smile. She produced two shot-glasses full of green, syrupy-looking liquid.

"Drink this now, it'll help."

"Where are we? What day is this?" Dag asked.

"Tuesday. The rest later—here's Dr. Halloway. Drink up."

They drank, looking over the rims of their glasses at a middle-aged, slightly rotund man with sandy hair and very bright eyes. The name on his lab coat breast pocket said *Charon*. A little like a big chipmunk, Dag thought. But his eyelids were very heavy, and before Halloway could finish checking the knee-bandage, he was drifting off. He had just time to hear Philippa call sleepily to him, "We're on a hospice ship."

Halloway smiled and nodded. "That's right."

But his patients were already lost in sweet, dreamless sleep, their bodies busy repairing the endless days and sleepless nights of *Sky-Walker*'s end.

At one point during the night, Dag woke to dim lights and saw, or dreamed, a tall man in gold-braided whites standing by Philippa's bed. This bothered him a little, until he saw that the man was looking, not at Philippa, but at something or someone beside him, by the foot of his own bed. A child? No—the presence moved away and became a blurred or veiled shape in a wheelchair. A vague sense of disquiet stirred in him, but then he remembered "hospice ship," and the wheelchair seemed somehow appropriate. The presence said something very deep and blurry. But Dag couldn't concentrate. Almost sure that this was all a dream, he let himself slip off the corner of consciousness, still grateful for their comfort and safety. Phil's okay, was his last half-thought.

Next day was blurry too, and emotional. One moment they thrilled again to their finding by the great hospice ship's lifeboat, and the next they collapsed into sadness and wept into their broth and custard at *Sky-Walker*'s fate.

"It was m-more than just an adventure," Philippa repeated. "We wanted to p-prove, to prove what one person can, to show you still can, that we c-could—"

"We were . . . crazy," Dag said in a bitter, flat voice. She'd never heard him so down. It roused her a little.

"That was a freak," she said. "Anybody can be hit by a freak thing. It doesn't *mean* . . ."

They were silent awhile, weighed down by reaction to the long nightmare.

Then Dag started to say something, but she got there first, in a tentative, little voice like a kid's. "We could . . . do it again."

He sat bolt upright, then painfully rose from his bed and moved over to hers.

"Do you mean that, Phil? Think. Would you really?"

She nodded hard, her lips set.

"We can. I mean, *we will*. . . . You can't have *two* freaks."

"You really would?" He reached for her, grunting with the pain of his rib. She nodded hard, hard.

"Even if we have *three* freaks. Dag, we're going to."

"Oh, my god, my darling . . . it'll be hard."

"So it's hard."

He choked up again.

"We'll call it the *D-defiance*."

"Yick."

"Okay, okay. The *Horatio H. Fish-Flattener*."

They giggled through tears, holding each other, thinking of the long hard year ahead—years, maybe. Raising the money. The talk-talk-talk. But they would succeed. Somehow they would. They'd start right away, while some of the stuff they needed to work with was still around.

Then Dr. Halloway descended on them with two nurses and a battery of tests, chasing Dag back to his own bed in mock scandal. He seemed extracheerful, a happy chipmunk. Halfway through the second tissue sample it occurred to them why. Typically, Philippa said it. "We must be some of the first healthy patients you've had in a long while, Doctor."

Halloway looked up, suddenly sobered. "That's right. My lifework is spent with the dying."

"People you can't help."

He grunted. "Well, I can help some. I don't mean save them, I mean we're learning a lot about how to make dying—also an important part of life—go better. For instance, we've come light-years beyond the old

Brompton cocktail, though we still call it that. Here on the high seas—great old phrase, isn't it?—we're not subject to the stupid drug laws of any nation. We can experiment with whatever seems promising for the patient. Only prejudice on our parts makes this gloomy work, you know. One of the last taboos. Because doctors hate what they can't fix. But I must say you certainly are a pair of splendid young specimens, especially after what you went through." He patted a bandage on Philippa's shoulder. "It does me good to see healing like that. One forgets."

Dag squinted at him, wondering if maybe Halloway would like to find and extract some kind of magic health-juice out of them for his patients—real mad-doctor stuff. But he didn't look crazy, just hard-working and pleased.

"When do we get up? It better be tomorrow or we'll start to go sour on you."

"Tomorrow you take a walk on the ward. With Miss Boyd."

"I want to see the ocean," Phil said.

"I'd think you'd have had enough of that. But okay. I guess I really have got into the habit of over-caution. I'll tell Anna Boyd to take you out on deck. If the weather's fine."

"Overcaution," Dag said sneakily, and Halloway laughed.

Next morning Anna Boyd brought them each a new blue hospital jump suit with *Charon* emblazoned in bright yellow on the breast pocket and presently led them through what seemed a mile's maze of corridors. Pleasant carpets, paintings ("By patients," she told them), doors ajar from which came normal-sounding voices and a laugh or two in the distance—nothing seemed like a hospital, except for the occasional IV stand or oxygen-breather outside a door and the number of nurses, male and female, passing by.

Only twice did they pass doors from which came sounds they didn't like. One was open; they edged gingerly past the rasping sobs and were startled to hear the weeping change to "Hello!" They looked in; a sobbing old woman in a dressing gown held the hand of an even older woman on the bed. She was sobbing too, but her free hand was waving to them. Nurse Boyd herded them to the doorway.

"H-hello," Philippa essayed.

The old woman peered at them. "You're not dying?" she asked hoarsely.

"No."

"Not yet," Dag added.

"Good!" She blew her nose and said, "So young! But you will someday. When you do, I hope it's as nice as this."

Her companion had pulled herself together enough to nod and add, "That's right," through a teary smile.

They stared helplessly, noticing a male nurse standing in the shadow by the port.

"I mean it," the older woman rasped. "Oh, we're just crying because of —somebody we both knew. He didn't have all this, you see. He . . ." She choked up, forced a grotesque smile. "Sometimes it's hard, remembering. But it's better to let it out."

"I see," Philippa said gravely.

"Bye now, dears. Thanks for stopping." Her companion lifted one age-warped hand in the ghost of a farewell wave. Her other hand clutched some knitting.

They went quickly on, into a sunlit lounge with someone's easel in the corner.

"I think I know what she meant," Philippa said in a low voice.

"Me too." Dag's tone echoed hers, and he took her hand and pressed it briefly. They needed no more words. They had in fact met each other in the visitors' lounge of the hospital where her father and his grandmother were dying of cancer.

The experience had been almost more than they could bear. The once-loved people, now helpless bodies who waked from inadequate "sedation" only to scream in agony . . . the gray back wards, where the nurses came ever slower and less frequently, and the doctors scarcely at all . . . the insane laws denying certain drugs on the grounds of preserving the dying from addiction . . . and deeper yet, the unspoken fear for self—that this was how one would end.

And now they were on a hospice ship—on one of the controversial death cruises itself, where no one but the dying were allowed. Immoral swindle or genuine benefaction? Well, they would see.

"They tried to keep them secret at first, didn't they?" Dag asked. "What was it—oh, yes, the *La France,* sixty thousand tons."

"The S.S. *Gabriel* now," said Anna Boyd.

"I guess it was very hard to get on then. They had quotas for rich people, and middle income, and charity. And no relatives."

"They still do. There *are* a few relatives, though, for the very young and very, very old patients."

They were passing a poster offering short shore trips at the upcoming ports of call. There was a photo of a green and white bus that looked familiar. Had they observed some of the "death trips" without knowing it?

"Hey, we're going to North Africa," Phil said.

"Yes, we've found people enjoy the tours—wherever the narcotics laws are, er, negotiable. The Sphinx is very popular, even with stretcher people." Anna Boyd smiled warmly.

"What happens if someone dies?"

"We do the best we can to handle the situation tactfully. S.A. Hospice Ltd. is good at that. Now—there's your sea!"

Strong glass doors opened onto a section of open deck that looked like a pleasant patio hung with live plants. Heavy storm shutters by the rail were folded back. It was a beautiful day.

They made for the rail and craned over, fascinated by the surge of water below along the great ship's sides. By peering they could just see the gleaming bow-wave curling out, and sternward, the tremendous churn of her wake. Refreshed by the breeze and sunlight, reveling in the huge ship's mastery of the element that had so nearly killed them, they didn't notice that someone else had come out, until a horrid fit of coughing made them turn.

The man was obviously a patient, a small, bone-thin man whose jump suit hung slack over his collapsed chest, with sunken, haggard eyes above his handkerchief. The coughing ceased; he grinned almost frighteningly and tottered to a bench.

"Hi! You're the kids who made the balloon trip, right?"

"Yes."

"Wow. Crazy. I like it." He turned away to complete another ghastly coughing fit. When it was over he gasped, "Told me—you were here. Sure am glad I met you." His eyes were going from Dag to Phil and back, hungrily yet somehow happily. "Rosenthal's the name, by the way. Not that it matters. Doc says I'll probably die tomorrow or Saturday, but I sure don't feel it. I used to be a CPA. Tell me, how was it? Was it worth it to you?"

"Oh, yes."

They went on to tell him a bit about ballooning, the wonderful part before the storm, the silent flights over waving people they could call to, the birds that came with them. Unconsciously they swung into the back-and-forth duet they had used so often in interviews, while their eyes tried to grasp the reality of the macabre figure before them.

He seemed delighted by every aspect, from the charm and wonder of this old-new way of flight to the smallest detail of their precarious financing.

"So you're going to try again, eh?"

"Yes, we are."

"Good for you. Geez, am I glad I lasted long enough to meet you."

A second, very small nurse had come out, carrying a nautical wooden tray of crystal wine-goblets. Anna Boyd, who had been listening from the rail, stepped forward.

"I feel pretty good, Shirl," Rosenthal croaked at the tray-bearer.

"And that's the way we want to keep you." She handed him a goblet. "Down with it, Mr. R."

"I was just kidding." He drank it quickly. "Great stuff, but they sure could improve the flavor."

"We're working on it. I brought you something to help." She set the tray down by Anna and produced a packet of Life Savers and something else which she slipped quickly into his breast pocket. It looked suspiciously like a cigarette.

"Ah, Shirl, you're an ange. When I get up there, first thing I do is make sure you're in the book."

"And how do you know you're going up there, Mr. R.?" Shirley asked mischievously.

"No doubt whatsoever. Can you think of any place they must need a CPA more?"

In the general laughter, Dag and Phil had been looking curiously at the beautifully set tray.

"Ah-ah-ah!" Shirley whirled and snatched it up again. "This you stay strictly away from, kids. The big no-no. Not even a lick at an empty glass. It's a Brompton cocktail with a few improvements that have side effects. One taste and you're up the wall for life."

She grinned at Rosenthal, took his glass, and trotted back inside.

Anna Boyd stepped back to the rail. "Hi, look. Porpoises!"

Rosenthal got up to see too. Self-consciously giving him space, they leaned out to watch the sleek olive bodies playing in the bow-wave, apparently scornful of the mighty ship bearing on them.

"Ah, glorious!" Rosenthal tried to breathe deeply and was doubled over by coughing. Back on his bench, he grinned ruefully. "Funny. Maybe you kids can figure it out."

"What?"

"All this." Feebly, he waved one bony hand around at the charming patio, the great ship in general.

"I can figure out ordinary costs. Top quality, every little thing. And the *Charon* used to be the *United States*, she's a fuel hog. Plus—I was on three or four hospital boards before I got sick—I couldn't begin to cost out this kind of care. And I know I paid full price—in fact I kicked in double, my heirs are richer than god and don't give a damn. Even assuming twenty percent of the others did the same, it doesn't begin to add up."

Phil and Dag looked about speculatively, but their work with *Sky-Walker* offered no basis for any such extrapolations.

"Plus—" Rosenthal held up bony fingers to count. "This Society Anonymous Ltd. has the S.S. *Mercury*, that was the *QE II:* the S.S. *Gabriel*, you know her; the *Queen Mary* that was once a museum is now under work as the S.S. *Saint Martha; plus* the old *Michelangelo* and the *Da Vinci* are in drydock for rebuilding. I think they have options on every damn thing afloat over thirty-five thousand tons. I know because I bumped into a couple of get-rich-quick medical outfits that want to jump in. This S.A. Hospice is not about to let that happen, no way. God knows, they may even raise the old *Queen Elizabeth*, she's down off Singapore."

He paused for a brief coughing bout.

"I tell you, it doesn't begin to add up."

The two young people could only frown thoughtfully.

"They must have an angel," Philippa offered.

"Hey, that's good." Rosenthal grinned. "Don't make me laugh, you trying to kill me?" He laughed anyway, and only coughed a little. "Well, just a thought to leave you with."

"Time you two *wunderkinden* went home," said Anna Boyd.

"Great meeting you, fan-tastic. And keep on flying, hear?"

"We will, Mr. R., and—"

Anna Boyd hustled them out before the farewells could become awkward.

As they walked back along the serene corridors, Philippa observed quietly, "*Brave New World?*"

"Huh? Oh, yeah. Remember the death ward—and roses and kids and candy, all sweety googoo. And some awful drug—I mean, weren't they all spaced out?"

"Yes. To think the mother didn't even know her son. Or didn't care."

"This place isn't like that though. Those old ladies, they weren't spacey, they were remembering. And Rosenthal was sharp."

"And their feeling bad about whomever, that was rational. But it's so hard to believe . . . Miss Boyd—"

"Anna, to you."

"Anna, is Mr. Rosenthal *really* going to die tomorrow?"

"He wasn't supposed to last to yesterday, my dear. We don't know *what* he's breathing with."

"Lung cancer, isn't it?"

"Yes, and badly metastasized. The only thing we've noticed is that people who aren't in pain, and have interests, sometimes seem to last just a little longer. Pain helps to kill, you know."

"Lung cancer," Dag said. "Look, I don't mean to talk out of turn, but, well, you had to have seen it too. . . ."

Anna frowned, then suddenly understood. "Of course. Shirl's cigarette. She slips him one every few days. Naturally Dr. Halloway okayed it first."

"But—"

"But why not? If he can have some pleasure. Mostly he just carries the thing around and finally lights it and sniffs the smoke."

"And coughs like mad?"

"Oh, yes."

"I'm starting to understand it," Dag said slowly. "Granted, these people really are all absolutely one hundred percent dying—they are, aren't they, Anna? No maybes, no cures possible?"

"No maybes," she told him. "There's a screening board. The decision has to be unanimous. I think there was one long remission case on the first cruise—it was a four-year-old girl; kids are the hardest to judge. But she went, on the second trip, while they were still arguing. Those whom I feel sorry for are the ones the board turns down, wrongly."

"Oh, my god, little kids," Phil murmured.

"Okay," Dag went on. "So they're absolutely one hundred percent goners. So then the rule is that whatever makes a person feel good is okay. If it really makes him happy—I mean, as herself or himself. Whether he or she goes happy on Monday instead of being miserable or hurting to drag it out to Tuesday doesn't count. Right?"

"That's right, my dear."

"Of course, it could be a problem," Phil said thoughtfully, "if, for instance, a person is an alcoholic."

"That's right too—in theory. Luckily we don't get alcoholics, so far. But even if we did—it's strange, but in practice, things are often simpler. You can always think up a good theoretical dilemma; but what we actually have to deal with just about solves itself, with common sense. . . . And now we have arrived at the practical issue known as your bedroom, and I'll bet somebody has trouble not going to sleep in his or her dessert."

She would have lost her bet—the dessert was delicious—but not by much. The wisdom of their young bodies took over, and afternoon merged into all-night in a sweet, dreamless, drugless blur.

Early next morning they discovered that all their own clothes, plus what few possessions had been salvaged from *Sky-Walker*'s pod, were neatly cleaned and stored in their closet. Even Philippa's bright scarf was there.

"Hey, let's get dressed! Then they'll have to let us out."

They were out of hospital garb and into their own in two minutes. Just as Philippa was cinching the belt that made her army fatigues a showcase for her tiny-waisted, healthy body, Dr. Halloway walked in.

"Well, well, well." He looked them over, twinkly chipmunk. "And where do you two think you're going?"

Dag stuttered for an instant, then inspiration struck. "Well, sir, we were going to ask you something. We met Mr. Rosenthal yesterday. Somehow he knew who we were, and he wanted to hear all about the balloon flight. He seemed to enjoy it too. So I thought I'd ask you if some other patients feel that way. If you like, we could stroll around the decks and chat with anyone who cares to. And of course it'd be better to do so in our own clothes. Or is that a no-good thought?"

"Far from it! In fact it's a delightful meeting of the minds." Halloway's merry grin contained only the faintest, most benevolent suspicion that Dag had just made up the whole escape plan. "It's amazing how word gets around this ship—I'll never understand it. You two are the sensation of the cruise. Everybody wants to see you, and half of them want to ask questions. Just strolling around wouldn't do at all. I've already talked to Captain Ulrik, and he'll be delighted to hear you're ready to give a little talk."

"Oof," said Philippa. "Some people are too smart."

Halloway winked at her.

"But it'll have to be done on a slightly more organized basis, to give the nonambulatories their chance. There's a nice big enclosed patio back of the main swimming pool; and it's obvious from your speed in getting dressed that you're both up to standing on a bench for a few minutes. There'll be a PA there too. Do you think you could be ready to give them a little story of your flight, and answer a few questions, by, say, four this afternoon?"

"Oh, *Dag*," Phil said reproachfully. "I can't, I just cannot."

"Well, why not, Phil? We've done it a million times. All but the storm part. And you can do that, it's fresh in our minds."

"Fresh?! Oh, you—"

"Now, now, now," chuckled Halloway. "Remember, my dears, this is one audience which"—his face sobered for a moment—"cannot take many postponements. Wouldn't it be a shame if a person who is very interested and able to hear you today should be, shall we say, too sick tomorrow?"

"Oooh," said Phil, and then muttered rebelliously, "That's blackmail. But—okay."

"Good girl." His twinkle was back. "Then I take it we're all agreed. I'll put the word out for four o'clock. But I'd like to collect you about three—there are a few very special people you should meet first. And now how about choosing a nice nourishing lunch?"

At three sharp Halloway and Anna Boyd ushered them out through still another corridor, which ended at the old main staircase, now largely converted to a wheelchair ramp. They seemed to be near the bottom; the hospital was evidently deep in the center of the *Charon*—for maximum stability, Dag guessed.

"Want the elevators?" Anna asked. "How's that knee?"

"No, thanks—he needs the exercise," Phil answered for him, a trifle tartly. She had not quite forgiven Dag for getting her into speechifying, which she loathed.

As they climbed up, they noticed that advantage had been taken of the high old ceilings to install a number of mezzanines. The first three landings featured a number of tastefully curtained-off chambers. Glimpses into some of those with drawn drapes revealed altars of various forms, the soft glow of candles. Chapels.

"We have provision here for nearly every faith," Halloway told them. "I would have said every one, but last voyage we had a Bahai, and a member of an obscure Albigensian sect, which required some speedy new construction. I've suggested to Ulrik that we better be prepared for an altar to the Unknown God, as the old Romans were."

"Or Goddess," said Phil.

"You'd be surprised what we have in that line already. What's the problem, Dag, knee acting up?"

It was, slightly, but Dag wasn't in the mood to confess in front of Phil. Instead he pretended interest in the heavy seals on the entrance to the mezzanine they were passing.

"The oxygenation ward," Anna Boyd told him. "We can do that another day; it only has two patients, both in rather bad shape now, and you have to wear special static-free clothing."

"Is—Mr. Rosenthal there?" Phil asked as they climbed on, "or . . ."

"No, he's still with us, believe it or not. We got him to carry a portable respirator, so he gets some oxy from time to time. He'll be there, you'll see!"

"Here are my first specials," Halloway said, leading them off the stairs and down a hall furnished with oddly low benches.

The "specials" turned out to be children.

About twenty of them were in the lounge; they ranged from toddlers to a girl and two boys who might be fifteen. Scattered through the group were four adult women and a man, all in civilian dress—doubtless some of these few parents permitted aboard.

Not many of the kids showed any obvious signs of illness; they were reading or drawing, or listening on earphones; two were constructing a wooden village, and one fat child was industriously disassembling a digital clock. Indeed, had it not been for the occasional roll-bed or wheelchair, and a certain quiet aura of maturity, they could have been any randomly assorted group waiting, say, in a dentist's office. Only the ravaged faces of the parents told another story.

Anna Boyd explained that Dag and Phil were the balloonists saved from the sea, and she introduced them around—so many Terrys, Kevins, Karens, and Jennys that Phil lost count. Dreadful to think that these ordinary names were soon to be inscribed on a stone headmarker or on the bronze plate of an urn.

"Phil and Dag are going to tell us all about their trip and the wreck in the big storm," Anna said. "It'll be in half an hour up by the pool. We can send some people to help you get there. Do any of you want to come?"

There was a chorus of assents, some very feeble. Philippa noticed that the plump little clock-dissector, whose name was Mike, only scowled.

A woman was sitting by a roll-bed containing one of the teenage boys. His assent had been soft-voiced, but his eyes were luminously eager. Now his mother spoke up.

"Dr. Halloway, I think this is most unwise. The exertion'll tire Terry much too much. He can't possibly go."

The boy on the bed turned a beseeching face toward her. "Mother! Can't you understand? It doesn't *matter.*" His voice, when he raised it, screeched and gurgled in his chest. "I'll be dead soon, *dead.* Maybe next week. Then I'll be getting all the rest there is. Meanwhile this is something I want to do. And it doesn't matter if I'm tired, it doesn't matter if I break both my legs. I can do anything I want to now, because soon I'll be dead! *Dead, dead!*"

"Ohhh—oh, *no*—my darling baby," the mother wailed hysterically. "Don't make jokes. Don't even think it. It's all a horrible mistake, you just need more rest and the right medicine. I'm going to take you off this dreadful boat. I won't let you die—I won't have it! You're going to live, my dearest! Live!"

"Die!" he croaked, grinning horribly, his voice a deliberate mockery of hers. He panted for a moment and then said, in his former quiet tone, "Dr. Halloway, you'll see I get there, won't you?"

Halloway nodded. He was writing swiftly in a notebook he carried.

"Not to worry, Terry. You may find your mother resting when you get back."

A smile of great sweetness lit Terry's face, and he lay back, exhausted.

Meanwhile there had been some interactions between Nurse Boyd and other patients, which Dag and Phil had missed. Anna said something to Halloway, and he made another short note in his book.

As they turned to go, the fat little clock-disassembler, who had so far shown no interest, presented himself somberly in their path. Philippa smiled at him; she couldn't tell whether his fat was normal or an outward sign of disease. He offered no response, but said to her in a surprisingly deep, loud, challenging voice: "I betcha don't know the pithagean therem."

Taken aback, Philippa replied, "Uh—do you mean the Pythagorean Theorem, Mike?"

"Betcha don't know it."

Phil glanced wildly at Dag, at Halloway and Anna. No help. "Well, if you do mean the Pythagorean Theorem, it's—wait a minute—yes: It's 'The square of the hypotenuse of any right-angled triangle is equal to the sum of the squares of the other two sides.'"

"All right," the child said, still scowling. "I'll come."

"Glad to have you," Dag said somewhat acidly. But the boy, who might have been around six or eight, had stumped back to his clock.

"That Mike," Anna half sighed, half grinned as they left the children's lounge. "You wouldn't believe it—I'll miss him. . . . Oh, wait; you go on ahead. They weren't all there. I better check on Tammy and Jane. Tammy's father may be acting up again."

They went on to the last of the "special" people, who turned out to be eight very, very aged and frail people in roll-beds. All but one were women. And beside each bed sat another of the relatives, in civilian clothing, and all extremely old themselves. Quite probably daughters—or in a few cases a son. Again it was the same scene: the grief-ravaged faces of the relatives— the first such faces Dag and Phil had seen on *Charon*, they realized— contrasting with the serenity or even gentle cheerfulness of the patients'.

Dr. Halloway introduced them around, his voice loud. "These are our near-centenarians," he told Phil and Dag. "Or wait, you're a real centenarian, aren't you, Mrs. Tombee?"

"I am," stated the old lady firmly. She appeared to be part black. "I made it. Last July."

"And have any of you heard of this young pair of balloon flyers we saved from the sea? They're going to be telling their story upstairs in a few minutes. If any of you feel like coming, we'll bring you up, or if any of your children here would like to go, I'll send someone in to take their places."

There was a general chorus of negatives from the "children."

"Oh, yes." Another old lady spoke up feebly. "Lucy tells us all about it. Come over here, girl, so I can see you. And you too, boy."

Phil and Dag moved from bed to bed, turning around self-consciously, and once or twice even bending over to be felt by shaking, gnarled old fingers.

"I'm glad I saw them," the lone old man said huskily. "But going upstairs—I don't think so. Can't see much, probably couldn't hear, might fall asleep."

This provoked a trembling flurry of laughter from the other patients.

"Tell you what," Halloway more or less shouted. "We're going to make a tape—a tape recording—of the whole thing. Now you've seen them. Any of you who want to can play over the tape with your earphones any time."

"That'd be just fine," a third old lady wheezed. "We'll probably never do it, but we'll always think we could. Good-bye, young people. Be careful."

This sentiment was generally echoed by those who had followed it, except for another aged patient who hadn't spoken before. "I want to go upstairs and hear it," she declared in a surprisingly firm voice.

There followed another version of the scene with Terry and his mother; this time it was her old daughter, at least eighty herself, tearfully, angrily, repeating, "It'll *tire* mother so!"

But the outcome was different. The aged patient gave in. "If I go up there, Effie'll have to come," she said crossly. "And she'll get exhausted and probably make a scene. And I'll have to leave halfway. You be sure and send that tape, won't you, Doctor H.?"

"I will," he promised her. "And maybe we can have a little chat about things."

"I'd be grateful," Effie's mother said and lay back, worn out, while her daughter fussed at her.

"One of our real dilemmas," Halloway told the young people as they returned to the stairs. "I'm not a man who often dreams of arranging fatal accidents, but—Ah, Anna, what news of Tammy and Jane?"

"Jane just wants to go on reading, but Tammy's got the problem with her father. You'll have to send Flink and his boys in there too."

Halloway made another notation as they climbed the last flight. "You carry on, Anna; I'll be along. Oh, you kids, that reminds me. I don't want you to get a shock. You know they fished up strips of your gas bag or whatever along with you. Well, you may see your raft, or maybe some hunk of *Sky-Walker* with the name, by the bench where you'll be talking. That bother you?"

Dag and Phil glanced at each other.

"Thanks for warning us," Phil said quietly.

Halloway took himself off, and Anna led them along immaculate sunlit decks to a large glassed-in solarium by the aft-pool. Inside was warm and light, and so jammed with arriving patients and their attendants and equipment—some had roll-beds, IVs, and oxygen tanks—that no individuals stood out.

They were grateful for Halloway's warning when they saw the huge red and yellow name-sheet of *Sky-Walker* hung above a large low bench at the center of one side.

"Hop on up," said Anna. They did so, and presently from nowhere a grayish arm stretched up through the throng bearing two hand-held mikes.

"You . . . cahn using these?"

"Oh, yes!"

The sight and accent of the little crewman brought back to Philippa in vivid detail their rescue amid the terrors of the great storm. She found it no longer threatened her badly, so perhaps she could deliver a good talk after all. Much as she hated speaking, it was her belief that audiences deserved the best she could do.

Dag led off with his usual fine balloon-enthusiast speech, spiced with his unquenchable zest and vision—and throwing in as many interesting figures and ratios as he could recall for little Mike's sake—while she faced and organized her memories: the hours of limping just above the wave-crests, throwing everything overboard—the fantastic updraft that carried them almost to the stratosphere and threatened to freeze or strangle them in vacuum even as it saved them—only to be followed by the more terrible smash-down finally, all the way into wild water, the butane heater drowned, the bell of *Sky-Walker* collapsing over them so they had to cut free for air—and then the four—four!—dreadful days and worse nights of sheer survival in the foundering raft; the last pause in the storm's eye, and then what would have been the end had it not been for the miracle of the hospice ship's lifeboat.

Apparently she did it well—she ended to clapping, cheers, pounding of canes.

In the after-chat, Dag added, "That transmitter must have kept functioning to the very end. When I get back I'm going to kiss the guy who made it."

"Let *her* kiss him!" An old voice cackled—and Phil was able to spot and wave at Rosenthal, now crumpled in a wheelchair and feebly waving back through his coughs.

Dag's eye had been caught by two figures quietly leaving through a sidedoor at the back—a tall, erect figure in whites, accompanied by someone veiled, in a motorized chair. He nudged Phil. "Captain Ulrik came to hear us."

"Who was that in the wheelchair with the captain?" he asked Anna on their way back, after over an hour of questions had finally emptied the solarium.

"Oh, some big shot on the permanent staff—Dr. T., we call him. Head of Multidisciplinary Research. Nothing to do with actual medical practice, like Halloway. The Big Think. He's the one we could get the use of a nuclear reactor from, or a super-computer if we needed it. Outside research projects come in through him, I believe. . . . He was in some bad accident, even his face is all messed up, poor man. He's always wearing those cover-ups the few times I've seen him. I imagine he finds the privacy of ship life more peaceful . . . Well, that was quite a show, kids. I think a good early supper and some beddy-bye are the prescription. Get those combat clothes off and have a tray in bed. How about it?"

They couldn't have agreed more.

When Halloway came in to congratulate them, Phil was drowsing over her pecan pie. Halloway seemed enthusiastic over the effect of the speech on his special people. "And the tape is *good,*" he told them. "You really get beautiful technical work here. Old Mrs. Brattle, the one who wanted to go, has listened to your part three times, Phil—hey, Miss Philippa, open those eyes a minute—and Mrs. Tombee is running hers."

"How about the kids? That little fat boy?"

"Great. Mike announced he is going to design an improved balloon. You know"—Halloway was abruptly serious—"I think we have a real loss coming there. He's only five, you know. Late five. He'll die too young for any serious work he might have done."

"Five!"

"Yeah. We had to give him the College SAT math section to get a score." Halloway sighed. "Speaking of losses, I don't know how this'll hit you, but you have to get used to remembering where you are. Terry—the boy with the mother, remember?—he died about an hour after he got back on the ward."

"He *died?* Oh—but did *we*—did we—?"

"Did you kill him? Of course not. His disease killed him—helped along by his mother. Almost his last words were, 'I'm so glad I heard them.' See? We always get a few people who go after any excitement. Often the more pleasant the event, the higher the after-rate. Terry was just one of four so far tonight . . . it's as if an unpleasant thing—like, say, the time a dead patient's mother got away and went berserk, dashing all over the wards, making scenes—it was exciting enough but it didn't satisfy people as a last experience. They seemed determined to outlast it. And then something nice gives them just the right feeling or memory; they feel they can let go."

Dag and Phil stared at him; this was something to absorb.

"Four people have died—"

"But we—"

"Not to fret." Halloway stood up and his voice took on a good-doctor authority they hadn't heard before. This was a new aspect of him: The friendly-chipmunk disguise dropped for a moment, revealing the strength at the core. "We all have to grow up, you know. The child refers everything to itself as cause. . . . And"—his tone softened—"I think it will make you feel better to know that the highest death-rates we have come after a really first-rate serious musical evening. You're nowhere near *that!*. . . . Good night, now."

They didn't talk it over much; Halloway had said it all. Serious, but in no way depressed, they sank into another night of marvelous sleep.

Sometime after midnight Philippa roused to use their bathroom. Automatically putting on her robe, she felt unusually alert—perhaps they really were getting "slept out."

In this she was not alone.

When she returned, Dag was in her bed, two muscular arms reaching for her. She melted toward him, and then an impulse of mischief rose in her. She laughed and bolted over behind his bed, which was near the door. He leaped after her onto that bed, erect and wild-looking in his inadequate hospital gown. Oh, god, she loved him!

But mischief still held her, and since she still wore her robe, she ran out into the corridor, expecting him to delay for his robe to give her time to hide. Instead he came bounding straight out after her into the empty corridor, making a horrible face as he lunged to grasp her.

"Rapist!" she called out, loving him in every fiber. But youth and some archaic zest of the chase carried her fleetly down the silent halls. If he didn't care, she didn't either; she tucked up her robe like Atalanta and flew giggling up a small ramp-way, pursued by her laughing and swearing naked incarnation of the male. Clearly, when he caught her there would be no return to their room—so, womanlike, as she sped she kept an eye out for a clean stretch of carpet, and at least a corner that would afford minimal privacy.

Up and up—he was gaining fast, and her own desire was gaining faster —the carpet was deep and unused-seeming here, and the next landing was a corner! She saw a shallow niche in the wall just as she came to it, stopped dead, and pressed herself into it, eyes shining, one hand to her mouth to stop her laughter, should he pound on past.

He rushed up the last bend after her, so aflame with love that to her eyes the absurd gown was the tunic of a running god. Oh! He was here, upon her—passing! She could all but feel his breath as she backed hard into the niche.

Just as he went by he saw her, whirled, and reached with a soft triumphant laugh. She pressed back to fling herself bodily at him.

—And the niche behind her gave way.

She half fell, half staggered backward, into what she assumed was a broom-closet, or something of the sort, and was amazed to find herself in a very large, palely lit space before a great translucent wall with double doors in it. The oxygen ward, was her first thought. But the air here was half gagging her—it was quite abnormal.

Then she found that the niche door had closed behind her. The whole wall containing it was curtained, or upholstered in some way. There was a set of large official-looking double doors much farther along in the wall, but that way would take her farther from Dag. She wanted the little secret service door. But her half-fall and spin had disoriented her, and she couldn't make out any edge outlines. She began to feel about and push frantically.

Just as panic started, she realized that Dag must of course be frantically searching for her on the other side—it was only a question of moments and he would find his way in too. She should warn him not to let the niche door close.

Meanwhile her sexual glow had receded a bit under the impact of strangeness, and curiosity—one of her dominant traits—was taking over. So she turned with her back to the wall and looked about.

Not ten feet from her stood a rolling bed, completely canopied in translucent greenish netting or plastic. Behind the curtains she could see a small dark figure—why, it was a black child, sitting up cross-legged and staring at her with white-rimmed eyes!

Evidently it was waiting to be rolled into the big closed ward. Perhaps she had frightened it terribly when she crashed through the wall?

She smiled. "I'm sorry. I just fell in. It's all right."

The child's mouth moved, but no sound came out. Instead she saw what seemed to be its arm, making a beckoning gesture at her.

Momentarily forgetting about Dag, she approached the canopied bed. The curtains were quite opaque, when light was not behind them. Was this some particularly difficult breathing problem? She raised a hand and waved hello to the child.

It continued to beckon. When she did not respond further, it reached up and parted the curtains beside it a crack, and she bent and looked in, smiling.

As she did so, she heard the sound of the niche door opening behind her and called out, "Don't let it close."

But her warning ended almost in a squeak—her eyes had taken in the creature sitting under the canopy, and her world was turning upside down. At first she thought the child was hideously deformed—so deformed as to be beyond even the most dreadful of side show freaks. Everted organs, extra limbs—she could scarcely bear to look. But it's bright eyes held her, and then she felt its touch—her hand, too, had been at the curtain-slit, and the child had grasped her wrist.

Had its grasp been rough or greedy, she would have jerked loose and run to Dag. But its touch was very gentle, delicate, and fragile-feeling.

Meanwhile her eyes and brain were busy, were bringing her one overwhelming, convincing message: this was no deformed human child, if indeed it was a child at all. Nor was it any earthly animal. Her breath choking in her throat, trembling from head to foot, she understood.

The creature before her, actually grasping her hand, was an intelligent being of no race that ever walked on Earth. An alien, an extraterrestrial. At her first full sight of it, the antique phrase "an imp of Hell" had flashed through her mind; and she almost screamed out. But that feather-light touch seemed to quench terror. Instead she simply looked.

The creature was not human "black," but deep blood-crimson, with bright vermilion spots, and accessory organs that pulsed. Its nose was an intricate red vertical slit; the mouth was sharply triangular, with an extraordinary number of tiny sharp bluish teeth; there was no chin or lower jaw. But the eyes! They were very large, and what she had taken for white rings extended threadlike into the pupils, which were great star-shaped black abysses, surrounded with flecked jewels of many colors. Beautiful . . .

In the short time she had to look, she was never sure how many limbs it had, save that there were far too many, of different lengths. Afterward she recalled one prehensile member that might have been a foot, holding a pen.

Meanwhile the creature was examining her wrist and hand with great but gentle thoroughness. It turned her hand, flexed and wiggled her wrist, fingers, and thumb, stopping at the slightest resistance: it put its eyes close to skin, nails, and palm-lines, smelled carefully between the fingers, even nibbled with exquisite delicacy at the forearm skin. Between its teeth something very hot—perhaps a tongue—touched her. It seemed prepared to continue up to her elbow and beyond.

At some point during the reeling and reshaping of her world, she realized Dag had come behind her. He bent to look in. As he did so, she heard his breathing change. As he went through the realizations she had endured, she could feel emotions jolting him. Almost at once he grasped her arm to pull her away.

"N-no," she whispered. "It's gentle. Listen—go look inside those big glass doors. I don't think it's any oxygen ward, I think I see . . . more . . ." A belated shred of common sense came to her. "Just take a peek. I bet we're not supposed to be here."

He walked over to the translucent wall, behind which moving shapes could be glimpsed as they momentarily came near the glass, and cautiously opened one door a crack. Instantly he began to cough. But still he stared in.

"Oh, my god—" she heard him explode.

"What?"

"Different—they're all different—"

A growing murmur of strange sounds began coming from beyond the open door.

"I want to see." She spoke directly to the creature who held her arm, pulling gently back. "Will you please let me go now?" It stared. "You have beautiful eyes," she said. "But please, may I go?" She tugged again, a little harder.

What the response would have been she never knew.

A squad of ten short, grayish crew members materialized through the "official" doors and surrounded them. "No-o, no-o," one said to Dag, pulling him from the glass doors. It was the only sound any of them made. Her arm was abruptly drawn from the red-imp's grasp—it made no protest —and its curtains were firmly closed. In instants they found themselves being marched up a curving ramp. No doors opened off it. Six led with Dag; four followed with Philippa.

Dag had made one or two attempts to struggle—he said afterward it was like fighting with an oversized granite bowling ball—and Phil tried to pull away from the hands on her arms. But their grip, though not tight or painful, felt like stone bracelets too.

Up and up they went, Dag becoming increasingly discomforted by his nudity.

"Listen, can't you fellows lend me some pants? Or even a towel or a rug?"

No response whatever.

"I think they're aliens too," Phil called to him. "Our clothing customs probably don't mean a thing."

"Yeah, but I have a feeling we're about to meet some humans," he called back. "Can you spare that robe?"

"I think you've just broken the chivalry record," Phil told him. "If they give us a chance, you can tie that gown thing around your middle. And if I can, I'll give you the one I have *under* my robe and we can build you sort of a dhoti."

"Oh, honey, I'm sorry. I forgot you don't have a real nightie under that, and I feel pretty weird. We're going to get some kind of chewing-out—it's a hell of a note to take with no pants."

"Just tell yourself you're Socrates or Alexander the Great—you'd be well-dressed."

"Hey, you realize we're way above deck level? I think we're being taken to the bridge. Oh, god."

"But we didn't do anything or hurt anybody. And we'll keep what we've seen a secret if they want."

"I have this feeling that they want just that, all right. We may get dumped in solitary, and disembarked in Macao. . . . Hey, I can see the top of the ramp around the next bend."

But at that moment they were turned aside and marched into a long, narrow, quiet, dim room, one seemingly just under the bridge. It was divided into two halves by a boxy enclosure which might have been a stairwell to the bridge. The end they were in was bare, save for a few unused-looking chairs and a table, but they could glimpse what looked like a highly functional office at the other end. It was empty of any other people. Two of their captors stationed themselves on each side of the central structure to block access to the office part. The rest left, as ever, in silence.

The tall, bronzed man whom they had first met in the lifeboat—whom they knew now as First Mate Ted Brandt—came in from the ramp.

"Well, youngsters, you've certainly bought yourselves a mess of trouble. Captain Ulrik and the professor will be along soon."

His voice was hearty, but indefinably lacking in some normal human resonance; it sounded in some way dead. They had both noticed this before, but put it down to the press of work and fatigue. Now they were not so sure, and it made them uneasy.

But Dag had a more urgent matter on his mind. "For god's sake, Officer Brandt, can somebody lend me some pants before the party?"

Brandt snorted, seemingly having just noted Dag's state. He said something very fast in a strange tongue to one of the guards, and the man trotted out the ramp door. Meanwhile Philippa was protesting to Brandt.

"I don't understand, sir. We didn't do anything at all—we only looked. I know we didn't hurt anybody. That—that person wanted to touch *me*. The only thing I can think of is that our breath or something spoiled the air—is that it?

"No," Brandt said. His face was flushing; his voice mocked hers savagely. "You didn't 'hurt anybody' . . . you 'only looked.'"

"And of course we won't say anything about their being there or anything they don't want us to. We really can keep secrets. I mean, important ones."

Brandt stared at her in explosive silence, his face changing complexly, as if something chronic had begun to hurt him deep inside.

"Oh, you'll keep their secrets, all right." He shook his head in mock wonder. "Babies! Oh, god, goddamn babies I fish for now! Listen—"

He was interrupted by the return of the guard, bearing, to Dag's disappointment, another hospital robe like Philippa's. But he put it on and at once felt better and more assertive.

"Officer Brandt, sir, I don't know exactly what you're saying or what we're into here. But there are a few laws, and plenty of people know we exist."

"Oh, yes. Human laws." He took a deep breath. "Now listen, kids, and listen good. In a couple of minutes the Captain and—another person are going to be talking to you. Catch every word they say and believe every word they say. It won't be repeated. Don't argue. Don't protest. You have some growing up to do, very, very fast. Start by understanding that our total human concepts of right and wrong, or what's important, don't apply here—any more than do a goldfish's. And that you're being talked to by a person who can eliminate this planet, or our entire solar system, and regard it at worst as a budgetary nuisance. There's only one thing that applies here, and that's whatever that person happens to want. As for your yatter about keeping secrets, he's not about to endanger one iota of one project by putting it in the power of any person—any person whatsoever—to mess up. Now, lesson one. You tell me: What kind of people are absolutely guaranteed-certain to keep a secret?"

There was a moment's pause.

"D-dead people," Dag said.

"I see at least one of you is getting the idea. You can also add in people with their brains cut out. Living vegetables."

"But that's like the Mafia!" Philippa protested.

"Little girl, compared with these jokers, the Mafia is a bunch of nursery delinquents. They could pick the Mafia up like a chicken and wring its neck tomorrow if they wanted. Unfortunately, they don't want. But that's not a bad place to start your thinking, baby."

"Wait one minute," Dag said. "You're alive, and I don't think your brain's been cut out. Are you telling us this bunch of aliens is taking over the world—and you're helping them?"

Brandt's face was now very sweaty, but it had lost its flush and was becoming clay-covered. He took out a bandanna.

"Take over the world? They couldn't care less. . . ." He mopped his face. "This is . . . hard for me to talk about, even when it's okay. . . . No. Just the opposite. They don't want to change anything. We just go right on, like always. Except there're a few things we can't do, like start a nuclear war. Or invent an FTL drive, maybe. . . ."

He mopped his pale face again, looked at his watch.

"Then what are they doing that's so secret they kill people?" Philippa asked.

Brandt drew a couple of painful breaths, and they could see the sweat spring out on his lips again. "Studying . . . just studying us. You ran into the students' floor, that's all."

"Then what's the big secret?"

"Use—use your heads. . . . I can't talk anymore. They'll be here in a minute or so . . . use the time to grow up all you can."

He half sat on a corner of the table as if recovering from an ordeal.

"One thing," Dag said. "Is the other person, the professor—is he that person in the wheelchair, all covered up?"

Brandt nodded tiredly.

Phil and Dag had drawn very close together during Brandt's speech.

"Remember, Phil," he said to her in their "special" voice. "We made it through the storm. This is just a different storm. Can you keep your cool and watch for every wave or break, like we did then?"

She nodded silently, Yes; her eyes large and grave.

"Time's up, kids." Brandt went to the central enclosure and opened it, revealing indeed a stairway. White-clad legs could be seen descending.

The two young people instinctively straightened their shoulders and stood side by side as Captain Ulrik entered the room. Quietly Dag's hand found hers and gripped it.

"Professor Tasso's on his way, sir," Brandt said.

The captain nodded and took up a position facing the ramp door.

"I've had a little talk with them, sir. They're of course very sorry, but I explained that's beside the point."

Ulrik glanced over at the pair, lips tight. "Good. I hope we need waste no time on emotional irrelevancies. Your apologies are registered. It remains for Professor Tasso to determine what he wishes done. I hope it has been explained to you that he's not kindly, nor is he cruel. In past instances, he has been as decent as he could be in human terms, given his priorities. His priorities and interests are simply not ours. And they are totally paramount."

"Captain Ulrik, sir," Philippa said shyly, "may we ask, are you human? I mean, not an alien too?"

The captain smiled frostily. "Why, yes, I am, little miss. But that won't help you."

"Oh, I realize that, sir. I was just curious. . . . And of course if you are, I wonder why, I mean, why you'd do all this for them."

He stared at her, and they glimpsed in his eyes a fanatic gleam, like a distant light across the waves of night.

"I have no family. . . ." he said slowly. "And I doubt if you can understand this, missy. There are men who would sail a load of devils to Hell for the permanent command of a ship like this . . . and I'm one of them."

"I think I do see, sir." Her voice was soft. "It's like *Sky-Walker* was to us." Dag covertly squeezed her hand. The captain's posture had relaxed ever so slightly. Dag decided against a question he was going to ask.

A brief moment of silence—and then one of the guards jumped to the big ramp doors and opened them wide. The large canopied wheelchair rolled into the room.

"Professor Tasso," Officer Brandt announced formally.

Even at close quarters, little of the alien could be made out behind the greenish translucent canopy, save that he seemed to be very tall and of superficially human form. The veiling material was a little thinner or clearer over the face region, revealing occasional glimpses of light, inhumanly long eyes, but no suggestion of nose. In the silence, a tank fastened beneath the chair seat hissed very faintly; there was a not-unpleasant chemical odor in the room.

The frighteningly long eyes had completed a brief inspection of Dag and Philippa. "Well, Ulrik," a cool inorganic voice said from somewhere near the wheelchair arm, "your impulsive act . . . has caused . . . trouble. You should have consulted . . . with me . . . first."

The voice was accentless, with odd pauses. Dag decided it was some kind of super-voder. He wished he could hear the alien's own voice.

"In this particular case, Professor Tasso, it would have made no difference." The captain spoke at normal speed, in his natural tone. "Their SOS —the emergency signal—was widely received. We were in a thickly traveled sea-lane, and the *Charon* was known to be the closest ship. Had I failed to respond, it would have attracted great unfavorable attention, possibly an investigation. It is an inviolable law of the sea to respond to such an SOS, and, for your information, one which I personally will not violate as long as I remain in command of this vessel."

"Perhaps . . . I should know more of these laws of your . . . sea before I receive . . . any more surprises."

It might have been only the voder, but there seemed to be a very faint donnish or academic humor to the alien's remark. The exchange did not seem to be really hostile. Dag and Philippa felt a faint revival of hope.

The next words dashed it.

"Now as to what is to . . . be done with . . . you. I can offer . . . you two choices. You may elect to die . . . as soon as you choose, but certainly before we reach the next port. When, Ulrik?"

"Next Friday. Eight days."

"And there . . . would be no difficulty, Mr. Brandt?"

"No, sir. Like the Doven case. A fatal accident."

"I would dislike too many fatal accidents on my ship," Ulrik put in. "Instead I suggest an apparent suicide. Motive, despondency over failure of their ambitious flight, and no finances or some other impediment to repeating the attempt. This would also be acceptable to human public opinion, of which they have attracted a great deal."

"Approved," said the voder voice. "Perhaps I should assure you two that your . . . actual—as opposed to reported—deaths would be—is humane your somewhat . . . curious term?"

Dag and Philippa were forcing themselves to remain unemotional, composed. In this they were aided by the growing conviction that they were in a nightmare from which they must soon awaken. In this state they were able to notice again the flavor of the academic in the alien's words. Philippa in particular was reminded of a professor she had long suffered with. Dag was reminded of another aspect of bureaucracy, and recalled that this creature was in charge of what must be a fairly major and expensive research project.

But could an alien—an *alien*—be compared with and treated like a human type? Each, in frightened silence, summoned courage to try the only clue each had.

Meanwhile the passionless voice was outlining their second choice. To be released freely, but only after a brain operation which would extirpate all memory of the aliens aboard.

"Officer Brandt mentioned this alternative, sir," Philippa said. "It appeared to us that an operation which would surely remove all traces of our memories would be so extensive that we would be in pretty bad shape afterward. Not ourselves. Is that correct?"

"There does appear to be considerable . . . deficit," the alien voice replied. "Four such operations have been done by one of our people—Dr. Halloway is not involved with us—and while all the patients lived, only the third appears to have been very successful. In this case . . . the individual achieved independent life in some form of . . . motor maintenance work, I believe. He had been previously occupied in . . . some aspect of your . . . music. The problem is that your brains, like some of ours . . . display considerable redundancy, so that extensive . . . separate incisions are required. . . . But doubtless I go beyond the limits of your understanding."

"On the contrary, sir," Philippa said bravely. "I have received some training in neurology while in school, and I understand exactly what you mean by brain redundancy. From the scientific viewpoint—the *human* scientific viewpoint, of course—it's a great pity that your student's actual experimental work could not be published. It would have created intense human attention and settled many theoretical arguments. Or started new ones," she added daringly.

From the canopied figure itself came a totally new sound—a sort of rhythmic squeak. Could it be laughter?

"Very good," said the voder. "Captain Ulrik, am I correct that this one of the pair is a young . . . egg-bearer, ah, female?"

"You're very expert, sir," Dag interjected, equally daring. "Many humans find it difficult to distinguish us without more clothing cues."

Again a brief, strange bell-note from within the canopy. But the metallic voder voice continued unchanged. "I had not been informed that your young, and females in particular . . . were intelligent enough to hold converse."

"Sir." Dag dared the ultimate—what was to lose? "If I may deduce that your human contact have been limited to humans like Captain Ulrik and Officer Brandt, that is, to mature males of highly specialized but very narrow interests, there may be much—uh—behavioral information about humans which has not been available to you."

"Possible," said the voder. "Um. Ahem. But now remains your choice."

"Sir, in order for us to choose more promptly, may I ask one more question? I can guess the demands on your time, and I hope I am not asking too much."

"Is it . . . relevant—and not too long?"

"Sir, we have already caused trouble, and we want to make amends by cooperating and being rational and helpful in every possible way. But we humans have a peculiarity—maybe a primitive weakness—and we find it almost impossible to function, to make decisions and do as we're told, unless we have at least a rough idea of the most important facts around us. You and your research group are the overwhelming mystery in our situation. Now, without some understanding of the simplest facts, we will deteriorate so quickly that it really would be a time-saver and a help to those who have to deal with us if you could spare a moment now. Because only you can do it."

"That seems rational—and you are not the only race with this need. What are your main unknowns?"

"Well, if we could have merely the barest outline of what you intend to do to our world, we could die or undergo surgery quite calmly. For example, we gather that you wish your presence here kept secret. Is this because you plan a massive change in our world, or, conversely, because you wish to observe us unchanged, and knowledge of your presence here would certainly alter our behavior? We see also that this is a very large, beautifully run, innovative project. Is it so large that all hospice ships carry your study teams?"

"And why our world?" Philippa put in. *"You* know countless other worlds, while we know only ours. So we're painfully confused: what could there possibly be about us worth your while to study? It must be just that we're so ordinary, a super-average. Or is there some unique thing here?"

"That too is rational, given your premises." The being paused and made an obscure movement beneath the canopy, then spoke rapidly over his shoulder to a guard, who left the room at once.

Meanwhile Dag and Philippa exchanged glances. Phil knew Dag's blood was running as icy as hers; he knew that the same knife twisting in his vitals was agonizing her. But he was proud of her. "Grow up," Brandt had ordered. Well, they had grown. From free human beings they had "grown up" to helpless captives, "specimens" of a world that itself had changed from being unique and free and its own master to being merely one of many planets dominated by alien powers. From life they had "grown up" to accept their own on-rushing deaths, for each knew that the other would never endure becoming a brain-cut zombie.

And they had grown even further—to the shared, tacit realization that their mere deaths would accomplish nothing but leave this outrage unchanged. Whereas their intact life, on any terms, might hold some crazy hope. So—from playing the game of nightmare, which had worn thin and abandoned them, they who prided themselves on free expression had grown into the courage of the slave's guile, and were playing for their very lives with only the weapon of sycophancy, likely to win nothing but the pain of encouraging a world-eating monster to explain its plans for cooking and garnishing their Earth.

"It's true that your type of world and culture is ordinary, but you are a unique find. In every other such world we know of, your *Wrrg*—let us call it your Alpha cycle—or the much rarer cycle we may call Beta—has run the full course. Apart from a very few tertiary late-starters where life is only just emerging, we have found usually only the Alpha remains: Blasted cinders, with perhaps a few surviving forms of no interests, such as your crab-grass. An essentially dead world."

"You mean, from nuclear war, sir?"

"Yes. They were self-destroyed. That's your most probable, or Alpha, cycle. Then there is also the rarer Beta, or entropic, cycle, where war has been somehow avoided, but where unchecked population growth has consumed all resources and destroyed all possibility of change. There the once-intelligent dominant species exists in some irreversibly degenerate form in huge, though periodically ravaged, numbers, with no other species left alive except a few simple external and internal parasites of no evolutionary potential. Some of them hang on for a surprisingly long terminal phase, but we mostly find the Beta planets dead too. They're quite unmistakable.

"Your planet is thus a unique find. Not only is it preclimactic, but the Alpha and Beta processes are both underway simultaneously, one might say, in competition with each other. And because of your unusual history, your development is so unbalanced that you show limited areas where entropic degeneration is almost complete, especially in urban enclaves like, say, Calicut—while in other areas, like North America and Roosh, the Alpha demolition is almost ready to let go. Additionally, a host of other areas in every conceivable intermediate stage, or combination of stages, right down to your so-called wildernesses. Unparalleled! The sociobiological equivalent of watching a star go through its climactic stages before our very eyes."

"Sir," Phil asked, "does this mean you plan to sit by and watch us destroy ourselves? Your interest is in seeing which of the Alpha or Beta deaths win out?"

"Oh, by no means. I am disappointed with your lack of vision—although I must say I've seen high-placed administrators make the same error. . . . Oh, my, no—that would be a terrible loss to science!"

At some point during this exposition, he had done something to the voder which caused it for moments to speak in tones throbbing with electronic emotion. Under different circumstances the effect would have been grotesquely funny. Here no one smiled.

"The proper scientific approach is quite the opposite. The incomparable scientific value of your condition dictates that we must maintain it intact just as long as we possibly can, so that generations of students may profit. Nothing fundamental must change—the delicately balanced potentials, with every variant tendency coexisting, must be preserved at all costs. And with very small, imperceptible interventions here and there, this is easily doable. For instance, maverick nuclear strike attempts simply encounter malfunctions. Fully entropic areas can easily be limited in spread. Lines of activity which totally deplete one resource or another can be diverted, or the supply covertly replaced. Massive conventional land warfare can be quashed overnight by disease. Overhomogenization can be checked in any number of ways. Interesting utopian efforts can easily be undercut if they become too successful. The accidental loss of pivotal culture complexes can be prevented. And all on a minuscule budget and with personnel requirements near zero. The only necessity is for constant, informed watchfulness—and most of this is achieved by the very activities which different student observers automatically provide! Nor is a hundred percent effectiveness required—changes within certain limits are certainly permissible, and desirable, as long as the overall balance is retained. One might say that never has as great a scientific object been presented along with virtually all means of observing and preserving it, at so small a cost. . . . 'Watch you destroy yourselves'? What an appalling thought!"

Midway through his speech, Dag—who had had some limited experience in obtaining grants—recognized what he was hearing—fragments of the oft-rehearsed expository enthusiasm of a high-level project application for a long-range, big-budget grant. Somewhere in the unimaginable bowels of an interstellar research hierarchy, was there a dossier, a computer address for a Project Earth, by whatever name or number it was called? The mere thought gave him the coldest shudder yet.

"And moreover"—Professor Tasso was wrapping it up—"your peculiar development has left a number of other interesting species still alive, some actually with evolutionary potential. It might not be beyond the realm of fantasy one day to observe man's replacement by an entirely different intelligent species! This would probably require some administrative assistance, budgetary considerations, and so forth; but since such events have been known or deduced to have occurred, to observe one actually taking place would be a scientific and educational event of the first magnitude."

"What wonderful vision!" Dag heard Philippa say, and made himself chime in too. "I shall be really quite resigned to dying tonight, after having heard such an inspiring plan, and even glimpsing it in action."

There was a slight pause before Professor Tasso's voice asked, "Your choice, then, is to die? But—tonight? It seems a bit abrupt."

"Oh, no," said Dag. "We could never be content with life as brainless subhumans—especially after having heard you. And it's characteristic of our race that this type of decision is best carried out quickly." He turned to Captain Ulrik. "We can write the suicide note right away, sir, and even let a few nurses or somebody see us being despondent and so on, if you wish. I'm sure you have something lethal handy. Or we could take some sleeping pills—break into Dr. Halloway's cabinet, if you wanted—and just jump overboard. Nice moon too." He turned back to Professor Tasso. "But you know, sir, I'll be a bit sorry to leave you, and all this. It's so wonderful. And that alien who felt Phil seemed really interested in actually touching a human. And of course we were fascinated too. It made me wonder for a minute if we could somehow find a role as specimens, on the same terms as Mr. Brandt here, not seeing any other humans. But you've undoubtedly considered all that, and no use bothering you further."

"That's right," Phil said. "And, my, it was interesting to feel his interest. A nice last memory. Oh—if it isn't one question too many, after you've been so kind. As Dag asked, are all the hospice ships like this?"

"No. Only this one so far," the alien replied. The voder voice sounded a little abstracted. "Although if the research interest continues to grow— you're a . . . very popular subject, you'll be glad to know—we may have to have another. And I may say the purely human interest in the hospice movement has taken us by some surprise—it's creating its own budgetary problems!"

"Well," Philippa offered, "if you're getting many big hospice ships, why not have a small, fast, all-alien ship and disguise it as a supply and service vessel? You could have a sister ship that actually was a support ship; you'll surely be needing one soon." She checked herself apologetically. "But of course you've thought of all that. Still if we'd been around, we certainly could have warned you to expect the human part to go like a bomb!" She chuckled shyly. "Maybe you do need an average specimen or two to give you access to typical human responses, the way our marketing researchers maintain a panel of human samples."

The alien made another of his undecipherable personal squeaks, or moans, all the while staring at her. The voder remained silent. After a moment or two Officer Brandt stood up, followed by Captain Ulrik. The alien guard moved toward the doors.

"Well, good-bye, sir. And the best of luck," Dag said, heart in mouth. There was another tiny pause.

"A moment, Ulrik." The voder was normally cool again. "Halloway's report . . . am I correct in recalling that these two young humans are of excellent health, intelligence, and so on?"

"First rate," the captain answered. "You couldn't easily find a better pair."

"And they're from a mutually compatible subgroup? Presumably fertile?"

"In theory, yes, sir. But they're untried. As you doubtless know, human fertility varies. In this case, all we can say is that there is no known impediment."

The alien's voder made an inconclusive sound.

"I believe I wish to discuss something, first with the captain and then with my staff. Meanwhile"—his uncanny long eyes slid to Dag and Philippa—"I wish you to allow me to revoke my permission to die as soon as tonight. Brandt will conduct you both to some comfortable place where you will have complete privacy, and see you get good meals and beds. It is possible, even probable, but *in no way definite*, you understand, that I may have a third alternative to offer you. That is to be evaluated and decided on its merits to us. Then I shall indulge in the custom of *my* race and visit you at sunrise to announce my decision. That will not defer your deaths unendurably, if my decision is negative or you still so elect, will it?"

"No, sir," Dag said. "I believe we can hold out. However, could I ask Mr. Brandt the favor of supplying some musical recordings, or reading matter? We aren't likely to sleep much."

"Mr. Brandt, you will supply everything they wish, excepting contact with any others. If this is all, you may go now."

"Good-bye, sir," they said in unison. "And however it turns out, good luck and thank you," Phil added.

Brandt said something quietly to Ulrik and received his assent. Then he led them out and down the ramp to a small unnoticed door, which gave onto a utility deck studded with ventilator shafts and gratings. They were startled to find it seemed to be midafternoon, a cheerless gray day.

Totally disoriented, tired beyond ordinary exhaustion, they followed Brandt numbly, barely aware that a squad of four small crewmen brought up the rear. These simply followed along, untouching, until Philippa stumbled over a cable and found herself being courteously and briefly upheld.

When it seemed that they must have walked at least a mile, they came to covered stairs leading up to a high, largely glass-enclosed crosswalk, a sort of shadow-bridge, across the stern. Their escorts opened the stair doors, and they climbed effortlessly behind Brandt, to come out into a long narrow white-carpeted room, not unlike the subbridge they had left, except that there was no office nor other signs of occupancy. Through the glass walls the great gray track of *Charon*'s wake was hypnotic.

Four more crewmen arrived, struggling in with a nonhospital bed. More largely white furniture kept appearing as if by magic before their benumbed gaze. The last load featured a stereo record player and sound system, and several attractive ferns and flowering plants in white pots. The sad gray day outside was now only a foil for summery coziness within.

"Fantastic," Dag said dully.

"Is this your doing, your selection, Mr. Brandt?" Phil asked. He nodded. "You have lovely taste." She stared at him hard; he didn't meet her eyes.

"Oh, Mr. Brandt, how did you ever get into this?"

"I was doing three ninety-year consecutives, in a max security federal brig." He looked directly at her then. "Ulrik knew me, and thought I'd work out. They fixed it so I died. There's a headstone back of Clintonville that's ten years old. I don't guess I'll ever get to see it, not that I care. We only do absolutely essential shore trips, see; most of the supply and refitting are done right at the pier. People come on, of course. Before every port they reinforce the hypnotic clamp; you may notice we're a little strange then. If you're around, that is."

"If we're around," Dag echoed somberly. "Listen, I wish we had something to leave you. Your getting us out of that storm will be one of the great things I'll think of at the end. Sorry we had to mess up on you."

"Take my scarf, Mr. Brandt," Phil said. "I'll try to get it to you. You can use it for a bandanna."

"Ah, for s—t's sake." He started out the door, then paused. "There's a better-then-even chance, kids. If you want it. You really did a job on the professor. I admit, I didn't think you had it in you."

"You did it, Mr. Brandt. We took your advice. If there is a chance of— of life as laboratory hamsters, it's due to you."

"Ohh, great flying turds of ducks—t!" Swearing hideously, he started down the stairs, turned back to stick his head in. "Since you like my advice, here's one last piece: if any of your thinking involves escaping, now or ever, forget it. Just save your skull power and forget it. *I know.*"

He was gone.

With one accord they turned to each other and simply held together, human heart to heart, in a long silent communication without words, without passion, while the room darkened around them. Ultimately Dag started, staggered, and discovered he had been sleeping on his feet, with Phil, asleep too, holding him up.

What seemed to have waked them was a soft, persistent knocking at the door. It turned out to be a crewman bearing a tray of steaming bowls of oyster stew and plates of big fresh strawberries.

They were young and stunned by despair; forced to believe, yet scarcely able to grasp, that the deepest premise of normal human life, the independence of their world, was a delusion. Now this reality had been turned inside out, revealing the great cancer of alien intervention. And for them there would be no more *Sky-Walker;* all dreams had died. Tomorrow's sunrise would bring only confirmation of their own imminent deaths, or— perhaps more dreadful—the offer of life as the study objects, playthings, of nonhuman monsters.

Life? Would it be even life, lacking all freedom, even all privacy? If they bore or were forced to bear young, their children would be for the prying fingers, lenses, noses of unknown aliens, subject perhaps to unthinkable experimentation. Their very acts of conception and birth would be open to the view, perhaps the interference, of their masters. Was this life?

They could almost find it possible to envy ordinary humans the pathetic freedom of their ignorance.

And yet—though it was far indeed from their dream of conquering the winds of a free Earth—they were not without one very small victory: all on their own and unarmed, they had met the enemy, diagnosed a weakness, and used it to manipulate the inscrutable, all-powerful master of their fate. They had made him acknowledge them as something slightly more than mere "specimens"; had at the least caused him to reconsider, to take unanticipated action recognizing their existence.

If sunrise brought only his refusal and their forced deaths, they would go knowing their killer was not wholly content. And if he brought an offer of life, they held it in their power to negate his plans, to die by their own free choice.

Such was their victory: a slave's triumph, tiny, gained by ignoble guile, but real—how very real, only those who have fought from total helplessness and nonbeing can know. They had no idea what they would choose or suffer, come morning, but meanwhile they were alive and young, and not without pride.

They ate the excellent oyster stew and strawberries, finding also crisp greens with vinegar, hot buttered muffins, cheeses, milk, and a small bottle of cold sparkling wine.

By tacit consent they didn't discuss their own plight then. Only with his mouth full of cheese did Dag say thoughtfully. "On the brink . . . that must mean they think it's a close thing with us."

"We all think that." Phil poured the wine.

"But how do they keep us that way?"

"Hmm. Hey—that earthquake in Iraq or wherever. Could they do that, to stop the wars?"

"Sure. What's a little pinch of earthquake-juice?" He sobered. "We didn't read enough news. Remember that big fire that got zapped in New York, and that crazy oil find off New Zealand? And those so-called nuclear misfires—maybe they were all them."

"And the fog-bank over the whales," Phil added. "He said something about saving some other species, remember? . . . And that funny place on, what, New Caledonia everyone decided was a sacred Moslem thing. Maybe that's where they land! Nobody's allowed near, and that big mosque-building could be anything."

"I bet you're right. My god. . . . Well, I guess that does supper. . . . Phil, come sit by the window. Let's just sit close."

"Oh, darling. My darling . . ."

There was of course no more sleep for them that night. For the first hours they sat with room lights dimmed, watching a magnificent full moon rise toward the zenith and simply vacillating. They were so deeply together that speech needed only fragments.

"Fertile," Dag or Philippa would say now and then, knowing that in the other's mind would unroll images of a laboratory hamster giving birth under the eyes—and fingers—of a dozen kids.

"Maybe not right away," one would comment.

"Hardest on you," Dag would add each time. Once he said, "No worse than human gynecologists, maybe. But what if it—if *they*—grow?"

"Pass along secret tradition?" Phil speculated.

"Possible."

"Or persuade them it has to be adopted out," Dag suggested. "My aunt could take one. . . . Lots of possible stories. Like, we had brain messed up by wreck. No oxygen. *Charon* kindly consented to let us end days here. Too far gone to visit. But you get pregnant, see. Kid's okay."

"But persuade them? How?"

"Tell them we all die, or kid dies, without humans. Get sick, starve like Gandhi. . . . If we're good little hamsters, they might not want to lose us. If it's perfectly safe for them, baby can't talk. Use it only for really major stuff, though."

"They don't know very much," Philippa said.

"Yet."

Now and again one of them would say simply, "It's cleaner."

And the other, sharing the overpowering yearning for a quick, near end, would agree with increasing relief. "Right."

Occasionally one or the other would say, "No friends."

"Interesting to meet aliens?"

"Medical students don't socialize with hamsters."

"Still . . ."

"Yeah."

"I don't think that Captain Ulrik really knows very much either," Philippa commented. "He's just a sailor."

"Brandt's got more to him. But he's morbid."

"Yes."

Considerably later Philippa said, "I can't get over that 'on the brink.' That's how they want us—*forever* on the brink."

"All the brinks," he said, reaching for her again. Sometime after midnight they had rather solemnly decided to make better use of what was either their last night of life or of privacy.

Later still, he made quite a long speech: "What's beyond the brinks is a lot worse, I gather. Maybe Earth should be grateful. Gives us time. Some people might find a different way."

"Wouldn't they stop it?"

"Only if they recognized it. Administrators get old, students get sloppy. We're the only representatives of our race here, maybe we could help. Unlikely, of course."

"But . . . it's the only game in town." Philippa was rubbing his sore knee. "After all, *they're* alive. Their worlds must be okay. How? Could we find out?"

"That could be really important," Dag said slowly. "I mean *really*. To us humans."

"But then what? Send out secret messages? Notes in bottles?"

"I don't know. Something. Oh, no use, I guess."

"No. . . . Regardless; it's still the only game in town," Phil repeated stubbornly. "Only it's dirty work. Like this afternoon, Dag . . . flattering them. Yassuh, Boss. . . . Dirty, dirty."

He reared up and caught her bare shoulders, looking deep into her eyes.

"Which is the real challenge, darling? An hour ago I was pretty sure we'd just go. If we get the chance to stay, you'd have to bear all the s—t part. Of course I'll be with you all they let me, but I might have trouble not killing some damn freak. But nobody can help you through some of it."

"They couldn't back home either. . . . I feel like you do about the challenge and maybe our duty. But I think it's pretty hopeless too. . . . But so was *Sky-Walker*."

"Listen, sweetheart"—only in their most serious moments did he use the old, old endearment—"this may all be beside the point. But if we get the chance, the toughest part falls on you. So I want you to decide which. I'm with you all the way either way."

"Oof. Okay."

When the first light grayed the ocean, they were sitting by the big windows, watching the phosphorescence fade slowly from sight in the wake.

"Cleaner." Philippa sounded final. "A clean good-bye."

"Right," he said slowly.

They held hands quietly. The light grew. The high top overcast turned pink. Suddenly it parted here and there to reveal bright blue beyond.

" 'That little tent of blue that prisoners call the sky,' " Dag quoted.

For the first time tears really threatened them. But suddenly Philippa drew herself up. " 'For each man kills the thing he loves'?" She took up his quote, sarcastically. "Stupid crap. An elderly faggot in Reading jail. F—k it. Let's stick to our own words."

He laughed, deep and free, even if for the last time. "My great woman. God, I love you."

"And me you. Listen—about the 'clean good-bye.' The clean part is okay. But I'm not sure I settle for the good-bye. Dag, I just *don't know.* You decide."

"Maybe we won't have to, is as far as I get. Hey! I just thought of another way to try: . . . which would you be most disappointed about if we had to do? Or maybe, if we couldn't do?"

Phil gave a surprised grunt, and they stared hard at each other, aware that the light was growing fast. The eastern horizon was clear; a great neon-orange blur showed where the sun would shortly rise.

"If we . . . gave up, I guess . . ."

Suddenly from the corners of their eyes they saw movement in the blinding glow on the deck. They wheeled and stared intently, hands gripped.

It materialized into a crewman trotting toward their staircase with a tray. Steam was rising from little jugs and covered dishes. He disappeared below them, and presently they heard him ascend and quietly open the door. The scent of hot coffee drifted to them. He went out.

Still they stared at the deck, only now and then glancing at each other, then back at the big white deck-well from which would come their fate: death, or the offer of deathly life. Behind it the orange glow changed to a blaze of gilded white. An intolerably bright diamond chip was suddenly on the horizon, blinding them momentarily.

When they could see again, a big translucent-green canopied wheelchair was rolling toward them. Their fate, but no clue. Suddenly, from the doors behind it, Brandt's arm appeared. He held his hand up, finger meeting a thumb, and the arm vanished.

"Okay," Dag said. They both breathed out hard.

They were human, and young and brave. They knew they would find a way to try something, to try some way out for themselves or others. Now they had their chance.

I'LL BE WAITING FOR YOU WHEN THE SWIMMING POOL IS EMPTY

Cammerling was a nice Terran boy, which is to say that his folks came from Groombridge 34 Nu and surprised him with a Honda 990 starcoupe for his traditional *Wanderjahr.* But Cammerling was one sigma off median in that he chose not only to travel by himself but also to visit the remoter parts of the ephemeris where the hostels were unrated or even nonexistent. Which is how he came to be the first Terran—or certainly the first for a long, long time—to land on the planet of Godolphus Four.

As his part opened, Cammerling's ears were assailed by a stupendous braying, skirling, and clashing which arose from an immense dust cloud in which gleamed many shining points. When the dust settled a bit, Cammerling made out that there was a barbaric festival of some sort in progress.

Two vast masses of men were rushing toward each other on the plain before him. From one side pounded phalanx upon phalanx of individuals clad in leather cuirasses and greaves and bearing obsidian lances decked with streaming hair and what Cammerling took to be dried nuts. Charging at them from his right came squadrons of reptile-mounted riders in dazzling glass mail who whirled glittering bolos. Just behind all these raced ranks of archers with fire-headed missiles on their bows, and the whole mass was being urged on by horn-blowers, cymbalists, and bull-roarers, and standard-bearers staggering under huge pennants realistically resembling entire flayed human hides.

As Cammerling stepped forward for a clearer view, the two hordes fell upon each other in primal fury, and the plain became a vortex of slashing, spearing, gouging, beheading, disemboweling, dismembering, and other unmistakably hostile interactions.

"Good grief," said Cammerling, "can this be an actual, real-live war?"

His presence was now noticed by several of the combatants closest by, who stopped to stare and were promptly clouted by those beyond. A head flew out of the melee and rolled to Cammerling's feet, making faces and jetting gore. Without pausing to think, he switched on his Omniglot Mark Eight voder and shouted, "STOP THAT!"

"Oh, sorry," he added, as he heard the sound of obsidian shattering all over the field and noted that numerous persons were rolling on the ground clutching their ears. Tuning the voder down, he recalled his panthropological semester notes and began to scan the armies in close detail, searching for their leaders.

To his gratification he located a group of banner-bearers on a hilltop somewhat behind the fray. At their head was a gigantic warrior mounted on an armored carnosaur, which was wearing a tower of jeweled human heads. This individual was magnificently painted and was leaning back in his saddle to accommodate a ham-sized triple-phallus codpiece from which spouted green smoke. He was alternately bellowing and shaking his fist at Cammerling and chug-a-lugging from a gem-encrusted skull.

On a similar rise across the way Cammerling observed a gaudy pavilion under which a very fat man reclined upon a gold litter upholstered with feebly squirming naked infants and languorously nibbled tidbits from a poignard while he eyed Cammerling. As Cammerling watched, the fat man wiped the poignard by running it through one of the meatier infants and snapped his jeweled fingers at his sides.

All these barbaric manifestations pained Cammerling, who was a good Terran boy, but at the same time he felt exhilarated by stumbling upon what was undeniably the Real Thing. Disregarding the flaming arrows and other missiles that were now arriving in his vicinity and being deflected by his invisible summer-weight nonabsorptive GE-Bilblas forcefield, he focused the voder to project directly at the two chieftains.

"Hi," he said. "I'm Cammerling from Groombridge Thirty-four Nu. How about coming over here where we can rap, if you aren't too busy?"

After a bit of milling, Cammerling was pleased to see the two personages and their retinues converging upon him, while the crowd nearest him drew back. Unfortunately, the delegation halted at a distance that Cammerling felt was too great for a really meaningful encounter, so he stepped toward them and said winningly, "Look, friends. What you're doing—you know, it's—well, don't take this wrong, but it's not nice. It's obsolete, truly it is. I don't want to put down your cultural identity in any way, but since you're going off this war kick sooner or later—I mean, studies prove it— why not stop now?"

Seeing that they were staring at him blankly, he added, "I don't recall my historical symbolism too clearly, but what I mean, I think, is that you two men should shake hands."

At these words the fat prince in the palanquin spitted three infants and screamed, "Me touch that lizard-fondling offspring of an untranslated defecation-equivalent diseased female organ? I shall serve his barbecued gonads to condemned thieves!"

And the dragon-chief threw back his head and roared, "Me handle that chromosomally imbalanced caricature of a feces-eating cloacal parasite? His intestines will be cruppers on my corpse wagons!"

Now, Cammerling could see at once that this was going to be quite a tough situation to turn around, and as he recalibrated his voder, which had begun to oscillate, he also reminded himself that he must be careful not to show disrespect for these people's cultural norms. So he said pleasantly, "If I could serve as a resource person here, I'd like to offer the suggestion that both modern science and ethical intuition agree that all men are brothers."

Hearing which, both chieftains looked at each other with instant and total comprehension and then wheeled back and hurled every weapon in reach at Cammerling, and their retainers followed suit. Amid the shower of missiles, Cammerling perceived that a poignard and a kind of broadax had penetrated his summer-weight forcefield, making nasty runs in the lining. He was about to remonstrate with them when two pale-blue blips floated down from the nose of the spaceship behind him and instantly reduced the two princes, the carnosaur, the infants, and most of the entourages to thin vitreous puddles.

"Good lord," said Cammerling reproachfully to the ship, "that wasn't nice either. Why did you?"

The voder printout came to life and typed in cursive: "Don't freak, dear boy. Your mother put in a few contingency programs."

Cammerling made a face and turned to address the assembled armies. "I'm truly sorry about that. If the seconds in command on both sides want to come over here, I'll try to see it doesn't happen again."

He waited patiently while some confusion died down, and presently two somewhat older and less flamboyant senior types were assisted to come forward, and Cammerling repeated and clarified his previous suggestions. The two viziers looked at Cammerling with the whites of their eyes showing, and they looked at his ship, and at the puddles, which were now cooled and streaked with beautiful colors suitable for intaglio work on a rather large scale, and finally at each other. To Cammerling's intense satisfaction they eventually allowed themselves to be persuaded to a distant brushing of the gloved hands. In his excitement he recalled an historic phrase:

"Your swords shall be converted into plowshares!"

"Madness!" exclaimed both viziers, shrinking back. "Ensorcel our swords into women!"

"A figure of speech," Cammerling laughed. "Now, look, I do want to make it crystal clear I didn't come here to intimidate you people with my superior technology created by the enlightened interplay of free minds in our immense interstellar peace-loving Terran Federation. But don't you think it would be interesting—just as an experiment, say—if you announced that peace has been declared, like in honor of my visit maybe"— he smiled deprecatingly—"and told your armies to go, uh, home?"

One of the viziers uttered an inarticulate howl. The other cried wildly, "Is it your will that we be torn to pieces? They have been promised loot!"

This made Cammerling aware that he had overlooked their concern about the emotional tensions, which were bound to persist in a situation like this, but luckily he recalled a solution.

"Look, you have to have some kind of big national sport. You know—a thing you play? Like shinny? Or curling? Tug-of-war even? Tournaments? And music. Music! My ship can put out fantastic refreshments. Isn't that the usual thing? I'll help you get organized."

The hours that followed were somewhat jumbled in Cammerling's memory, but he felt the encounter was, overall, quite successful. Some of the native sports turned out to be virtually indistinguishable from the original battle, and he did regret having inadvertently triggered the ship's vaporizers once or twice. But no one seemed overly upset, and when dawn broke over the plain, there were a goodly number of survivors able to accept his good-bye gifts of inertia-free athletic supporters and other trade trinkets.

"That rugger-type thing you play has a lot of potential," he told the viziers. "Of course, I'd hope we could substitute an inanimate ball, and perhaps tranks instead of strychnine on the spurs. And the eviscerating bit, that's out. Here, try another Groombridge Jubilee. I want to explain to you sometime about setting up a farm system. Little Leagues. By the way, what was the war about?"

One of the viziers was busy shredding his turban, but the other one began to recite the history of the war in a sonorous singsong, starting with his tenth grandfather's boyhood. Cammerling set the voder to Semantic Digest and eventually decided that the root of the matter was a chronic shortage of fertile flood-plain from the local river.

"Well, look," he said. "That's easy to settle. Just throw a dam across those foothills there and impound the water so everyone will have enough."

"Dam?" said one vizier. "He who chokes the father of water," said the turban-shredder hollowly, "his gonads shall become as small dried berries, and his penis shall be a dry wick. Aye, and all his relatives."

"Believe it," said Cammerling, "I have nothing but respect for your cultural orientations. But really, in this one instance—I mean, from an existential viewpoint, although I'm aware that we should do this on a more participatory basis, man—look!"

And he took his ship up and vitrified a couple of miles of foothills; and after the river-bed had overflowed and filled up with mud and dead fish, there was a big lake where none had been before. "Now, there's your dam," said Cammerling, "and the water will flow all year, enough for everybody, and you can go forth and dig irrigation ditches—I'll have the ship make a contour map—and the land will blossom."

And the viziers looked all around and said, "Yes, Lord, I guess we have a dam." And they went back to their respective peoples.

But Cammerling was a sensitive type, and after he thought it all over, he went down to the nearest village and said, "Look, you people shouldn't get the idea that I think I'm some sort of god or whatever, and to prove it I'm going to come right in and live amongst you." He felt confident about this because his whole class had been on the pangalactic immunization program. And so he went down and lived amongst them, and after they got over his diseases, most of them, he was able to get right inside their heads and experience all their mind-blowing cultural practices and perceptions, and especially their religions. And although he knew he shouldn't do anything to mess up their ethnic reality, still he was pained in his good Terran heart by certain aspects of it.

So he called on each of the two viziers, and as diplomatically as possible he explained how deeply he respected their cultural outlooks, and that he wanted to help them along the inevitable evolution of their present religious phase into the more abstract and symbolic plane that it was surely headed for. "Those big statues," he said, "I mean, they're absolutely smashing. Major works of art. Coming generations will stand in awe. But you've got to protect them. I mean, those caves, and drip-drip. Oh, what a good light man could do. And you know, burning up babies in them is corrosive. Incense would be much safer. How would this grab you: *one* religio-cultural center for *both your nations,* where all the people could dig them? And while we're on it—you know, this bit of dropping babies down the wells to bring rain has to be a joke. I mean, existentially, that's why you all have squitters."

And so he went about and opened up different lines of thought for them as unobtrusively as he knew how, and when he detected signs of tension, he eased off at once—for example, on his project of persuading the men to do some of the plowing. He himself laid the first stones for the Culture Center, and waited patiently for the idea to take. And presently he felt rewarded when the two head priests actually came together to see him. One was wearing a white and black death's head twice as tall as he was, and the other was wreathed in ceremonial snakes. After the greetings were over, it turned out that they had come to ask a favor.

"Delighted," he said, and he was. They explained that every year about this time a fiendish man-eating monster ravaged the villages in the hills, and they were as straws before it. But he would undoubtedly be able to dispatch it with one hand.

So Cammerling gladly agreed to take care of the matter, and he set off next morning feeling that he had actually been accepted at last. And since they had stressed the negligible difficulty of the task—for him—he went on foot, carrying with him only a light lunch, his Galactic Cub Scout kit, and a target laser his aunt had given him when he left. And the high priests went back to their peoples rubbing their hands and pausing only to urinate on the stones of the Culture Center. And there was a great deal of smoke around the caves where the idols brooded.

Cammerling noticed some consternation when, two mornings later, he came whistling down the hill trail, but he put it down to the fact that behind him crawled an enormous shabby saurian with one leg in a plastiseal and a tranquilizing collar on his neck. Cammerling explained that the creature's vile habits had their origin in impacted tusks, and treated everybody to a practical demonstration of orthodontistry from the ship's Xenoaid. After that he spent several mornings training the beast to serve as a watch-dragon for his ship, which had sustained a few attacks of high-spirited vandalism. And the Culture Center suddenly began to shape up.

But Cammerling was thoughtful. On his mountain trip he couldn't help noticing that this planet had really terrific potential in other ways. And so, after chewing it over, he gathered some of the more enterprising common-ers into an informal discussion group and said, "Look. I'm keenly aware, as studies have shown, that too rapid industrialization of an agrarian culture isn't a too good idea, and I want your frank comments if you feel I'm pushing. But have you thought about a little light industry?"

And so—well, pretty soon one of the nations had a small metal-siding plant and the other had a high-quality ceramic operation. And although Cammerling was careful to keep hands off local native customs and never to override native initiative, still, by his enthusiasm and participation in their life at the actual village level, he did seem to be having quite a catalytic effect. Certainly there were a great many activities available for everyone, what with laying out the irrigation system and collecting the kaolin and the materials for ore extraction and so on.

And so it came about that one morning, while Cammerling was helping someone invent the spinning jenny, the high viziers of the two nations came together in a secret place.

And one said, "While in no sense renouncing my undying enmity to you and your horde of agrarian defectives whom I intend to exterminate at the earliest possible moment, it's plain to see that this blasphemous usurper is grinding both our generative organs into skink soup and we ought to get rid of him." And the other replied that, while he did not wish to convey the impression that he was befouling himself by communicating on equal terms with the irrevocably tainted offspring-of-a-chancrous-scrotum represented by his present interlocutor, he would be glad to join in any scheme to get this interstellar monkey off their necks. But was he a god?

"God or not," the first vizier responded, "he appears as a young man, and there are certain well-known ways to quiet such prick-mice, more especially if we pool our joint resources for maximum effect." To which the other assented, and they began to count.

And so a few evenings later, hearing his watch-dragon snirkling hysterically, Cammerling opened his port to behold twelve dainty shapes swathed in brilliant gauzes, but not so well swathed that he failed to glimpse delicate belled toes, eyes, limbs, haunches, waists, lips, nipples, et-triple-cetera, such as he had never before beheld on this planet. Which was not surprising, since he had been gamely rubbing noses with the gamier squaws of the village level.

So he hopped out the door and said eagerly, "Well, hi there! What can I do for you?"

And a girl veiled in smoldering silks stepped forward and parted her raiment just enough to dislocate his jaw and said, "I am Lheesha the Bird of Passionate Delight and men have killed each other for my merest touch and I wish to do to your body caresses of which you have never dreamed and which will draw out your soul with unforgettable bliss." And she showed him her little hands with the breasts of hummingbirds implanted in her tender palms.

And another stepped forward and swirled her vestments so that his eyes popped and melted, and she said, "I am Ixhualca the Burning Whirlpool and I have thirty-two hitherto undiscovered muscles in my thing and I desire to inflame you to madness by means of unbearable pleasure indefinitely prolonged."

And a third knelt down demurely and whispered, "I am called Mary Jean the Cannibal Queen and I have been forced all my life to take nourishment only by compressing and vellicating my lips and gullet upon a certain shameful device, and mortally wounded princes call for me that they may expire in joy."

And by this time Cammerling could sense that they were all thinking along the same general lines, and he said, "Well, you certainly are some superchicks, and to tell the truth, I have been kind of horny. Please come in."

So they trooped in through his doorlock, which had also been programmed by Cammerling's mother, and on their way in it imperceptibly relieved the girls of various blades, gimlets, potions, amulets, poisoned rings, essences, fangs, stings, garrotes, ground glass, and so on, which had been installed in interesting recesses of their anatomies. But even if the high viziers had known this, they would not have been discouraged, because no man had ever enjoyed any two of those girls and lived.

When all twelve of them were inside with the door closed, it was pretty crowded, but the ones closest to Cammerling set to work on him with the hummingbird frottage and the tonguing and the spice-inflamed apertures and the thirty-two new thing-muscles and every kind of indescribably intimate and exotic stimulation so typical of upper-class feudal debauchery, while those who couldn't get at him just then indulged in unspeakably erotic and obscene activities, which he was able to observe in close detail. And so they went on all night, finding refreshment not only in Cammerling's youth and vigor but also in the chance to pick up some cross-cultural technical fertilization, since they were half from one nation and half from the other.

And the morning light shone in upon an expanse of totally intertwined and exhausted bodies. But it had not shone long before a gentle heaving started from below, and Cammerling crawled out.

"Well, now," said Cammerling, "that was truly rewarding." And since he was a nice Terran boy who had been raised on wholesome Terran orgies, he bounced out the lock of the spaceship and did thirty-two push-ups, one for each muscle. And he poured water on his head and whistled and sang out, "Hey kids, when you get yourselves together, I'll show you how to make some pizzas. I have to go help lay out the new sewage-filtration pond; we don't want to pollute the ecology."

But the girls straggled out, very upset, crying, "Lord, we dare not go back because we have failed in our mission, and we will be dispatched with excruciating and bestial tortures."

So Cammerling told them they could stay with him, and he showed them how to work the stove. And they all settled down happily except the girl Ixhualca with the whirlpool thing, who said, "W'at ees dees batsheet peetzas?!" and stamped back to the executioners.

And Cammerling went out to participate in the filtration project and the water-wheel project and the Voltaic cell project and numerous other projects, becoming more involved than he really felt good about, because he could see he actually had dislocated the native cultural gestalt some. And he got flak from people who couldn't do their thing because their thing was, say, shrinking corpses, which there weren't enough of now, or holding sticks to make the women plow straight, when the women were now plowing with lizard-drawn plows that went too fast. And he began to understand what his group vocational computer meant by acquiring maturity of outlook.

But he learned to cope, like when the metal workers came to him and said, "Lord, we've made this devil-machine for vomiting out this unholy hard stuff. What in the name of the sacred iguana egg do we do with it now?" So he said, "Look, let's all vote. I vote we make water pipes." And when the kiln-workers said, "See, O Lord. These fire-bellies which we have constructed give birth to these unbearable tile pots. What use are they?" And he said, "Well, let's all kick it around. I'll throw in the idea that we make ceramic flush toilets." And a high priest said, "By this you know that the new religion is to put water in one end of the body and take it out the other with maximum effort."

Meanwhile, all the babies that had not been put down the wells or into the idols continued to pile up and drive everybody into the walls. And one day Cammerling heard strange sounds and opened the door of his ship to find the watch-dragon surrounded by hundreds of roaring infants. So he walked out to look them over and said, "Good lord, these are cute little buggers."

So he turned to the eleven houris who were mucking about with strudel dough and said, "Here! We have a perfect opportunity to raise a whole generation free from prejudice, fear, and hatred. Let us build a schoolhouse, and I want you to teach these kids."

But the girls exclaimed, "This isn't our area of specialization, Lord! What can we teach these larvae?"

"Why," said Cammerling, "everything!" And he went over and switched on his old teach-panel, which was in his ship. "Look: Montessori method, Holt stix, Allspice Avenue, Parsley Place, Dill Drive, Betelnut Boulevard—we can make that Lizard Lane—Mr. Spock's Logic Book— the whole bag. We'll have like a kibbutz; studies show that has its drawbacks, but it's an optimal form for situations like this."

And in a very short while they had a kibbutz, and the girls were teaching Montessori set theory and creative hygiene. And more and more babies arrived, and more girls too, because it turned out that Ixhualca the Burning Whirlpool had busted out and started a women's lib movement, and many of her recruits opted to teach babies as an alternative to making ceramic flush toilets.

And time passed—actually quite a few years, although to Cammerling they seemed only weeks, because he was a nice Terran boy with a life expectancy of five hundred years and he was only into postadolescence. And behold, there was a whole high-school generation of marvelous kids in well-cut tunics riding around on tractors labeled WAR IS ICKY and COOK PIZZAS NOT PEOPLE, with the sun shining through their eyes. And they were restoring the land and helping the people and organizing truck-farm cooperatives and music festivals and People's Capitalism and community dance-ins and health clinics. And though a majority of the older people still seemed sort of silent, Cammerling gazed upon the unstoppable flood of Montessori babies pouring out of his kibbutzim with middle-Terran values plus pioneering macho and knew that it was only a matter of time.

And one evening, as he sat watching his sabras setting up a transmitter, practicing karate and laying the foundations for a supermarket, there came a flash in the sky. And a spaceship shrieked in out of nowhere and sat down daintily on the beach. And Cammerling saw it was a supersports model of a style that was unfamiliar to him but obviously very heavy indeed. And he went over to the alabaster lock full of strange stirrings.

And it opened, and there stepped out that indescribable being, a nice Terran girl.

"Well!" said Cammerling. "I must say I haven't seen a nice Terran girl for some time. Would you like to come in my spaceship and visit?"

She looked at what was visible of Cammerling's sportster under the passionflowers and the pizza shells and replied, "Come in mine, Tonto; I have low-gee conditioning and a couple of six-packs of Groombridge Jubilee."

So he bounced into her ship, and she opened her arms and he lunged right at her in the good old Terran way. And after missing once or twice because he wasn't used to a quarter-gee, he made it.

And afterward she asked him, "How was it, baby?"

And he said, "Well, there's like a muscle or two I could show you about, but I do believe that's the Real Thing."

"I know," she replied fondly. "There's nothing like a nice Terran girl. And now, Cammerling, it's time you came home."

"Who says?" said Cammerling.

And she said, "Your mother says."

"In that case, I'll do it," said Cammerling. "Things are going down pretty smooth here."

So he opened the door of the spaceship and called to all his friends and followers and all the great young people and anyone else who cared to listen. And they came and stood before him in a loose but jaunty formation expressive of individual creativity blended with empathic sharingness. And he said to them, "All right! I have served you as a humble communication link with Terran interstellar enlightenment, although I hope I haven't screwed up your native cultural scene too much; still, it's done now. Now I go back into the sky. Feel free to get in touch with me at any time via my ship's transmitter if you have any problems. Carry on, Godolphus Four! Farewell."

And they replied, "Oh, great pink friend from the sky, we realize you are not a god and all that; you have taught us freedom from superstition. Nevertheless, bless you. We will carry on. Farewell."

And so Cammerling went away; and as soon as he took off, all the old hairy chiefs and priests and tribesmen came out and rose up and started joyfully hacking everybody and everything in the name of their sacred Godolphian way of life. But the young sabras, whom Cammerling had thoughtfully instructed in the use of advanced weapons as well as Ixhualca's karate, were easily able to handle them. And in no time at all they had the situation totally under control and were able to proceed with energy to fixing up the planet truly nice, all over.

And after many years had passed, a faint message reached Groombridge 34 Nu by sublight, saying:

"Hey, Cammerling! We have fixed up this planet all over truly nice. All is blooming and participatory and ecological. Now what do we do?"

Well, Cammerling was out when this message came, but his secretary got hold of Cammerling's wife, who passed it to his therapist, and when the therapist thought Cammerling was ready, he gave it to him. And

Cammerling and the wife and the therapist conferred, and at first nothing much came of it, but finally Cammerling got off by himself and messaged back, saying:

"Suggest you now proceed to develop an FTL drive and offer the option of Terran enlightenment to other planets in your vicinity. Computer program on FTL-drive theory follows by faxblip. Carry on. Love, Cammerling."

And so, many more years passed, and passed, until one day a new, quite strong message came in from Godolphus Four. It said:

"We have built an FTL drive and we have gone forth and communicated Terran interstellar enlightenment to four thousand three hundred and eighty-four planets. That's all the planets there are. Their peoples join with us in asking: WHAT DO WE DO NEXT?"

But Cammerling never got that message.